The

CW00404400

Teacher's

Cook Book

JAMES HUCK

Twisted Chalkboard Press

Copyright © 2020 James Huck.

All rights reserved.

No part of this book can be reproduced in any form or by written, electronic or mechanical, including photocopying, recording, or by any information retrieval system without written permission in writing by the author.

The moral right of the author has been asserted.

This is a work of fiction, Names, characters and incidents

are the product of the author's imagination, and any resemblance to actual persons, living or dead, is entirely coincidental.

ISBN 9798677877247

*For Liz who has always encouraged me
to try to be better than I am; and Jet,
without whose company on long walks
this would never have begun.*

Only the illumination of the monitor pierced the darkness of the semi-detached house where she lived, alone. Aileen's face and neck were bathed in this glow, floating in the inky blackness of the smallest of the three bedrooms she had converted into her study. Her clothes absorbed the weak light, making it appear that her body had vanished into a black hole that occupied the office chair.

Vague shapes of files and folders orbited a gently humming tower on the desk in front of her: a plastic monster that glared into space with the single indifferent red eye that indicated existence, without consciousness. Around it, on the desk, that had once been fastidiously and obsessively neat, as only a teachers could be, printed sheets and scribbled papers lay as disorganised as her rapidly deteriorating grip on reality.

Aileen leaned closer, her eyes fixed on the accusatory, blinking cursor, aware that a ghostly apparition was visible and returning her gaze. The careworn wrinkles and lines around the face were invisible in the reflection, only bitter eyes and a fixed scowl burned out of the empty page of the document that she was determined to write.

The electronic apparition's neck appeared to be adorned by the colourful icons that were displayed along the base of the screen. A multicoloured collar of international news broadcasters, where a deluge of cherry picked, guilt and anxiety breeding content rained and poured out. Every click and hyperlink led to an atrocious, voyeuristic video or photo slide-show of a new war, famine, flood, tyrant or assault.

Night after night, Aileen and her unblemished digital phantasm, devoured the litany of civilised monstrosity where truth and fact had been incrementally demeaned, disproved and twisted. She was just one of many who were groomed accidentally and unknowingly by the short-sighted and ambitious merchants of media in the bubble of the capital city; her eyes were pierced by needles of condoned violence as the world shrugged, day by day.

Aileen knew she couldn't rely on fact and truth, they could no longer hold up a shining light to expose the lies of the elite and politic. Every calamitous global event had become a point of debate for talking heads who argued and tried in desperation to appeal to the consuming public's communal opinion. Meaning was constructed out of the ephemeral egos of the insecure, spawning clashes of cultures, counter-cultures, generational cultures, political cultures. The terrifying enquiry of the multi-channel, twenty-four hour news cycle meant a race towards banality. Her eyes, and those of untold thousands of others, were gouged by this information, agonising electrical impulses to torture offended morals.

In the muddy light of the small room, she considered whether to write in the style of a diary or a memoir. The ghostly head scattered its fixed features with an electronic twitch and formed the words that hissed from Aileen, 'A confession.'

Fingers caressed the familiar keys smoothly, the capital letters and numbers almost invisible on the small buttons after hours and years of overwork. It was no matter, the sequences of words and sentences were well known to the Head Teacher commanding them. She typed a title first: *The Sick Teacher's Cook Book*.

'Forgive me Father, for I have sinned. It has been thirty-five years since my last confession,' Aileen's lyrical voice disturbed the silent gloom of the sleepless night.

She reflected that she had been a good Catholic girl, growing up in Waterford, in Ireland in the 1960s. Her family had worked in the world renowned glass factory. The lush green land and charismatic town had provided her family with security, stability and happiness.

Admitting her transgression aloud in the midnight space surprised her in an unexpected way. She reached down under the chair to recover the half filled glass of whiskey. The liquid first tingled her lips and tongue as she took a sip, then lit a gentle fire as she swallowed the rest of the glass in one. The fingers returned to their work typing: a plan, a manifesto, a justification, perhaps more importantly for Aileen, a confession of her struggle.

Letters appeared, hesitantly, nervously. Guiltily.

Those of us alive today, mistake the seeming solidity of our existence, our daily business providing a collective tectonic plate on which we all stand; where we are balanced precariously, endlessly stumbling through the moments of our life. We fail our ancestors and descendants, those we have loved and those we love still, through determined ignorance.

As the words appeared on the screen and became cathartic sentences, Aileen's invisible shoulders began to relax in the shrouded blackness of her jumper.

No warnings or signs are convincing enough to penetrate bourgeois delusions of luxurious permanence. Seasons, natural and human, become confused. Wars spread like the wildfires that consume our grasslands and forests all over the world. Storms rage, water dries out, pollution has become a desirable and trade-able commodity and opinions and popularity have become more important and reliable than fact, truth and morality. How has all this happened?

The glowing whiteness of the screen became dulled by the electronic black letters; the spectral reflection dimmed and faded. Dark thoughts bubbled around Aileen's head like blobs in a lava lamp. Now was the time. Her fingers tapped on the keyboard, an irregular rhythm bearing a cadence for ephemeral ideas. Her introduction continued.

It is known that the motion of the moon creates the oceans' tides; the ebb and flow of the water over our planet's surface: a placid and serene benefactor, encouraging life to flourish in glorious diversity, or by turns a vengeful hammer that indiscriminately smashes anything in its path against a rocky coastal anvil. Could it be as simple as tiny changes in magnetism, altering the flow of underground water, changes that make people ebb and flow? Kindness and cruelty in equal measure, as the form and structure of the non-linear god-like biological machine in our heads is influenced and changed. Axons and Dendrons formed and joined into ley lines by new thoughts and experiences like mystical monuments to barbarity and civilisation. The planet that bore us broadcasts a plan for our thoughts and actions like a nightly shipping forecast.

Outside the first glow of the dawn of a new Monday morning smudged onto the horizon. A lifetime of stifled anxiety, stress and mental illness was bursting through the shackles of professional respectability into the world with the radiance and glory of the rays of the Sun through a stained glass window.

2

'Sir? Sir...I'm writin' a story about you,' Will sneered, as the parting in his mousy hair fell over one eye, providing him with an accidental squint that added to his unintentionally insolent demeanour.

'Really?' Mr Carpenter feigned interest without missing a beat, his face contorted into a gentle smile. Knees cracking, he lowered himself to the child's level to inspect the day's offering in the exercise book. 'That's interesting, Will,' he glanced at the scrawling, spider-like writing on the page: two dozen poorly formed words, some made up of quite random letters that required considerable effort to de-cypher, 'what's it about?' he sighed with renewed disappointment.

'Well...well it's about you and your tie sir. The tie's an alien and it controls you. Sometimes it gets bored, tightens around your neck so you get a bit strangled,' Will's eyes widened with the obvious pleasure this idea gave him, 'and makes you mean and grumpy.'

The child earnestly waited, a finger dragged the errant strands of hair back across his unwrinkled forehead. His eyes flicked nervously between the striking exercise book on the desk, made up of pages of bright green paper, a result of an overeager Irlens diagnosis, and Mr Carpenter's ear. Will noticed that Mr

Carpenter had tiny curls of white hair growing around the hole of his ear. He wondered how much it would hurt if he pulled one out, and hoped that nothing that gross ever happened to him. Revulsion of adults and adulthood crashed over him like a breaker on the shore and he vowed never to become one himself.

Robert Carpenter gave the story due consideration. His face was an inscrutable mask to the child, who thought that his teacher was thinking long and hard about the merits of his writing. However, Mr Carpenter was merely counting down from five – slowly. He taught at the Thresher Street Primary School in Falmbourne, a mid-sized town in the south-east of England.

The school itself stood between two very different districts of the town. To the north and east, was a fairly affluent estate of period properties hugging the train station that had a fast line to the city of London. To the south and west was one of the most deprived regions of social housing in the south-east. Will, the pupil whose work Robert was evaluating, was from the poorer district.

Robert had once been a man of lofty ideals and patient political activism. At university, he had chaired a respected and lively debating society. His steely gaze and whiplash wit had been known to silence arrogant undergraduates and pompous visiting speakers alike. An amorous admirer, a man named Miles who studied astrophysics, had likened Robert's eyes to the Helix nebula: stellar, deep, multi-tonal and fluorescently shimmering in a certain light. Although flattered, perhaps egotistically so, Robert deflected Miles's advances in favour of an intense

Philosophy post-graduate called Elle. Nevertheless, a photo quality print of the 'Eye of God' in the constellation of Aquarius had adorned a wall wherever he had lived ever since. It had seen him read, drink wine, and seduce Elle. It was a spectator to the comical, yet sweet moment, where he had knelt on the floor in a dressing gown, next to the futon they shared, and opened a small velvet box, pleading the time honoured cliché, 'Please, marry me.'

It had been twenty years since his heady days in university, fifteen of those had been consumed by teaching, the last seven at Thresher Street. The lofty ideals had been tempered by what he called 'compromise'; Elle alternatively called it a 'mortgage', and his steely gaze and whiplash wit sparred pointlessly with innocence and naiveté.

'That sounds really exciting, Will.' Robert had managed to overcome the impulse to be sarcastic to children years before, despite some of them clearly deserving it, and Will was no challenge for his hollow compassion. 'Perhaps you could cast your eye over your work and check it to make sure that you have used your capital letters and full stops properly.'

Will nodded sagely, Mr Carpenter's acceptance of his otherworldly narrative masterpiece was duly noted. He knew that punctuation and grammar was his Achilles heel.

Robert continued with the same note of indoctrinated sincerity in his voice, 'You might want to use a dictionary to check those words that you're not one hundred percent sure of, too.'

He paused to make sure that his advice had garnered a response from Will before he rose slowly, swivelling as he stood, to survey the other children in the room. He saw the stuttering movement of the clock, as it meted out temporal sanctions and rewards to those under its auspices in his peripheral vision, and realised that the small hand had indeed reached the ten, and the long hand had reached the three.

Inhaling slowly until his lungs were full, he boomed: 'Finish the sentence you are on. Tidy your tables and fold your arms 4C.'

The classroom was filled with the clattering sounds of ice-bergs colliding as chairs scraped, desk drawers opened and pens, rulers and dictionaries were submerged into the dark purgatory below the tables' tops, before a preternatural stillness washed through the room.

'Stand quietly behind your chairs,' Robert knew that this instruction was unlikely to be followed to the letter, unless he was willing to waste his own precious fifteen minutes enforcing the strict discipline he espoused, 'have a great break time!'

With this salutary dismissal, the room erupted as children dived for the exit; watching, Robert was put in mind of a wave cascading from a broken dam. At the back of the room, a child with poorly shaved brown hair bobbed in and out of sight, collecting the class ball from the shelf, as the door jammed with eight year olds who all wanted to squeeze through it to the freedom the intermission offered.

Moments later, the maelstrom ebbed away out of earshot. Robert Carpenter stood alone in his Lilliputian fiefdom, rocking gently between the balls of his feet and his heels and back again. Through the long, arched Victorian paned window, he could see the branches of an oak tree sway, slowly and gently divesting itself of its patchwork green and brown cloak, leaf by leaf, as Autumn had suddenly replaced Summer.

Robert often pondered about the history of the room he occupied. How many 'teachers' had been custodians there? Gone were the inaugural days where mortar board and gown were required uniform, instead he wore a plain black v-neck pullover, with a white shirt and grey tie that matched the streaks of hair on his temples, black trousers and black Derby shoes. The only charismatic display of his camouflaged personality were his homage to the Channel 4 newsreader Jon Snow. His socks, bought for him last Christmas by Elle, were grey with stripes of neon pink, cerulean blue and lipstick red. They flashed secretly, as he strode purposefully towards the Staff Room and his caffeine fix.

Each step Robert took was accentuated as he imagined his imperial march to the staccato orchestral sound of Holst's Mars. His dark, brooding alter ego, inspired by the iconic villain of a popular galactic movie franchise, as it provided a welcome retreat during his daily contact with children and his adult peers alike.

3

A pause, a blink, and with a practised non-committal smile, Robert pushed open the Staff Room door and entered.

This was always a risky time of day to go. Would Mrs Simpleton, who taught the Reception class, want to swap duties? Or even worse, want to sit and talk to him about her hilarious morning rolling around on the floor with her five year old 'mates' and getting covered in yoghurt, glue or – something else – she always had a slight smell of ammonia about her.

Robert quietly nodded to a couple of Teaching Assistants and moved over to the coffee machine, taking a nondescript cup out of the cupboard and pouring a tall, black coffee. He closed his eyes and took a sip.

He imagined his route back to the door, avoiding the boorish school leaders' table and timing his pass through the cloud of young, eager staff all desperate to tell him how they had avoided a disastrous encounter with a parent with their quick thinking, or their enthusiasm for a positive can-do approach to classroom behaviour management. He turned and took the first step, straight into the Great White shark.

Mr Syndale, the Deputy Head, loomed and blocked Robert's path with an insincere smile and a sheaf of colourful printouts, beckoning for Robert to follow him across the room towards the younger staff. His shirt was an expensive way to demonstrate that he was different and separate from the rest of them. First among equals, he would say. However, it failed to hide the calories that were stored around his considerable frame from too many rushed lunches and dinners and too much comfort eating to compensate for the stress of needing children to attain arbitrary generalised statistical targets, irrespective of their interest in achieving them at their age.

'Mr Carpenter,' he began with a voice that Robert couldn't help thinking would do better if it uttered several lines from a Carry On movie – more Kenneth Williams than Sid James, 'would you be so kind as to join us? Miss Tallister tells me that you have revolutionised marking!'

Charles Syndale stood opposite to Suzy Tallister, the new Year 5 teacher, next to the low, uncomfortable, cushioned, armless seats designed specifically to give anyone who sat on them for too long a backache. These chairs were exclusively found in staff rooms throughout the country and were provided to help staff to relax and discuss important pedagogical developments. Charles sat down gingerly and Robert noticed that he was wearing the same socks.

Without hesitating, Suzy flashed pearly white teeth and a wide, open, friendly smile, 'I think Robert would agree that we worked on this together! Isn't that right, Rob?'

Robert leaned on a table covered with glossy leaflets advertising an after school sports club and took another sip, nodding and smiling at Mr Syndale.

Suzy turned to pick an exercise book out of a box that had just been marked. As she bent over, her fashionable knee-length skirt rose slightly, uncovering an inch of thigh.

Robert watched as the flat, hard, shark-like eyes of the Deputy flicked lower in small steps. Past shapely hips, toned thighs and over the young woman's well moulded calf muscles, taking in the raised ankles above the shiny heels of the fashionable, but uncomfortable shoes. The Deputy's eyes tracked down to the ground, before his head slowly rose as Suzy turned with a swish of blonde hair, above flashing eyes and attractive features, to provide evidence of the efficacy of the simple marking method.

Robert wondered if Suzy knew, or even intentionally encouraged Charles Syndale's regular mental defilement of her body. He felt sorry and slightly ashamed, knowing that he was certainly no better. He wished that he had the same super powers as his alter ego and imagined squeezing the breath out of Charles with his force grip, before returning to reality and realising that both Charles and Suzy were waiting for him to speak.

Suzy sat down next to Syndale, being careful to leave a few inches distance between their arms, before looking at Robert expressively.

'I'm sorry, but I have to get back to class. It was mostly Suzy's ideas,' he lied, 'so she can fill you in on how it works.'

Without waiting for a response, Robert swam through the crowd with the grace and urgency of a seal escaping a pod of

Orcas, leaving Suzy behind as she moved closer to the Deputy with a book open in her lap for Charles to scrutinise.

He emerged, hoping to return to the relative safety of his classroom without further incident, walking purposefully and gazing intently at the floor three feet in front of him. He did not see Aaron Parminster approaching.

'Hi Rob!' chimed Aaron, with the camaraderie of a fellow excavator at the chalk face. His permanent childlike expression, on his slightly flaccid face, gave Aaron the appearance a 1970's children's TV presenter. Somewhere between Brian Cant and a young Chris Tarrant. 'How's it going in the old four by four?'

'Sorry Aaron, I have children in my room and I have to get back. It's going great, how are you?' Robert sidestepped and carried on walking, maintaining his momentum, raising his cup of coffee in greeting as he passed him.

'Oh fine, you know me,' Aaron's voice rose on the last syllable as if he was a cheerful cockney chimney sweep in a period drama, 'here, 'ave you heard about London?'

Robert slowed his pace and turned slightly as he shook his head to indicate that he had not heard, trapped into extending his interaction beyond a simple salutation, and wishing that he had not bothered with the coffee at all this morning.

'Been another attack! In London,' Mr Parminster unconsciously stepped forward with one leg to deliver this news, dropping one shoulder, giving the impression that he had delivered a killer punchline in a 1920s vaudeville act, 'people have…died.' Aaron mouthed the last word, not wishing to actually say it, in case a vulnerable child overheard their conversation.

'Oh.' Robert mouthed back. He raised his coffee cup in farewell and then continued on his way back to the classroom to enjoy the last few moments of peace before the maelstrom returned for the next preprepared and pre-digested TV dinner of a maths lesson.

Outside in the early Autumn warmth, basked the school of children. Girls bounced, crossing and uncrossing their legs to an unknown beat.

Herds of boys dramatically swept around the field, never wanting to be more than a couple of metres from a ricocheting ball, oblivious to team tactics or strategy. The spaces in between were filled with children of all sizes: running, jumping, chasing, squealing, eating, crying, talking and shouting. The din was symphonic.

On the playground, on an area marked out as a netball court, stood Will and his best friend Toby. Together they carelessly tossed a ball back and forth, remembering their epic weekend building a tree shaped like an elephant in Minecraft. Neither wanted to draw attention to themselves. The boys always made sure that they were never too far away from the safety of the duty teachers. Proximity to the adults provided shelter like an umbrella from the rain of verbal insults and physical intimidation by the confident and popular children. Today that was provided by Mrs Maguire, a wise and experienced senior teacher of twenty-five years, who taught Year 2, and Miss Aileen Byrne, the Head Teacher.

The two staff stood near each other, but not together. There was an empty area around Miss Byrne whose perimeter of personal space was rarely breached. She stood today, dressed in her preferred long black overcoat, a splash of peacock colours provided by the neck scarf tied loosely around her neck, the breeze tickled through her raven black hair. Imposing.

Aileen's eyes danced with the merriment that she saw before her and her demeanour was far from unapproachable. Her sweet smile delighted the small children around her, as some danced and cawed, flapping their arms as they circled around (the children, and the parents, had nicknamed Miss Byrne 'Blackbird' long ago).

The last of the morning passed uneventfully for Robert, as twenty-nine eight year olds learned all about equivalent fractions by drawing out their own versions of a fraction wall in their maths books, differentiated by challenge, of course.

After he had dismissed them for lunch, he closed the door behind the last child to leave and sat at a table at the rear of the room, hoping that he would not be visible to any casual passer-by. He arranged the books he needed to mark in front him like a child's barricade to fend off any unwanted intrusion into his solitary hour.

Before a daily ascent up Mount Formative-marking, Robert decided to investigate the trouble in London. Elle worked in London, as a PA to a marketing jerk, and although he was not overly concerned, Robert thought it best to make sure that the trains would still be running.

He remembered that the morning digest of sound-bites and preachy newsreaders had been pretty standard from the news he caught before leaving for work. More war in the Middle East; how we should all be ashamed for not helping 'migrant' asylum seekers to escape their misery in another country; how we should be ashamed for not providing more aid to the starving, the hungry and dispossessed. All of this Robert felt to be true, but he ruefully reflected that there was always an 'us' and always a 'them'.

Politicians, bankers and corporate tax-dodgers had released a new tiny scandalous snippet of their continuing corruption, dishonesty and fraud. Not too much to anger the mob, just enough to keep them sneering and smouldering. Enough to keep everyone at their posts, taking the moral high ground. Letting the wealthy conspirators keep all the spoils.

As always, there had been a segment about the imminent collapse of the global ecosystem and our need to mend our profligate ways. Additionally, time was allocated to how we needed to donate to a worthy charity, tidying up the mess that the corrupt, dishonest and fraudulent politicians, bankers and corporate tax-dodgers had promised us was the future, using products and technology that would make our lives easier, instead of shorter.

Finally, there had been a large report about the sport. Robert wondered whether the producers of televised rolling news made the sport segment as long as the rest of the news put together on purpose to keep most of the working population ignorant of what was actually happening in the world. A coffee, bowl of cereal and shower meant that most people saw less than 20 minutes of the news. If there was an even split between the news and sport then there was a good chance that all we would find out is whether Andy Murray had managed to develop a sense of humour, or if any one of a number of European football managers in the Premier League had made a humorous faux pas in stuttering, pigeon English.

'His shit - was best I have seen!' a famous Portuguese celebrity manager had remarked that morning, after another unremarkable ninety minutes of ball kicking.

He read the news headlines on his smartphone app and realised quickly that something was different this time. The tide of terror attacks by rogue suicidal religious fundamentalists and right wing isolationist nutters, committed by individuals in vans, or with knives or even the rare co-ordinated attack with explosives, had been going on for years. A perpetual risk. A common thread. Predictable. Avoidable.

He clicked onto the live thread where reporters provided a timeline of developments using the reduced syntax and word count afforded by many social media platforms. Rob was shocked by the first line – *Terror plot kills 100s in co-ordinated attack across capital* – and read on: *Schools in several London Boroughs targeted by bombers and lone wolves in morning massacre.*

Aaron's face rose around the door, flushed and moon-like, 'Staffroom briefing: two minutes.' Aaron intended to emphasise a sense of the importance to the unusual event, yet he singularly failed to communicate this as his voice rose on the last syllable. Instead, Robert rose and followed wondering if the school office had received 'the call'.

The two men strode along the corridor returning to the staffroom silently, each pondering the meaning of the meeting. Separately, they had come to the same conclusion that it must be the Ofsted Inspection that was due.

Each of the men were hoping that they would be passed over by the anticipated inspectors, in whose hands clipboards carried attached sheets, with tick boxes and assessment criteria, by which the adults would be tested against.

Robert had been through three inspections and had survived them all with a 'Good with Outstanding' grading, and a series of targets to improve his practise that he had no intention of implementing. The last time had been the worst as the four middle aged inspectors stalked around the school like the Gestapo. They disguised themselves by dressing like air-line stewards, rolling their small luggage bags behind them in formation.

The Inspectors spent their time interrogating children, parents and staff at will using short clipped questions and wearing a disapproving sneer at all times. He felt like the teachers had been separated during the process – you go to the chain gang, you go to the 'hole'. Several long standing members of staff had vanished soon after, never to be seen or spoken of again. It had been this way for years now.

Robert weaved towards the corner of the staff room and tried to look inconspicuous. When? He wondered. When did someone decide that the adults who had passed all of the tests and exams in their childhood, adolescence and young adulthood to gain the qualifications needed to be able to teach, needed to be tested even more? It had become a surveillance regime of almost monthly testing through lesson observations, book monitoring - to ensure that teachers provided detailed feedback and development targets for children on a daily basis in all of their English, Maths and foundation subject books - pupil progress meetings and termly data analysis, that surely made teachers in the UK the most over tested people on the planet.

It didn't matter how many years service had been dedicated, or the circumstances of the teacher's life. If one of the monitoring methods detected a hint that the delivery of the proscribed learning did not meet 'national standards', that could be it. The madness of this always overwhelmed him, so he missed the entrance of Miss Byrne, the enigmatic and slightly chilling Head Teacher, as she floated towards the notice board, which she always stood in front of, to address the staff. The memory of her standing in front of the board covered in festive graffiti last Christmas, framed by red and green tinsel and appearing to have had reindeer antlers drawn onto her head made Robert smile every time.

She stood stark against the whiteboard, her raven black hair and pale white skin was emphasised as she was dressed in a formless black turtle-neck sweater, that hid any curves to indicate femininity and an expensive, grey, pencil skirt that ended below the knee. Only the neck scarf proved that there was a personality within the clothed shape.

'Between Eight thirty and Eight forty-five a.m. this morning,' the Head Teacher immediately began, 'around twenty separate terrorist attacks took place targetting schools in London.' The hum of the room was silenced.

'White vans packed with explosives were driven at school gates and detonated in crowds of children and parents. Individuals in masks also gained access to school buildings and attacked pupils and teachers with knives and bottles of bleach.'

Aileen let every word drip from her lips like grease from a roast chicken. She feasted on the impact of her blunt, matter-of-fact delivery and felt vindication for what she was about to do course through her veins. Each member of staff were left to their own horror and personal outrage of this event.

'I have been in contact with the relevant authorities and other local schools to arrange a staggered end to the school day. Of course we do not want panic, but an orderly evacuation. The closure of all schools nationally has been arranged due to this unprecedented event.'

She went on calmly and impassively, her soft almost musical accent belying the gravity of the information that she was sharing. She knew that all they wanted was to leave as soon as possible and collect into their gossip groups and chatter about their own 'feelings' or conspiracy theories. Being in the room with them disgusted her.

She went on: 'It has been agreed that we will be closing the school at two forty-five p.m. today and a text message has been sent to parents informing them of this. There will be no wraparound care or clubs. It is essential that the children are aware of the early closing today, but all they have to know is that we are undergoing essential maintenance to the school boiler.'

The staff remained hushed and all eyes were on Aileen. Some were wet with tears, others looked grave and pale. It's not happening to you, she thought, you haven't suffered anything. They weren't your children, or your brothers or sisters, your mum or dad. It never is. She knew she needed to wrap this up.

'I expect all staff to escort their classes out today. No child leaves until you have confirmed who you are releasing them into the care of. I don't expect you to stay on the school site later than Three p.m. Go home and watch the news.' Watch others' pain, she thought.

'The Governors have requested a meeting to discuss the site security measures, but I'll see you all in the morning. Mr Carpenter, could I see you in my office?' As she walked back out through the stunned staffroom, she tied her hair into a bunch with a demure grace that surprised Robert.

'I think she enjoyed that,' he said to no-one in particular, but he received a grunt from Charles Syndale who had sidled over unseen.

'You have been summoned to the chamber of secrets, Robert. Best you go quickly.' Charles had somehow managed to make the Head Teacher's request into his instruction, to reaffirm his authority, despite his jealousy at not being forewarned of this himself, or being invited into the inner sanctum now. He sulked off to find Suzy.

Robert weighed up whether he should first go back to his room so he could text Elle and make sure she was OK, or go and find out what the Head Teacher wanted. Ordinarily, he avoided any interaction with her like the plague. He respected her, she ran a tight ship and left everyone to get on with their jobs. There was an economy about her, like the way she had delivered the information today, straight to the point without wasted time or effort. Robert noted the rare quality time and again and appreciated the forthrightness. Still, there was something about her that left him cold, disquieted.

He decided to bite the bullet and go straight to Aileen Byrne's office and then get back to his room to rush through the marking so he didn't have to take it home. He began to mentally prepare a change to his planned afternoon lessons to ensure that it was an activity that required no marking at all – perhaps some research on Henry VIII or some times tables maths games on the laptops. As he opened the door to leave the staffroom, he noticed that Suzy and Charles were sitting together, shoulders touching. She crossed her legs quickly allowing the heel of her shoe to tap against his shin.

Robert quickly turned his head away and walked through the threshold into the corridor feeling guilty at observing the private moment and something like disgust and envy well up in his stomach.

6

Aileen had returned to her office as quickly as she could. The events in London were presenting her with the opportunity to put the plans that had been developing like a cancerous tumour in her belly for years into action.

No-one would be watching, or expecting an inside job like this. All eyes would be turned outward towards the extremists. It was so exciting that her hands shook as she filled the kettle and prepared the cafetière and the cups.

Robert liked coffee, she knew that. She made sure that the little cartons of UHT milk were carefully arranged and had been correctly labelled with the small green and red stickers that she had placed on them. Red for safe and Green for danger. She checked to make sure that she could find the small pin prick in the green labelled cartons.

It had been years since she had collected up all the old thermometers in school and 'disposed' of them by taking them home and emptying their mercurial contents in an airtight beaker. Waiting for the time to be right. She had purchased medical syringes online – it was amazing, the things you could buy without a certified need – she had meticulously measured out doses of mercury and the newest, most concentrated rat poison she could find, and added them to a group of the UHT cartons that she had begun to insist were used in her office. She added little coloured stickers, to group them by use-by date, she had informed her cock of a Deputy, Charles, and Ruth Maddison - the President of the Parent Teacher Association - during a meeting a year ago. Charles had joked that the school was operating so well, Aileen had to time to waste on such an endeavour. Ruth saw it as another strange ritual from an oddball Head Teacher; she wished they could just have someone normal.

Aileen's silent, brooding presence at the regular fundraising events had lost the PTA so much money that she was no longer expected to attend them. Ruth had recalled the last empty Valentine's disco with Aileen standing with arms folded, passive-aggressively watching over the small, determined group of Year 6 girls dancing the 'Macarena', wringing every last drop of fun out of their last year in Primary, no matter what. Instead, the ladies of the PTA had turned to the charming Deputy, Charles Syndale, who had proved to be a hit with the stay at home, and single, mums of the school.

Aileen scooped the second dessert spoon of coffee powder in to the cafetière precisely, when an irregular knock on the door of her office disturbed her. She looked over her shoulder and saw the portrait of Robert in the small square window.

'Come in, Mr Carpenter,' Aileen jerked her head to invite Robert in and watched her hands and body complete the task of making coffee autonomously. Her mind raced to plot the possible responses to her initial gambit like a chess champion.

Finding as many branching pathways as possible and planning move and countermove to ensure that the game reached the required destination of check mate.

'What have I done wrong?' Robert sighed as he entered the sparsely decorated office.

In the corner, by a window overlooking the school car park, was Miss Byrne's perfectly neat and ordered desk. No personal effects cluttered the space. No pictures or funny pencil pots adorned the Head's workspace. Apart from a single folder laying squarely on the corner, it was clear and efficient like a Camp Kommandants should be.

Behind it stood two grey four drawer filing cabinets that housed, in alphabetical order, folders on each child and adult in the school. Foolscap biographies of surveillance describing, sometimes in detail, the life and times of each individual during their stay in the institution. Every incident, every fight, argument or element of perceived misconduct, even if it was only suspected by someone, was logged in these folders. It was the closest thing to the secret police that the government could afford. Robert imagined that they were regularly and secretly examined in dark smoky rooms by faceless fascist stooges. Little did he know that the last inspection had required Miss Byrne to do just that. Two of the inspectors requested seemingly random files and interrogated her on their contents.

In the middle of the room, stood the oval meeting table and adjacent to the door, was the office mini-kitchen that had been installed when Miss Byrne had taken over. The thought of actually sharing physical cutlery and dishes with the staff made her vomit in the staff toilet, which of course she cleaned and disinfected herself before and after her every use.

Robert shuffled forward, stepping with his right foot twice in a nervous manner and moved to the meeting table. Aileen always sat at the head of the table and staff had discussed what placement in the other five seats could possibly mean. If you were told to sit at the foot of the table, facing Miss Byrne, you were sacked and would probably be made to 'disappear'. Presumably, to the gulag that all 'disappeared' teachers were removed to, out of sight for the collective good.

Elle had joked that there must be a school in Slough where pupils ate their way through all the crap teachers who got sacked, like zombies gorging during the apocalypse. Robert did not find it at all amusing at the time and pointed out that she wouldn't think it was funny either, when his turn came, as they both knew it would with a sad certainty.

If you were seated by Aileen's left hand, she wanted something from you; by her right hand, you were going to be promoted; the far left seat indicated she favoured you; the far right seat, the nearest to the door, was a neutral seat and indicated neither favour or displeasure. Just business.

Robert hesitated, waiting to be invited to sit. Miss Byrne turned, carried the tray of coffee and cups, which she placed on the table then sat in her usual chair.

'Well sit down then, I am very busy today, Mr Carpenter,' she indicated the seat nearest the door.

Just business, Robert thought with relief.

'You're not in any trouble. Not today, anyway. There are more important things than your insolence and incompetence happening you know.' Aileen thought that this levity would set him at ease.

'Yes, of course,' Robert was totally thrown off balance by the attempt at humour. He wondered if she was really joking about the injury and death of hundreds of children and parents?

'I need a coffee,' Aileen poured herself a generous amount and held the cafetière over a second, empty cup, 'would you like one, Robert?' she mustered what she thought was the most disarming and welcoming look and tried to twist her features to match.

'Yes, thank you ... Aileen,' Robert replied stutteringly. The informality of coffee and first names with the Head Teacher alerted him to danger. He reminded himself that he was in the 'Just business' seat and prepared himself.

'You're welcome.' Aileen was desperately trying to contain her excitement.

The anticipation of this moment almost overwhelmed her. She concentrated on controlling her arms and hands to ensure that the coffee did not dribble, splash or miss the cup. Maintaining a steady flow until the liquid filled two thirds of the volume the container, she lifted the cafetière with a flourish to indicate that the process was complete.

'Help yourself to milk and sugar,' the moment had arrived and she calmed her voice, 'the little green stickers tell you that the milk is still in date.' She smiled benevolently and picked up a carton with a red sticker. 'I'll finish off these. They went out of date last month, but I don't like to waste.'

With a well practised flick of her thumb, she snapped the seal and looked up to make sure that Robert had taken the correct carton. Staff respected Robert, and beginning her campaign by poisoning him slowly and watching him degenerate as the heavy metal broke down his nervous system and insinuated itself into his brain, inhibiting neurological chemicals that sustained healthy, intelligent brain function would be devastating to morale. She thought of the recipe title for the cookbook that she would write during the night's sleepless hours. *Heavy Metal Americano for King Rat*. The smile froze as she saw Robert lift the steaming cup to his lips.

'Are you sure you wouldn't take a milk with that, Mr Carpenter?' Aileen poured her own measure of the unadulterated ultra-pasteurised liquid into her cup and examined Robert coldly.

'No, thank you. My wife is dairy intolerant, so I've had to give it up too! Solidarity. You know. Soya milk just isn't the same, so I've just got used to it.'

He looked at the contents of the cup and took another sip. It was a cheap blend that left a tang like oily fish in his mouth and he was disappointed.

'It's great, thank you again.' He smiled and asked, 'How can I help you today, Miss Byrne? I'm sure you're really very busy, especially with everything that's going on in London.' Robert placed the cup down. 'I don't want to take up too much of your time.'

He looked at Aileen meaningfully having returned the exchange to a less familiar, more formal and business-like footing. He felt more assured by the direction the conversation was taking.

'Right.' Aileen folded her arms.

A disappointment. Her grand campaign had not got off to a good start, as none of the avenues that she had considered minutes earlier lead to this conclusion. Was she really clever enough or worthy enough? She considered just stopping her great confessional work there and then and find another way.

For a moment her face betrayed a sense of confusion and bewilderment. Chaos reigned in her eyes, and Robert gained a brief insight into the slow dissolution of the Head Teacher's sanity. He didn't know whether to run from the room or jump to her side to help her.

Before he could make a decision, Aileen continued, 'We were scheduled to meet with Miss Tracey this afternoon, about Lewis's appearance and you know, general hygiene.' She had regained her composure and resolve, her manner was crisp and economic. The crisis was over and Aileen knew what her next steps needed to be to get things back on track. She was in control.

'Yes...that is today isn't it?' Robert had forgotten and wondered if he had remembered to fill in the paperwork that he found last week in his pigeon hole.

Aileen reached over to her desk and picked up the folder that was three inches thick labelled in the top corner 'Lewis Tracey' and opened it. Robert was relieved to see the green safeguarding form that he had filled in last Thursday as the first page.

'We were both going to meet with Miss Tracey. As I understand from this form, you have significant safeguarding concerns beyond the clothing and hygiene,' Aileen paused and read back through the description of the odour emanating from the child, the food stained clothing and the appearance of four small bruises on his shoulder, one on his collar bone – a hand grip - the body map indicated their exact location.

'You saw the bruises as the boy changed for PE as I understand it, and you have already tried to call the mother in, but she didn't turn up.' Aileen turned her cold, hard penetrating gaze upon Robert. 'Is that about it?' Aileen had stopped modulating her voice and the monotone question sounded more like a threat to Robert.

Robert was struggling to process what he believed he just witnessed. Had he just seen behind the curtain of the Head Teacher's unflappable and competent professional mask? The wild-eyed manic expression seemed to cross her face like a cloud that briefly covered the Sun on a windy day. His heart had begun to pound in his chest in sympathetic response; he felt a clamminess in his palms and a line of sweat had emerged on his forehead.

Robert tried to answer the question, but the bitter coffee had dried his mouth out. He willed his thick tongue to move and looked at the cup. Something about the reported safeguarding concern had triggered an anger in the woman sitting at the end of the table that left him feeling vulnerable and sick. He wanted to leave the room desperately.

'Yes,' was all he could manage as he pushed the cup of cooling coffee away from him and sat as far back in his chair as he could.

'I see,' Aileen's voice had become musical and magical once more, but she noted that Robert's face had grown ashen and his eyes darted from the cup, to the folder and to her face, then away again. He seemed nervous, she thought. Does he know? A paranoid whisper insinuated itself into her mind, a wisp of smoke through a crack in her psyche.

'Well, I see no reason to change the time and I will conduct the meeting with Miss Tracey personally. The safety and well-being of the children in this school is paramount and this case clearly needs escalating beyond you.' She wanted him out and hoped the insult would hit home. 'Is that a problem for you?' Aileen's threatening monotone returned and she fixed her attention on the folder on the table in front of her.

'No problem at all,' Robert replied without a hint of feeling insulted, grabbing the opportunity to escape in the hope that the meeting would now come to a close so that he could return to the classroom and his barricade of books.

'Then, that will be all. I will update you tomorrow if I need to.' She slammed the folder closed and pushed her chair back in dismissal.

Robert took his cue to leave instantly and almost jumped from his chair, needing only one step to reach the door. There was no hesitation now, and without turning he whipped open the portal and stepped into the cool of the corridor.

It was like stepping back to Earth from another dimension. The atmosphere in the Head Teacher's office had been heavy and foreboding, menacing even. Here, amid the sounds of children clattering plastic plates and chatting through mouths, half-filled with food, Robert felt his sweat dry, his heart rhythm return to its regular pace. He took a steadying breath and straightened his shoulders.

Already the encounter seemed distant and dream-like. Surely his imagination had tricked him. He began to walk back towards his classroom and dismissed his emotional reaction as a delayed response to the shocking news of schools less than seventy miles away being the target of terrorists. There was the terror, the madness and inhumanity, he told himself. The day must have been more than trying for the Head Teacher too, he realised, as she was responsible for the safety and security of all the children and the staff in the face of a real, tangible threat. Was there really any surprise that her mood was changeable? She was a bit obsessed with Safeguarding and Child Protection. Had his reporting of his concerns and attempt to meet with the child's parent been interpreted as his failure? Did the unpredictable head teacher hold him personally responsible for the suffering of the child in his class?

The door to the staffroom opened with a turbulent gust of warm air just as Robert reached it and Charles Syndale burst out, walking in the direction that Robert had just come from. He looked Robert in the eye with a smug 'cat got the cream' expression and gave a single snort of derision as he registered that Robert looked like he was the lone survivor of a terrible accident.

7

Aileen sat looking at the wasted effort on the table before her. The unused milk cartons with little green stickers looked lamentable on the tray. What on earth had she been thinking? She had wished Robert Carpenter harm for so long. His laconic deportment and pretentious air had always irritated her.

She recalled the interview seven years ago, where he had impressed her with his lack of understanding that a man could not find any liberation from within feminist doctrine. His patronising, patriarchal attempt to adopt, appropriate and undermine the radical philosophical and political movement that meant so much to her, enraged her so much that she decided to hire him; if only to crush his soul. To provide him with an opportunity to experience the gender based oppression that she and women all over the world throughout human history had suffered first hand. She wanted him to feel the frustration of a stagnating career, of being passed over for promotions that he clearly deserved and being arbitrarily belittled on a regular basis with no way to gain redress or respond.

He had, frustratingly, always managed to resist her attempts to deconstruct his natural teaching talent. She had failed to disrupt his innate strategies due to his consistent 'good' lesson observations and his meticulous recitation of the teacher standards in feedback meetings. Then, three years ago Charles Syndale had been hired, the governors had insisted. She considered Charles to be the epitome of male boorishness. Using the term 'misogynist' didn't really seem adequate. He was a total cock. Her need to inflict pain on Robert Carpenter had had to be put on hold.

She stood, collecting her thoughts and the remains of the failed poisoning attempt when Charles's face appeared in the window with a rat-at-tat-tat tap on the door that interrupted her covering tracks. He walked in without being invited and sat down in the chair that Robert had recently vacated.

'So Boss,' Charles began with just a hint of sarcasm and insouciance, he knew she hated the gender specific term. Picking up the cup that sat in front of him, he wrapped his hand around it to test its warmth.

'What's the big picture?'

Charles knew that his observable lack of deference towards Aileen grated on her. He may as well have walked into the office with an old fashioned chalkboard and begun scrapping his fingernails down it, over and over again. Reaching over, he spooned two sugars into the cup and picked up a carton of milk.

Aileen remained quiet, but slowly sat back down, a Cheshire cat grin spreading from ear-to-ear. The carton had a green sticker.

Oblivious, Charles poured the contents into the cup and stirred. Unsatisfied by the muddy colour of the coffee, he reached back over and emptied another, then another of the small UHT cartons into the coffee. Finally happy with the consistency, he raised the cup in a salute and drained the contents in a single gulp.

8

Sitting alone in Reception on an uncomfortable sofa, Maggie Tracey waited nervously.

The school had long since emptied; the children and staff had beat a hasty retreat to the safety and security of being anywhere but near a school. Maggie had seen the reports on the news app on her phone. Grainy images of blue-light emergency services surrounding the smouldering remains of a decimated vehicle outside the iron railings of an unknown school, somewhere in London. The report described scenes of utter 'carnage' akin to the bombed out streets of Kabul, Baghdad or downtown Aleppo. Certainly not what the news expected to be describing in Wandsworth or Enfield. She did not want to be in the school, she felt like the building was in the cross hairs of an invisible giant sitting above the clouds, waiting for the moment to strike with a lightning shock and devastating speed.

Her knees appeared through her ripped jeans over the edge of her phone screen, alternately bouncing as if she was preparing for a hundred metre sprint. Her jaw clenched and unclenched, then continued to furiously chew at the nicotine replacement chewing gum.

She seemed to be constantly fighting someone to keep her son with her. Lewis was the only thing that she had that she felt she had any ownership or control over. He was her son. They had taken him away before. This Miss Byrne, she was one of them. Why did everyone always seem to pick on her? Maggie had decided some time ago that she was fed up with the shit end of the stick. She wasn't going to take it any more.

As a means of coping with abusive partners, a violent pimp, a lecherous dealer, who never left her alone, nosy neighbours, the 'Old Bill' or social workers, Maggie had developed a range of strategies. She watched family feuds and confrontational ex-lovers on morning TV shows for examples of how to behave both passively and aggressively, but always vilely: she could shout and scream and keep repeating a single personal insult or accusation; she could sit or stand silently and sullenly, ignoring every other party around her and rudely focus her attention on her phone; she could wear a fixed smear of a grin and inform everyone around her that she 'knew her rights' over and over again, no matter whether that was a relevant or pertinent statement; finally, if all else failed, there was the acceptance of wrongdoing and the redemptive plea that things would change, be different in the future somehow. She would no longer fear anyone. The world would bend to her way.

She sat and considered how to play the bitch of a Head Teacher this time. Lewis had been a pain recently. Always complaining of being hungry, or that his friends played on Fortnite all the time. Why couldn't he have a games console like them? He stilled pissed himself in his sleep, the little shit. She worked hard every night, risking a beating or worse, and she came home to a flat stinking of his fear. She thought he needed to toughen up. Charlie, her dealer, had already asked if he was ready to do some muling around the town for him. Be a nice little earner for her too!

'Thank you, Harry, we would have had a freezing cold winter if you hadn't spotted that.' Miss Byrne had been in an ebullient mood all afternoon, despite the urgent crisis and sense of imminent danger that had beset Head Teachers all across the country. She strode beside the county sponsored gas engineer with a bounce in her step that surprised the diplomatic tradesman, who had just diagnosed an expensive malfunction in the school heating system.

'How long will it take to get the parts you need to fix it?' Aileen's mood could not be dimmed, even though she knew that the cost would put a large dent in her already tight capital spend budget that she could allocate to maintaining the Victorian era building.

Budget cuts had meant that she had not been able to replace the previous caretaker, Mr Carmichael, when he took early retirement due to a lung condition two years earlier. Waiting for the diagnosis had given Aileen sleepless nights.

The Boiler Room had contained Asbestos, and she had put back the removal by three years when she was first appointed in an attempt to get the school out of deficit. She would be responsible. When he told her he had COPD she almost cried with relief, but she did not sleep again. Insomnia had become her most reliable companion.

'Difficult to say Miss Byrne, I'll get it ordered right away and be in touch,' he replied, lifting the Visitor badge over his head, dropping it on the Reception counter and pressing the Visitor's button on the touch screen in one swift, deft move. Wasting no time, he found his name on the screen, signing out with an experienced and practised motion. He seemed eager to leave.

'Would you like to come this way, Miss Tracey?' Miss Byrne didn't miss a beat, but immediately turned her attention to the parent waiting uncomfortably in the harshly lit corridor next to the reception desk. Without waiting for an answer, she walked away down the corridor, towards the the meeting room situated around the corner, silently.

Harry pressed the green button marked 'Exit' at his shoulder height, disabling the magnetic security lock, facilitating his release from the school. He spared a look back at Maggie and with a shiver, walked purposefully towards his van in the car park. His gait a little quicker, his steps a little longer than usual.

Silent treatment, Maggie decided as she watched the Gas engineer leave hurriedly. She took a deep breath and walked quickly to catch up with Miss Byrne. The sweep of her arms rubbed the nylon material together on her green Modish bomber jacket, making her sound like an oversized duck waddling along the corridor.

In the distance, the hum of the vacuum cleaner's motor indicated that she was not alone with the Head bitch.

9

Aileen waited, holding the door open to the meeting room and watched as Maggie Tracey approached. Cheap, strappy, white high heeled shoes, toenails with chipped pink nail polish and clearly painful bunions. Ripped, bleached, skinny denim jeans. A small checked cowgirl style blouse that was too small, Aileen thought. Hips and cleavage were clearly visible. A green bomber jacket was the only sensible item, in Aileen's opinion. The evenings were certainly drawing in and getting colder, she thought.

As Maggie drew closer, Aileen appreciated how much make-up the single mother had plastered on. Too much foundation gave her face a distinctly orange tinge, at odds with the pale skin visible in other areas. Maggie's right eye seemed to have had more than its fair share of application. The blue and purple bruise that had been evident days earlier had been easier to mask once it had become yellow.

The fingernails looked unnaturally long and rectangular, the false nails were coated with shellac, the same colour as the toes. She had big hooped golden earrings and her long mousy hair was pulled tight into a pony tail, stretching the skin of her forehead and cheeks taught. It reduced, but did not eliminate the bags under her eyes. A shame, Aileen considered, she could be pretty.

'Please, take a seat Miss Tracey. May I call you Maggie?' Aileen offered her hand in greeting, 'You can call me Aileen, please," she indicated a seat.

Maggie shrugged and collapsed into the chair, hooked an arm over the back rest and struck a pose, placing her large smartphone on the table in front of her. The screen displayed a chat was open on a social media platform. She chewed loudly and wondered why there was a plastic shopping bag, a biro, a length of string and a soapy looking used jay cloth laying neatly in the middle of the table in front of her.

Aileen moved the slider on the door to inform the cleaner that a meeting was taking place and let the door slowly swing closed with a satisfying 'click' to indicate the fire door was secure, but unlocked. At the internal window, she twisted a rod to close the blinds to ensure that they had complete privacy. The hum of the cleaner's hoover was no louder than the quiet drone of a bee, signalling that it was over the other side of the school. The Key Stage 1 break out area, she thought.

Aileen took her place at the table, her back to the door. She noticed the puzzled look on Maggie's face as she looked quizzically at the oddly assembled items.

'Year 3 have been making kites with Mr Parminster,' Aileen dismissed the pile and moved on. 'Do you know why we are having this meeting, Maggie?' Cool, calm, collected and consummately professional, Aileen began the meeting the same way she had with countless other neglectful and abusive parents.

With a measured, friendly smile; she was determined to give Maggie a chance.

Maggie gave a much practised haughty shrug to indicate that she didn't know, or care. With a casual flick she turned the phone to stand-by and dropped it, screen down, on the table in front of her, turning her gaze to her finger nails and admiring the high sheen. It had taken just a glance at Aileen's black turtle neck sweater and shapeless grey skirt for her to decide her opinion: lesbian.

'Well,' Aileen focused all the empathy she could muster, 'we're concerned about the well-being of your son, Lewis. How have things been at home?'

Maggie sighed petulantly, the silent treatment wasn't going to work, 'Fine, why? What's Lewis been sayin'?' She shook her head, whipping her hair first towards, then away from Miss Byrne, with a wiggle of her chest that was intended to be a tease.

'That boy lies y'know? I do my best dunni,' she sucked her teeth, 'He won't go t'sleep when I tell 'im to. He don't eat what I tell 'im to.' Maggie raised her hands imploringly, 'What am I supposed to do?'

Aileen's thin veil of empathy was instantly pierced as Maggie's insolent attitude wasted her good grace.

'Well, you could start by washing his clothes, providing varied and interesting meals, spend time making stimulating experiences and paying him some attention so he knows he is loved! The child is your son, not an inconvenience that interrupts your life. In short be a mother, you moron.'

Maggie waggled a single index finger in front of her face intermittently, but sat gobsmacked, the months of watching idiotic morning TV had not prepared her for brutal honesty. Her mouth hung open, the chewing gum sat visible to Aileen on her molars.

'Lewis's hygiene has deteriorated, there is a an unpleasant odour about him. His clothes are visibly dirty and his teacher identified a series of stains on his tee-shirt and trousers that were evident for three days in a row. He believed that they would have been there longer, but they may have been superseded by a large tomato sauce stain from the baked beans he had at lunchtime,' she looked at her notes briefly, 'last Wednesday. The teacher also observed,' Aileen went on without stopping for breath, undaunted by the brutality with which she was speaking to the increasingly agitated mother opposite, 'that Lewis's hair seemed to have been shaved by a blind goat and the filth that caked his body last week upset the other children and isolated him from them, as they did not want to sit next to him.' Aileen began to enjoy herself and interwove heavy sarcasm into her polite, professionally lilting voice.

A single tear washed down the dry Martian-like landscape of Maggie's face, scoring a pale pink floodplain through the foundation caked cheek.

'How da...who d'ya fink....you 'ave no idea...I'm a single muvver, yeah, its hard. You have no idea of what I go frew ev'ry day, ev'ry night,' Maggie stammered through her indignation, her breath catching in her throat.

Aileen closed her eyes and recited from memory, 'Maggie, you are a suspected prostitute and you are certainly misusing drugs. I would imagine you are a habitual user. Social Services have removed Lewis from your care on two separate occasions in the last three years. The first when you were found soliciting. You took clients home to your flat, to the room next to the one your son was sleeping in...' Aileen gently shook her head disapprovingly, eyes still closed, she was preparing herself.

'The second time because you were arrested with a quantity of cocaine in your bag at the port of Dover.'

She opened her eyes and stood quietly. She stepped soundlessly around the table and stood behind the weeping mother. Maggie had her hands over her eyes and was panting to catch her breath.

Aileen placed her hands consolingly on her shoulders, 'Miss Tracey, you are not fit to be a mother.'

This last insult was like red rag to a bull and Maggie swivelled and stood in a single motion, pushing Aileen's hands away from her.

'Not fit?' Maggie snarled, the tears and the shame forgotten. 'I'll tell you who wasn't fit to be a mother. Mine.'

In full flow, Maggie spoke rhythmically, her arms gesticulating wildly like the fighting ex-lovers that she admired on TV.

She pushed her face close to Aileen, 'She used to bring her boyfriends 'ome. Laughed when they got me drunk or stoned. Then let them use me for thirty quid.' She stood back to let the impact of her abuse hit home on the impassive Head bitch. 'I was fifteen years old!' Maggie sank back into the chair.

'When they beat me, yeah, she told me not to argue wiv 'em. Do what they wanted. Take the money. I would never let anyone harm Lewis, no-one raises a hand to him,' she turned imploringly.

'A member of staff has witnessed four bruises on his shoulder, Maggie. Can you explain how he got those bruises to me?'

Maggie turned away and faced the door, she leaned her elbows on the table and rubbed her fingers into her temples. She began to chew loudly again.

'What bruises?' She couldn't look at Aileen any more. This was worse than the bloody Pigs interviewing her. This crazy Irish bitch was tearing her apart and judging her at the same time.

'Don't know any bruises,' she repeated.

Aileen remained standing, her pose and countenance closer to that of a Stasi inquisitor than Primary School Head Teacher.

'A hand gripped your son's shoulder so tightly, that there are bruises where the fingers pressed.'

Maggie tilted her head to the side, her tied back hair fell across her thin delicate neck, 'Well he's not a good boy, is 'e? 'E needs to tuffen up. 'Cos life's hard, innit.'

'It is indeed, Maggie. You're such a fragile thing yourself aren't you?' Aileen placed her hands on the back of the chair and looked straight down at Maggie's china-doll neck.

'I am so very sorry for what happened to you. That shouldn't happen to anyone. No-one. But you see, you are not my concern, Maggie. You are an adult. You make your own decisions. Your destiny and fate are in your own hands. You are free to choose. Now, you have the responsibility of raising a child yourself. You are accountable for Lewis.'

Maggie sat upright and could feel Aileen's hands on the back of the chair. The truth of what she was hearing could not be argued with.

'I know I did wrong, Miss Byrne. I know it. I'll do better I promise. It'll never happen again. I love Lewis.' This was the last throw of the die for Maggie. This lesbian bitch had turned her inside out in minutes. She hadn't admitted what her mother had done to her to anyone since she had told her pimp, who promised to protect her all those years ago. Another lie. She had just stopped trusting any one at all. Should she trust this woman who was charged with educating her boy?

Aileen had reached the denouement and reached over the seated mother, taking the biro in her right hand and flicking the orange plastic shopping bag open with her left.

'You just don't understand that the welfare of the child is paramount. His well-being is all I am concerned with.' She raised her right hand up. 'He will be housed with a caring, loving family.' She drew the biro down in a stabbing motion and sent the plastic shaft deep, through the orb of Maggie's right eye into the brain tissue beyond.

Aileen's head pounded, the sound of her heart blasting blood and adrenaline around her body filled her ears. Just to be sure, Aileen shoved the end of the pen hard with the heel of her hand. As Maggie's head snapped back with the force, she swiped the bag down over it. Clutching the handles of the bag tightly around her neck, Aileen deftly looped the string around the neck twice and tied a quick hitch knot to ensure that the bag was sealed.

She leveraged the twitching and heaving body under the table and quickly wiped the clear liquid that had squirted out of the eye, and the red flash of the single pulse of blood that had managed to escape Maggie's body before the protective helmet of plastic had been secured. The rushing, pounding, thumping, beating, drumming sound in her ears subsided, and was replaced by the zushing of the vacuum cleaner as it whooshed up to the door, then flowed away. Only to return and retreat again. It made Aileen think of gulls at the seaside.

Shaking the random memory aside she moved fast, placed the jay cloth in the pocket of the bomber jacket worn by 'the body'. To her, it was no longer a person. Just something that she had to take responsibility for. Like a report or staff meeting. A task to be completed. She picked up the smartphone that had been discarded on the table and pressed what she hoped was the 'off' button, then stripped the back off, removing the battery and Sim card. She wasn't sure why, but she had seen Idris Elba do it on a TV show, so thought it would be a good idea. She walked over to the door and opened it with a smile.

The cleaner, Doreen, squealed and leapt back, dropping the hose of the hoover.

'Miss Byrne!' Doreen stated the obvious, 'You scared the living daylights out o' me, Oh!' She waved both hands like a Cocker Spaniel or a boxing Hare, breathed heavily and bent to pick the hose up.

'I'm like a ninja, Doreen, you know me!' Aileen made light of the situation, and noticed that she felt great. 'Don't worry about this here meeting room tonight, Doreen. I'm getting it ready for a Governor's meeting in the morning.' She rolled her eyes to indicate how tedious and boring this would be.

'Righto, Miss B,' Doreen waved again to indicate she had understood and got on with hoovering the last corridor, before going home.

Once the school was quiet and she was alone in the building, Aileen carefully logged out the deceased parent from the electronic visitors register, she noted that it was forty-five minutes after she had signed in. She made sure that the school CCTV cameras were inactive. The body was then wheeled out to her car, after the school buildings were locked up and the alarm was set, in a shopping trolley pilfered from a local supermarket years before. It was still regularly used to cart large volumes of books from classrooms to cars at the end of term by most of the teachers in the school. Now, it was, in effect, the hearse carrying the remains of Maggie Tracey on her last journey.

10

The drive home was uneventful and Aileen parked her car, as always, in the garage.

Once the garage door was locked she did not have to leave the security of her property again until morning. A door opened straight from the utility area into the kitchen. Alone and without any pressing need for pace, Aileen moved the cadaver into the kitchen and laid it on the floor.

'Alexa, play Radio 4,' she instructed. It was almost six thirty and she hoped the 'The Unbelievable Truth' might soon be on.

Alexa responded, 'Playing, Radio 4.'

A further female announcer's voice informed Aileen that she was listening to the BBC Sounds App, as she released the hitch knot and lifted the wet, sticky shopping bag from the corpse's head. It was messier than she imagined it would be. The hoped for theme music played with plinking strings and the introduction of the host, David Mitchell, a favourite of Aileen's.

She began to search through pockets in order to collect all personal effects for disposal. In a concealed, inside pocket of the jacket, she discovered a bag containing several smaller bags and three blue pills, loose. One bag contained a white powder, another a green herb. This was going to be more fun than she thought. She sat back on her haunches and considered tonight's title.

The body was skinnier than she had hoped it would be. The meaty pies she was planning, and had been practising with all manner of roadkill was not going to work. She surveyed the shelf above the microwave containing recipe books. One stood out: Merry Oatley's Buffets. *Cannibal Canapés* struck her as appropriate.

She stood and walked to her fridge, taking an open bottle of Petit Chablis from the inside of the door. Walking to the shelf and taking the required recipe book, she pulled the cork that had been stuffed back into the neck as a makeshift stopper with her teeth, and after spitting the cork onto the worktop, took a swig. The cold, crisp, dry white wine tasted especially delicious this evening. A glass waited upside down on the drainer, by the sink. She turned it over filled it to the brim, reaching for her apron in preparation for a gruelling and gruesome nights work.

11

The ragu bubbled gently.

Robert had taken out some beef stock to defrost before putting the weekend's dirty washing through the machine and hoovering the whole house, bottom to top. It felt good to get ahead of the curve.

The stock was a left over from a slow cooked stew, the remains of a Sunday Lunch some weeks before. The secret ingredient had been a bottle of Merlot that Robert had sneaked into the slow cooker without Elle noticing. It had provided a deep, berry richness to the braised pot roast.

After reducing the left over stock for ten minutes, to concentrate the beef and red wine flavour, he added Passata, and half a dozen ripped up basil leaves, which he cast in to the stainless steel pot on the gas hob. He watched the bubbling brown broth as it muddied and thickened, transmuting into a mouthwatering, voluptuous consistency. He smelled the sharp tang of concentrated tomato and the leafy freshness of the basil as they were released, combining their flavours and textures in the sauce.

Pasta was the ultimate comfort food for both of them. Today had been a testing day. Robert had got home by Three thirty that afternoon. He hadn't wasted the opportunity to leave work early.

It was a widely held misconception that teachers only worked between Nine a.m. and Four p.m. Robert was regularly in school preparing for the day by seven, and rarely got out before Five-thirty, what with after school clubs, meetings with parents to explain why their child had been disciplined or the interminable 'twilight' training sessions; that was before the work that went into marking pupils' extended writing and the weekly planning that could easily go on into the night and often took up a majority of the weekends. It was a life that was not advertised in the glossy social media campaigns to get young undergraduates into training. Although, to be fair, the government couldn't be honest about a teacher's life.

Elle had left him a message to tell him that she would be home late. Two of the executives in her firm had children in schools that had been attacked and it sounded like the city was in pandemonium. She had volunteered to stay and help cover the desks, and she wanted to go for a drink with her friends to decompress after the day ended. She would get into the train station by Nine, where she would get a taxi home. She had also begged him to make some pasta, ready for her when she got home, and blew him a whole bunch of kisses.

Chairman Miaow, the couple's tabby, rubbed himself around Robert's legs purring loudly. Food love, he knew. They had found the cat in the back yard of their terraced Edwardian townhouse a year after moving in.

The place was situated in a fashionable area of the town. They had a view over the park opposite, a welcome green space commemorating a variety of royal occasions and used by the local cricket club to play badly on Sundays on hot Summer days. It was surrounded by beautifully maintained period properties and dotted with non-chain coffee shops, independent convenience stores and the onmi-present bistro pubs sponsored by the dominant local brewery.

Robert had thought it twee when they first came to view the house. Joking about greasy spoons and the awful Gypsy Tart, the local speciality of the county. He had remarked that the delicacy looked like a dodgy turd after a particularly hot curry had been smoothed into a pastry base. One mouthful had confirmed his suspicions.

It was probably the lack of the metropolitan, globalised, homogenised feel of the town that had attracted Elle so much. It was the complete opposite of her life in the city, the airbrushed global outlets that made every where seem familiar and the same. A tonic compared to the places in London they had frequented, that had been robbed of their unique identity.

The cat had looked lost and lonely, when he was discovered by the shed on a cold, rainy evening, with greasy looking fur and a limp. They had wondered if it had been hit by a car. Elle had searched on social media and he had walked around the surrounding roads looking for photocopied posters placed by desperate owners looking for their lost cat. But the search had drawn a blank. They kept the cat.

After feeding the Chairman, to the grateful approval of his feline dictator, he felt inspired to return to the children's book that he had been trying to write for the last ten years. He had read George Orwell's *Animal Farm* as a teenager, studying for his 'A' Levels. It had changed his life like no book before. He had loved the fact that it seemed to be about a group of farm animals that freed themselves from human subjugation, only for the pigs to turn traitor and sell the other animals down the river. It took a while for him to discover that the story was an allegory of the Russian revolution. Each of the animal characters had in fact been based on the principle political actors in the fall of socialist ideals and descent of Russia into another tyranny.

He began to read all of Orwell's work and found *1984* just as he had had to make a decision about his degree application. It had to be politics. He wanted to be active. Change the world and make it better, fairer.

He discovered Orwell's vague plagiarism during a random meeting in the University Union Bar with an attractive Russian Literature undergraduate, in his first year. She was studying early Russian dissident literature, especially that of Yevgeny Zamyatin, a naval architect who was exiled and came to the UK after the October Revolution. The dystopian plot of the story, as she described it, centred on the exploits of an unimaginative male 'hero' in a totalitarian state headed by the 'Benefactor'. The man is seduced by a woman who breaks all the rules and offers him a view of a life free from the constraints and fears engendered by the 'Benefactor' and the all seeing and all pervasive secret police. They are of course caught and tortured, only she refuses to be broken and does not tell her torturers a single thing. The male 'hero' of the story breaks almost immediately and desperately begs for 'correction', after blabbing every sordid detail and consigning the woman and her fellow conspirators to death.

The parallels with Orwell's seminal work were blindingly obvious. Robert had reflected, drinking another pint after the rather lovely Literature student had left with her boyfriend, that he had learned all of this too late. These narratives really should replace the bland, simple modern tales that were being churned out to children. After all, the origin and the messages in the original fairy tales were often far grittier than they were credited with. He was determined to try to write a children's novel that told a modern fairy tale of political upheaval, collective responsibility and the role everyone had to play to make the world a better place.

Robert sat and opened his laptop reaching for the bottle of Negroamaro wine on the table, removing the ornate ceramic stopper, decorated with a brightly painted gecko that the couple had found while on holiday in Seville.

He poured himself a glass while waiting for the machine to boot up. The red wine had a chocolately, plummy scent that wafted to his nostrils and he took an appreciative sip. He and Elle had made a 'pinky promise' never to buy wine from a supermarket, but to always go to an independent wine merchant after sampling possibly the best wine they had ever had at a friend's dinner party. They had been informed that 'Perseus's Wine Emporium', a warehouse just outside Falmbourne, could be relied upon to supply out-of-this-world wines at reasonable prices. The bottle from Italy that he was currently drinking had become a favourite of the pair, yet it cost less than Ten quid. They had never looked back.

As the ragu simmered magically on the stove, he read through his great work. In it, a medical mouse called Cheesy G had witnessed his fellow rodents being terrorised by the greedy Fat Cats on the small idyllic island of Qooba. One day, Cheesy was helping an old mouse called Miguel collect some grains to store for the winter, when the Fat Cats struck.

Miguel had to abandon his home in the race to escape and lost all of his possessions as they were stolen by the greedy Fat Cats. His family was scattered all over the island and some younger mice were captured by the Cats and forced to work for them for mouldy old grain that no-one wanted.

Cheesy was incensed and organised a rodent revolution to overthrow the Fat Cats and replace them with a fair egalitarian government for all mice and cats to live together in harmony.

He scrolled the screen up and down. He knew every dire paragraph of it. He knew that it was a steaming pile of crap. But after he had seen a children's TV show with a Rastafarian mouse he wondered if he should still peddle it around, hoping it might find a sympathetic executive looking for the next crazy crap idea to make money out of. The irony was not lost on him.

He closed the laptop, without adding to, or editing the manuscript, as he always did, and took his wine into the sitting room. He switched on the TV and selected a news channel. Miaow joined him and snuggled in for a tummy tickle.

On the screen, grave looking on-the-scene reporters provided their eye-witness accounts, that added little or no new information to the news cycle. No-one had claimed responsibility for the morning's attacks in London. The usual international terrorist organisations were strangely silent on the matter.

A security expert in the studio commented on the indiscriminate nature of the attack. Families from all sectors of society had been victims of the attacks. Christian, Muslim, Jewish, Hindu – all fell during the attacks, as did English, Scottish, Welsh and Irish nationalities, even those whose ancestors hailed from the four corners of the globe. Similarly there seemed to be no class barrier in the targetting of the schools. There was no pattern, except that school children and their parents were the intended victims.

A senior ranking police officer appeared in front of a disorganised mass of journalists and cameras to reiterate that 'all avenues of investigation were open and being pursued', but 'no, they didn't know the identity of the attackers', 'yes, some of them got away but arrests were expected imminently'. There was the usual appeal for witnesses or anyone who might have information to contact the police immediately.

Next, a high ranking military officer appeared informing the public that due to the nature of the attacks the Prime Minister had requested that the military assist the police with public order. He informed the journalists that the public should not be alarmed by the visibility of military vehicles on the streets and outside strategically important sites. They were there for our protection.

Robert was sceptical of this last point. He did not feel particularly protected, considering the historical record of the military in 'civilian' scenarios in the British Isles. He tried to recall examples other than 'Bloody Sunday' from the last half century and couldn't, so he was not mollified by the assurances of the officer on the screen. He wondered if he would find a tank sitting outside the school in the morning. Squaddies searching through the pupils bags to make sure that they had their Reading Record on them, parents interrogated on the streets to make sure that they had signed them to indicate that their child had read to them the night before. In numb acceptance of this new reality he flicked over to watch the sports channel, hoping to catch a re-run of the final round of the PGA championships that he had missed. It was Moto-GP.

Robert absent mindedly stroked the cat's belly as he recalled the events of that day. His meeting with the Head Teacher had not been right. He knew that she was stressed and her blunt, almost rude behaviour, was an acquired taste. There was something today that was out of place.

The coffee, the first name familiarity and the anger at the reported safeguarding concerns and the parent meeting. He didn't think that professional diligence had ever resulted in rage like that in any meeting, anywhere in the world. Except, perhaps in North Korea.

Chairman Miaow flicked his paws blissfully, the deep, regular purring began to slow down as he fell slowly into a relaxed and deep sleep. Robert looked at the cat and thought about Lewis. He knew that Lewis had a troubled home life. His mother was emotionally and physically neglectful and surrounded herself with bad people. He wasn't sure if the physical marks he had seen were from her, or one of her coterie.

Robert had tried his best to help Lewis to make friends with children whose parents would be supportive and hoped that some of them might take Lewis 'under their wing' so to speak. Lewis was tolerated, so long as there was fresh air and a football to play with. Other than that the children in the class avoided him. They were never mean or nasty to him. They were a little afraid of his mum and the people she hung out with.

She had resisted all attempts to help her. He had managed to get the school's part-time SENCo to arrange for Early Help, but Maggie Tracey had refused. Any attempts by social workers to intervene brought back memories of Lewis's removal into care.

He had acted appropriately, in a timely and professional manner. Although the Head Teacher's manner with Robert today had hinted otherwise. He knew that she had never really liked him, but she had tolerated him due to his ability to get children to genuinely learn. The data charting the children's progress was never inflated or exaggerated and they always accelerated after a rather duff year with the well meaning, but dull Aaron Parminster. Robert decided that he was going to keep his wits about him and pay close attention to the actions and behaviour of the erratic Miss Aileen Byrne. He gently tipped the cat off onto a nearby cushion, to the total indignation and disgust of Chairman Miaow, and went back to the kitchen to fry off some minced beef to be added to the ragu, with a splash of balsamic vinegar to finish it off. The fresh pasta itself could wait till Elle got home.

12

The long nights of practice on dead badgers and foxes had paid off. Aileen butchered and sliced her 'prime cuts' quickly and neatly, although the quantity of some of the meat was lacking, leading to mini-sausage rolls instead of the pies she had hoped for.

The body was dismembered and wrapped into grease proof paper. Each parcel neatly and carefully placed into black bin liners for disposal at a later time. She stood at the sink, washing out the food processor. She scrubbed every curve, corner and blade carefully and methodically, before placing it in the dishwasher for a final blast of detergent and heated water.

On the worktop were assembled neat lines, cooling and ready to be packed for transport, of vol-au-vents, crudites, mini-meat rolls, crostini and tarts that all contained the camouflaged cannibal delicacy of Maggie Tracey's butchered kidney, liver, tongue, buttock and thigh meat.

Aileen mopped the floor with a weak bleach solution while she waited for the marijuana and cocaine infused chocolate brownies to finish in the oven. She had made too much of the normal brownie mix. Not wanting to dilute the drugs too much, she had already baked an untainted test batch of brownies that sat on the kitchen table, cooling down. She popped one in her mouth and chewed with satisfaction as she passed it, mopping vigorously. Delicious. She didn't remember the last time that she had had an appetite like this in the morning.

'I think I'll have scrambled egg on toast,' she declared to the world outside the kitchen window.

The morning was dull and overcast, with an early morning mist rising from the dew. A pigeon sat on the fence and cast its superficial glance into the industrious interior. Aileen paused and watched as the pigeon turned on the fence like a marionette in a music box. Slowly completing the circumference in jerky, clockwork steps.

'You're a cheeky one,' she remarked, with a sway of her hips as she set about collecting cooking equipment that was unsullied by her unsavoury baking assignment, in order to cook her celebratory breakfast to prepare her for the arduous, but rewarding day ahead.

13

Robert arrived at work early on the overcast and leaden grey Tuesday morning, expecting to be relatively alone in the school for at least twenty minutes. He knew that it was being opened up by Mrs Maguire, the Year 2 teacher.

She was an early bird and would have the school open by Six thirty, but she rarely ventured out of her room the rest of the time. She was 'old skool' and was struggling to maintain the pace expected of modern teaching. Counting down the months until her retirement, she spent all her time and energy on her classroom displays and her marking, ensuring that the children were well prepared for the Key Stage 1 standardised tests. She wasn't going to get caught out and be made to 'disappear' into the limbo of Supply teaching like so many of her contemporaries. So she stayed in her room and kept herself to herself, only leaving when absolutely necessary.

Robert discovered that he had been beaten to it, as he pulled up in the car park. The Head Teacher's car was already in its designated and reserved spot. He parked in one of the three spots he usually parked in.

He liked to pretend that he wasn't the creature of habit that the others were. It was surprising how many of the staff lost the plot when someone parked in 'their' space. Even though the only spaces assigned were for the Head Teacher and Guest. If a child behaved in such an irrationally obsessive way about an inconsequential part of a daily routine, they would be sent straight for a diagnosis of Autistic Spectrum Disorder. So, he liked to mix it up.

One spot was under the young oak tree, close to the pedestrian gate. Although he rarely parked there in the Summer and Autumn terms because of the falling acorns and leaves. Birds had a tendency to sit in the tree too, and he had returned, on several occasions, to find large dollops of pigeon shit on his windscreen. The wipers never managed to get rid of it, instead smearing the white gloopy excrement over the rest of the glass. In the end, he always just got out and wiped it with tissue paper.

A more regular spot to park, was next to the playground fence. It was a straight line drive, once you had turned the corner to get in the automated gates to the car park. This space was competed for by himself and Aaron Parminster. But the Year 3 teacher never arrived at school early enough to block the space.

Today though, he took the spot opposite to the Head Teacher's. It was a hotly contested space as both Suzy Tallister, the Year 5 Teacher, and either Hailey Price or Megan Billings, the job share in Year 6, tried to occupy the coveted parking position.

Robert locked his car and walked through the chilly morning air, the increasingly gusty wind blew the recently fallen leaves around his feet, to the main entrance where he waved his key fob over the reader beside the door.

'These aren't the droids you're looking for!' he said in his best, worst Alec Guiness voice.

With a whirring buzz, he was granted access. He pulled the door open and proceeded to the Reception area. He logged into the electronic register using the touchscreen on the desk. As he walked past the Meeting Room, he noticed that the light was already on and he could hear the room being vacuumed. The blinds were down and closed so he couldn't see in. He guessed it had something to do with the Governors' meeting that was scheduled today regarding the tragic events the day before in London. They were due to discuss how well prepared the school was for an incident of that nature. He wondered if Doreen had been sent home early last night as well.

He followed the corridors to his classroom and deposited his coat and laptop bag by his desk. Picking up the empty coffee cup, that he had left from the break time the day before, he returned to the staffroom. The daily morning duty of emptying the dishwasher and putting the first of many pots of coffee through the percolator was a worthy sacrifice for Robert. He knew that no-one else wanted to do it and that his efforts were known and appreciated.

He observed, without much surprise, that the notice board had been wiped clean. The information written up on the Friday of the week before, to inform staff of the school diary of the upcoming week: who would be in and out of school, who had a visitor in, that sort of thing, had been removed. The normal routine of the school was being interrupted. The only item left was written in the row dedicated for Tuesdays: *STAFF BRIEFING 8:15am*. The large blue capital letters were in contradistinction to the usual convention of adhering to standard formal English punctuation and grammar, it stood out like a pustulating sore.

Robert completed his morning contribution to staff well-being, then opened the cupboard containing the jumble of unwanted cups and mugs that staff had deposited and contributed over the years. He wavered, looking at the coffee in the pot and then up at the mugs, back to the pot. An odd shiver worked its way from his neck to the base of his spine, but he didn't understand why the icy sensation struck him. Closing the cupboard door, he took a step back.

'Not today,' he murmured and walked out of the staffroom to return to his room and his preparations for the teaching day.

As he walked back through the empty corridor, he breezed past the Meeting Room's open door and witnessed Aileen Byrne's back as she fussed around the table, laying out what seemed to be a buffet for the Governors' meeting. Robert was stunned, but couldn't decide what it might mean.

14

Lewis awoke to find that he had had the bad dream. His legs and belly felt warm and wet. Looking down, he put his hand on the front of his pants to confirm that he had wee'd himself again.

He got up off the plastic sheet covering his bed, that his Mum had made him sleep on, and stripped off his wet clothes. He looked around the room to find a dry pair of pants and t-shirt to wear. Over on the radiator, there were the pants that he had wet a couple of days earlier and left there to dry. There was a big yellow stain and they felt stiff when he put them on, like they had been ironed in too much starch. Not that he knew what ironed clothes felt like. Or what starch was, or why it might be used.

He slipped the school shirt that he had worn the day before over his head. He hadn't heard his Mum come in the night before, so she must be at someone called Charlie's having a party after her night at work. She had told him that she did that sometimes.

He had not eaten the night before and he was now ravenous. He went to the kitchen and picked a dirty bowl out of the sink. The washing up had not been done since sometime last week. Lewis searched around looking for something edible.

Eventually he stood on a chair, reaching for the cupboard that his Mum stored all her 'special treats' in, that was out of bounds for Lewis. He was not normally allowed to eat any of this. He hoped she didn't choose this moment to walk in. Shaking as he opened the door, he found only a loaf of bread that was beginning to go stale, cup-a-soups and some peanut butter. It was all that was left from Maggie's last trip to the foodbank.

Lifting the bread and peanut butter carefully and silently down, he sat on the floor and used his fingers to smear the spread on the dry bread. Once his belly had been quieted, Lewis tip toed to the toilet. The door to his Mum's bedroom was slightly open and Lewis confirmed his suspicion that she had not been back at all that night.

'Dai off school!' he cheered and ran and jumped onto the toilet to have a Number Two. It was only after he finished his faecal assignment that he noticed that there was no toilet paper left on the cardboard roll. Lewis sat briefly with his head in his hands. However, with a shrug, he stood and pulled the already soiled pants up, flushed the toilet and leapt freely and happily around the empty flat, pretending that he was a character in Fortnite; eliminating unseen adversaries until he was victorious and left alone, the last man standing.

15

The meeting in the staffroom had been pretty uneventful, but Aileen lead a prayer and suggested a minute's silence be observed for the victims and their families of the atrocities the day before.

The staff were instructed to keep a keen eye on the notice board for any announcements or changes to the regular school day and were to 'Keep Calm and Carry On'.

Any questions from children were to be sidestepped and referred back to their parents. The best thing to do, the government strategists had decided, was for everything to carry on as normal.

For Robert, the only pronounced change was the buoyant mood of the Head Teacher. She sailed through the delivery of the messages expressively and with relish. She wore the same dark turtle neck sweater and pencil skirt – her uniform – but today the colourful neck scarf was jauntily tied into her hair a la Amy Winehouse. It reminded him of the American propaganda posters that were used in the Second World War. The ones with the woman in a boiler suit, flexing her biceps. 'We can do it!' The resemblance was a little startling. There was even a moment where she placed a sympathetic hand on Charles's shoulder when he began to get a nose bleed and had a coughing fit during the minute's silence.

Aileen had looked directly at Robert during this. The pair had made eye contact. Even at some distance across the crowded room, he thought some form of telepathic interaction occurred. He was sure he heard her invite Charles to her office for a coffee, as she linked her arm in his, to discuss a strategy for dealing with the Governors' meeting. Something that he had never heard her do before. She usually just skulked out with a glare at Charles, daring him to follow her.

Robert cast about to see if anyone else had smelled a rat. However, no-one else to seemed to think that anything was amiss or awry and everyone went their own way, back to their own preparations for the school day.

As the crowd cleared, only Suzy Tallister looked troubled. She strutted over as if she were on a catwalk to join Robert at the photocopier, as the rest of the staff made their exodus in twos or threes.

'You don't think they're...,' Suzy nudged Robert's elbow with hers, 'you know...at it, do you?'

She looked over towards the door where the pair had left, leading the procession of teachers out the door moments earlier. She looked up at Robert and he realised that she was hurt by the intimacy between Charles and Aileen. It hinted at the possibility that the married Charles Syndale might also be betraying her.

'I don't know,' was all Robert could reply, even though his own thoughts considered that the uncharacteristic physical intimacy from Aileen towards her detested Deputy, might reflect a much darker act might be taking place. The pair stood together pensively, looking at the door as the arithmetic worksheets Robert was copying clunked through the machine with a dull repetition.

16

Toby lived on the same street as Lewis. After Will was dropped off by his Dad, the pair would often drift towards school with Lewis tagging on. Always a couple of steps behind though.

Toby's Mum was a bit of a liberal hippy, dressed in tie-dyed t-shirt and jeans, with flowery Doc Martin boots. She always chatted to Lewis as she escorted the trio to school. She kept encouraging Toby to spend more time with him, as part of their social duty, but Toby didn't really want to. Lewis smelled. If he and Will were seen with Lewis too much, they would get picked on at school. Especially by the girls. They were the worst. They always made up a song, or a rhyme that caught on, and soon everyone in school would repeat it to them. There was no escape from the girls' teasing.

As they approached the block of flats that Lewis lived in, they noticed that he wasn't there waiting for them with or without his Mum, as he usually did. Will pointed up to a window on the first floor, and started laughing.

'There's Lewis,' he said and doubled over.

Lewis was jumping up at the window and waving. He looked a little like an inmate in a mental asylum, with his unevenly shaved hair, dirty t-shirt and clearly visible pants that flashed into view with every jump.

'He's still in his pants!' Toby screeched.

The two boys were in hysterics. The chance to say the word 'pants' on the street was the icing on the cake of seeing Lewis being mad. Toby's Mum was not impressed with the boys and she shushed them while signing to Lewis to open the window as if she was in a giant game of charades.

'Morning Lewis, hasn't your Mum got you ready for school today?' Toby's Mum called up once the window had been levered open the few inches it would move.

'Mum's not 'ere. She ain't bin awl nite,' Lewis informed the street gleefully and began jumping up and down again. 'I'm n__ Go__g to sc__ol __day.'

They all guessed that he wasn't going to school today, but couldn't hear it all clearly, as his voice was obscured every time he jumped.

'Stand still please, Lewis.' Toby's Mum instructed. 'When your Mum gets in can you ask her to call me, please?'

'I'm hookin' off the hole dai,' Lewis informed them. 'I will, Mrs 'edgecock.'

With that he slammed the window shut and vanished from sight.

'Mum, can I hook off the day too?' Toby looked hopefully towards his Mum. 'We could hang out with Lewis, you always say you want me to spend more time with him!'

Toby's Mum harrumphed, 'We're getting you two to school, now. I don't want you being late, again. I don't need another letter from the them telling me that because you've been late ten times, I'm going to get a hundred quid fine!'

She placed a hand squarely on each of the boys backs and shoved them in the direction they needed to go, setting the pace for the rest of the hike to the school.

Later, during registration in class, when Mr Carpenter issued his usual instructions: 'I'm taking the register, only two people in the room are allowed to speak, that's me and the person answering their name!' and raced through the alphabetical roll call, he hesitated and glanced up at the chair where Lewis should have been when silence met his call.

'Lewis?' Will and Toby bit their tongue's but shared a knowing look, 'Lewis?' he repeated and the pair inwardly giggled at the memory of Lewis jumping up and down in his underpants.

17

While Toby and Will were struggling with their arithmetic, Lewis was left alone in a big, cold and untidy flat.

Maggie always kept the remote control for the TV in a secret place so that Lewis could only watch TV when she allowed it. After twenty minutes of searching in vain that morning, Lewis had given up. Instead, he did his best to clean both himself and the kitchen.

He knew that the other kids didn't like being around him because he wasn't as clean as them. He stripped and used a flannel to wipe his body with soap and cold water in the bathroom, then brushed his teeth without toothpaste. He didn't realise that putting the same clothes on straight away meant putting the smell back on like the stink was a designer label that he chose to wear.

After that, he set about washing the dishes. He moved the chair over to the sink and knelt on it as he washed and rinsed the dishes and cutlery dumped there in cold water. He did his best to stack the cleaned utensils next to the sink, making sure he didn't drop anything that might break if it fell to the floor.

He was interrupted in these chores by a knock at the door accompanied by some unintelligible shouting. He waited to see if the person at the door went away. His Mum had told not to open the door to anyone, ever. But she was not here and he was alone.

Lewis walked towards the door that was being continuously thumped by what sounded like a man outside. Whoever it was sounded angry. The voice kept repeating his Mum's name and threatened to knock the door down if she didn't answer.

'Maggie! Maggie you useless, lazy bitch! Open this door naow, or I swear I'll kick it in!' The voice sounded familiar to Lewis, the closer he got to the door. He could see it rattle with every blow.

'She ain't 'ere! Stop it, and I'll open the door, Mickey.' Lewis shouted, hoping that he was right about who was at the door. The banging stopped.

'Alright Little Man? Open the door to your Uncle Mickey, now. Let me in, there's a good boy.' The gravelly voice instructed Lewis.

Lewis reached up and unlocked the door, twisting open the night latch, letting the door open inward.

'Allo, Oncle Mickey. Mums not 'ere. She ain't bin 'ome all nite. Promise.' Lewis apologised and covered for his Mum.

Mickey was 'bad news' and 'not to be trusted', that's what his Mum had told him, but Mickey had probably been the most consistent male adult in Lewis's life, outside of school.

'Why aren't you in school, Little Man? Why 'asn't your Mum got you dressed and got you to school? That's where you should be.'

The bald, heavy-set Mickey 'Two Fists' Butcher, a man now in his sixties, had as distinctive an appearance as he had a voice. Thick-set, bald and tattooed. The man had a tree trunk for a neck and small, mean eyes, like a stoat or a weasel. He was the 'Mr Big' of the town. Nothing happened in Falmbourne that he didn't know about, or get a cut of. His accent was still true to the East End of London, where he heralded from. His youth had been a tale straight out of a Sixties Michael Caine movie.

He got the moniker, Mickey 'Two Fists', on account of his training as a boxer in his teens. He had always been big for his age and he discovered that, on most occasions, a left – right jab combo was enough to lay his opponent out cold. This was a useful skill to have, and he quickly gained notoriety around the clubs in less salubrious areas of London, as an enforcer for the local crooks. He had been farmed out 'to the sticks' as a reward, after helping a particularly lucrative jewellery heist in the Seventies.

Dressed in his signature suit and leather jacket with wool lining, he did his best to honour the legacy of the Krays, in terms of gangster style, if not the violence. He had found that he didn't need to use actual violence any more, just making reference to it was enough of a deterrent. The films of the Nineties by Guy Ritchie had worked wonders. All he had to do was act like Vinnie Jones and people did whatever he wanted. He made sure not to seem like one of them poofters out of that shoddy Soap Opera set in the East End on the Beeb.

He had only once had to call on his 'Old Firm' connections. It was like a reunion for Mickey – the 'Old Times'. Some jumped up Eastern Europeans, Serbs, he thought, had tried to muscle in and peddle their dodgy gear and set up a brothel. Mickey, and a few of the staunch fellas from up London, had paid a visit. Soon the trafficked girls were shipped off to Eastbourne, the Serbs had been 'informed' of the rules and told that the old duffers in Sussex had money, and were too old to get it up anyway. Easy money. With the Serbs paying a cut going to the London bosses, to be respectful, like.

Mickey strode through the flat, examining each room as he went. The smell made him wince.

'I'm 'ookin' off ain' I, Oncle Mickey,' Lewis proudly informed the larger than life character before him, as he stood in his wee stained pants and dirty t-shirt.

Mickey felt pity for the skinny wretch before him, he could have been a character out of Oliver Twist. He looked Lewis up and down, disgusted that one of his girls would leave a child in this condition in this day and age.

Lewis's mum was a worry to Mickey. She was a good earner, but the girl was unreliable. She had a habit of missing bookings and couldn't keep regular clients, no matter how hard Mickey tried to arrange them. The trouble was - her habit. He knew where to go looking for her and decided it was time to give her another short, sharp, shock.

'Get some trousers on, Little Man, we're gonna go find your Muvver,' he decided, running a grizzled hand over his bald pate. 'Oo cut your 'air son? It's a travesty!'

He walked back out the door and waited on the landing. Pursing his lips in paternal contemplation as he waited, considering where to take the child for breakfast first, then to a barbers to get that mess shaved off.

Lewis didn't reply, but ran into his bedroom to find his school trousers. He lifted a dry, crusty sock to his nose and almost choked. Slipping into his trousers, he jammed his unsocked feet into his scuffed, black shoes as quickly as he could. He had the feeling that he shouldn't keep Uncle Mickey waiting too long.

18

The sounds of a busy school bustled around.

Children were sent on errands, classes of five and six year olds were paraded around the field in their search for mini-beasts. Older children ran between temporary stations on the playground, indicated by different coloured cones, searching for the right numbers or mathematical symbols to produce the solution to their puzzles.

It was silent in the Head Teacher's office. It was as if the walls and the door absorbed all sound to ensure that it was a space for contemplation. A monk's cell.

At her desk, Aileen reached down to her simple, M a& S handbag under the table. From it she took two items. The first was a wooden cross. It bore the image of Jesus's crucifixion etched into it. The second was a set of rosary beads. Ornate, little wooden spheres had been attached to a string that had been speared through holes that pierced the bead's wooden poles, connecting the hearts of each little ball to the small, plain cross that sat at the end of the loop.

She had been given these religious artefacts, along with a battered and beaten Bible, by her Grandmother on the day of her twelfth birthday. The wizened old lady had given her a hairy kiss on the cheek. Aileen had thought, at the time, she had a deeper moustache that her Da.

'Dese are the most important gifts that you will ever receive from me, girl. Dey will get you true the bad days.' She had whispered into the young girl's ear.

The Bible had vanished in one of Aileen's many moves during her adult life, but she had kept these keepsakes safe through all these years. She came across them again at the bottom of a kitchen drawer when she was looking for a tea towel last night, but had no idea how providence had placed them there.

Aileen placed the crucifix in the centre of her empty desk, and took the rosary in her hands. She held the small cross that joined the beaded loop loosely between her thumb and index finger. Reaching up to to the scarf tied into her hair, she pulled the knot, and dropped the scarf into her handbag. She genuflected to begin the sacrament, and began with the Apostle's Creed.

'I believe in God, the Father Almighty...' Aileen paused, stunned at how easily the words returned to her. Her prayer began to flow like the drips of rain in an April shower, but soon became a torrential deluge of emotion, like a thunder storm in July. She raced through the Creed, moved her fingers to the first bead and blurted out the Lord's Prayer, willing God's redemption to find her.

The shame of what she had become coursed through her; she struggled to maintain composure as bolts of recognition flashed through her struggling mind. Her head slightly bowed, she rocked in her chair to provide a rhythm, a beat to her recitation. Just like Maggie Tracey had the night before during their heated exchange. A cadence that had led to the young mother's murder.

Aileen's adult life had dragged her, step by step, away from the faith of her youth. She became aware of her sexuality in Sixth Form.

She had always been studious and quite sporty and she sought the company of other like-minded girls her age. Saoirse Kilkenny was a close friend. They played in opposite positions in Netball, and often played against each other. Although it was a non-contact game, they both found themselves bumping into each other regularly. Aileen became increasingly aware of her friend's body beneath the uniform. The curves, the contrasts between the firmness of toned muscle and the softness of burgeoning womanhood. It first confused, then excited her. Their competitiveness was not just fuelled by the desire to be on the winning team.

Time after time, their eyes had met, pupils dilating. The changing rooms after each of the games were a minefield to Aileen. Heady scents after a frantic game filled her nostrils and the increasingly charged, playful banter in bra and knickers turned into Aileen's first full blown kiss after a particularly feisty match. The other girls had laughed knowingly.

'I hope you'll be confessing that there, girls,' the Captain of Aileen's team had joked.

'Hail Mary full of grace. The Lord is with thee...' Her fingers moved onto the next bead.

Aileen had always struggled with her sexuality not being in alignment with the expectations of her church. How could genuine, caring and full love be sinful? Her fall from grace had continued steadily, throughout her years at University; as her attendance at Mass became less frequent, her faith lapsed.

She left Ireland with a degree in Literature and as a qualified teacher, arriving in the UK ready to make her marque, filled with feminist zeal. It was her mission to free the minds of all of the oppressed and repressed young women that she encountered.

She quickly gained attention as an assiduous, bordering on obsessive, practitioner, with a clear passion that ignited imaginations and aspirations with pupils, both boys and girls. She was the absolute image that the glamorous TV advertising campaign had portrayed at the time.

Due to her efforts she had been noticed, and rewarded, and praised and lauded. She had been promoted. Her ardour was not dimmed by the bureaucracy that the dedicated generation of teachers, that she was a part of, encountered. She sought to master the various responsibilties that schools in England accumulated; the funding for the various institutions in Civil Society were slashed again and again by governments of all persuasions over the decades. Their roles collected and concentrated into the tiny number of senior staff in schools, who were then convinced that they had a legal obligation to replace social workers, mental health professionals, youth workers and parents.

'...Blessed art thou among women..' Aileen recalled the confessions of her sexual awakening to the priest, Father Murphy O'Riley, who had always asked for more detail. A little breathlessly, she recalled in hindsight.

Aileen had taken the responsibilities as a school leader seriously and extended her mission, initially to save all of the world's girls, eventually to all of the world's children. As each year brought a new policy, a new requirement, a new legal responsibility, Aileen found herself retreating from her life.

The school became the gravity well that pulled her into ever closer revolutions, a supermassive black hole that trapped all of the light in her life into a frozen event horizon. Nothing seemed to change.

The ladies choir that she had sung in, as a clear and sweet soprano, missed her initially. They kept messaging and calling on her, desperate to keep their best soloist. But, after a time, they had given up on her.

She always seemed to be writing something called a SEF (she had tried to explain that it was a Self Evaluation Form, a way for school leaders to reflect on the progress the school was making) or SDP (she would tell them it was a School

Development Plan, a way that Head Teacher's could fix all the problems in the school). Anyhow, they seemed to take up all her time. Friendships and relationships fell away as Aileen first rain-checked, then cancelled and finally gave up, trying to meet with friends, lovers and acquaintances alike.

Year after year, the responsibility increased. Not only was she there to ensure that her teachers were delivering an increasingly demanding range of curriculum requirements, but she also became responsible for replacing the withdrawing, underfunded state institutions, as well as progressively detached parents, who cared less for their own children than they did for their own virtual, social media avatar. Even this did not dim Aileen's vision, or mission.

With the focus and strength of a titan, she stretched every ligature and strained every sinew to hold on to the two worlds. One the apocalyptic aftermath of the disintegration of families, morals and values. In the time it had taken for Aileen to grow from adolescent to woman, the world had mutated and she found herself in an era of irrational greed, conspicuous overconsumption and the end of the truth. Lord knows what might happen in the time it took for a child born at the dawn of the new millennium to grow to school age.

The other world, the impossible, the unchanging, weekend colour supplement imaginary world, the glossy celebrity Instagram 'Hello' magazine world, with its airbrushed image of the perfect nuclear family of two and half kids, a dog a cat and an iguana that politicians tried to convince themselves, and everyone else, was the goal of their 'Good Society' that hovered at the edge of everyone's peripheral vision. Providing aspiration. Providing expectation. Providing an illusory bear trap that caught unsuspecting Gen Xers and Millennials into a depressive cycle of failing to achieve the spray tanned Stepford plastic polluted fairytale life.

With a fuzzy, shimmering chimera in each hand, Aileen had forced the imperfect jigsaw together, time and again. Year after year, children were 'protected'.

Adults who had stumbled into grown-up responsibility without any idea of how to succeed when they were a child themselves in this developing global, digital age, were guided towards a 'better' future.

Over time, the strain took its toll. Her heart had been broken, over and over again, sometimes by the depravity she had witnessed. She asked herself, how could so many children experience so much neglect, abuse and poverty? How can there be so many broken people out there? So many fractured families?

Sometimes she was hammered by the implacable and faceless professional bureaucracy that dictated actions on people, with widely varying experiences and problems, determining a future based on standardised child protection flow charts and risk assessments, forms and multi-agency contacts.

As her heart hardened, as it had to, she became guilty, as many in her difficult position did, of over-proscribing interventions into families that could have got through their bad times with hope and a little time and care.

Children were wrenched from loving parents who just couldn't afford to feed and clothe themselves, let alone their children. In Aileen's eyes, parents became demons in a world where success and failure could, and had been digitised, monetised and measured.

Many worry filled days, Aileen had left work, alone, to return to the empty shell of a house containing her few possessions. These were times when she pressed her hands tightly into her eyes, desperately trying to push the tears back in, hoping for sleep to welcome her into a black abyss of peace and annihilation. Eventually, the tears and the worry stopped. So too, though, had the healing balm of sleep.

'...and blessed is the fruit of thy womb...' The rocking stopped. The recitation ended.

Aileen closed her eyes and all she could see was a Marvel comic version of the fury filled face of Maggie Tracey. Mascara smeared down her cheeks, a pyroclastic flow of fear, disappointment and frustration, released in a final sacrament to a life filled with hate and frustrated disappointment. Dreams abandoned and promises broken.

The dead mother's eyes screamed for some form of mercy, before Aileen's right hand, holding the biro, had fallen and the final paschal ritual smoothed the waters as she had transitioned into the ever after.

'Well, I suppose the pen is mightier than the sword after all!' she said to the empty room and was shaken by deep, guttural heaves as she let go of the last threads holding her to her past self. Her younger, hope filled life.

Low, longing filled laughs erupted. She barked as the tension and guilt of the past twenty-four hours dissolved in the emptiness of the room.

19

The morning had gone well, she thought, once she had regained some composure. Placing the rosary on the desk, next to the discarded crucifix, she recalled the days events so far. Charles had looked ill, she remembered, and hoped he looked sicker still tomorrow. He had meekly accepted her invitation to her office for refreshments, after what she considered to be one of her finest staff meetings ever.

She had made sure that he received another dose of the poisoned milk with a smile on her face. In hindsight, she realised that she had missed a trick though, as he always had sugar to sweeten his drink (she didn't, because she was already sweet enough), it provided her with an opportunity to add one of those little blue pills she had recovered from Maggie Tracey's jacket. If she crushed one of those up and slipped it into his coffee too, not only would he be increasing the concentration of mercury and rat poison into his system, making him sicker than a parrot, but also getting a raging erection to boot! She considered whether this might be too much, then caught herself, reaffirming that he was already a total cock anyway. He deserved that and much more too!

'In for a penny, in for a pound! As my old granny used to say,' she smiled as she swept the religious artefacts back into her handbag disdainfully. The old articles of her faith had been soundly replaced by a new unholiness and deviant ritual behaviour.

Over by the office mini-kitchen, were the silver foil platters that she had used to deliver her buffet for the Governors' meeting. The bite-sized culinary delights had gone down a storm. So distracted were they, that they spent more time complimenting Aileen than discussing how to improve the security of the children in the school.

She had delivered a delicious variety of mouthwatering delights - she must have been up all night - one of the governors had exclaimed appreciatively, stuffing a vol-au-vent in her mouth before she had finished chewing a mini-sausage roll. The cooking revealed a new dimension of the Head Teacher's talents. This was the beginning of a new tradition in the forward march of the school, the quorum decided, providing quality home cooked food to liven up what they all agreed could be a rather tiresome chore.

They chatted over their respective specialities: baking cakes, baking biscuits, baking bread. One of the younger members of the governing body, a stay at home mum, declared that she was a dab hand at making sushi, to the approval of all at the table.

A rota was drawn up, allocating each member of the body to a future meeting with a varied suggestion list of possible baked or unbaked delicacies, that would be shared on the Governors' webpage. They then discussed whether they were happy to share their recipes, with each other and the school community as a whole, by posting them up on the school website, too.

Aileen had held her counsel throughout the entire exchange, watching as each of the disposable platters were emptied of their offerings. When asked whether she was prepared to share her recipes she had merely smiled.

'A lady must have some mystery, surely.' she offered teasingly, then assured the group with a short and humble clarification, 'I am sure that I would be breaching Merry Oatley's copyright if I did.'

Only one platter still offered cannibalistic canapés. The left-overs were condensed in an effort by the parasitic committee to convince themselves that they hadn't actually, gorged themselves entirely. They crowded the remaining parcels onto one of the foil platters, heaping the meaty bites on top of each other in places. An offering for the troops they had joked, intending to deliver the tray to the staffroom later. They then got on with the actual business that they had gathered for and discussed the awful events in London the previous morning.

20

Jo, the governor who oversaw the school's finances, an old fox, who had spent her years working in Accounts, for a local department store - long since closed - dabbed at the crumbs on the table before her. She thought that Aileen must have used shop bought pastry, but she was too polite to ask.

'I saw them talking about it on the BBC this morning,' she spoke with the gentle quietness that years of unhurried and patient retirement brought.

'They said the Police were confused,' she raised her painted on eyebrows expressively and glanced skyward, a gesture implying that she was not in the least surprised. If anyone had asked her, she would have happily spent an hour explaining how it had been different in her day. No-one did.

'Yeh, something about the suspects not matching any of their terrorist databases,' chimed in Tom, a data analyst and church parish council member, who told his wife that membership of the school's Governing Body, where their children attended, was his Christian, community duty. However, secretly he just wanted an excuse to ask his employer for a day working from home, so he could take the dog for a long walk in the spectacular countryside, including a hearty lunch and a couple of pints in his favourite pub. He didn't think that God would mind.

It was true, Aileen had been listening to the Today programme on Radio 4 that morning. Investigation into the previous morning's attacks in London was leading to some strange conclusions. The work of tracing the vans used had not taken the police to the expected religious fundamentalist suspects that they were gearing up to arrest and prosecute. Instead, the credit card records for the rental vans had been traced to a retired police inspector in Newcastle, a physiotherapist in Grantham, two were traced to a married couple, foster carers with a spotless criminal record, from Oxford. In fact, all of the events were pointing to unlikely suspects with no previous links to extremist groups or tendencies to violent behaviour. There seemed initially to be no link between any of them. None of the suspects could be found and no trace of them could be recovered from the crime scenes. The atrocities remained a mystery.

'Our business today,' Aileen had needed to bring the meeting to a close, these things could drift on for hours, she knew from long, bitter, experience, 'is to assess the school's current security arrangements and consider what further actions we need to take, to ensure the safeguarding of the children's, and staff, welfare during their activities in term time.'

She paused briefly to ensure that she had their full attention, without providing an opportunity for an unwelcome interruption.

'At present the site is secure during the school day, with automated gates that operate on a timer. The school Secretary having the ability to open the gates for individual callers at her discretion, with a CCTV monitoring and recording system.'

She looked at each member of the assembled body inclusively as she spoke.

'The school building, playground and field are surrounded by steel fencing that meets *School Premises Regulations, 2012* and access to the building through doors is restricted using RFID technology.' Aileen knew that none of her assembled overseers had the faintest clue whether what she was saying was true, they had to take everything she told them on trust, using the minutes being recorded to protect themselves in the event she was lying.

'However,' she had continued, 'a window could be broken, or an intruder could gain access to the building under false pretences, or lord forbid, a child could become a danger to themselves and others, and we have no policy or procedure in place to deal with that. So, I propose that we put in place a policy that clearly states the purpose, and actions required by staff, in the event of a school lock down in response to a critical incident. Either in our local community or a national emergency.' Aileen was brisk, business-like and straight to the point. The assembled governors murmured their agreement to this eminently sensible action.

'I also propose that we begin practising a lock down protocol, similar to our fire drills, later this week.' The proposals were quickly seconded by Tom, who looked at his watch ruefully. He had better things to be doing. The meeting ended with a gentle ripple of applause.

21

Mickey parked his vintage Jaguar XJ6 in a bay outside the 'Catch o' the Day!' fish and chip shop.

The corporation housing estate it served had been built in the 1950s. The idea had been to build affordable homes for low wage workers, especially those who had sacrificed so much for the war effort. Now its denizens were rarely working class 'heroes'. Instead it had become a sort of ghetto for those lost by, or those seeking to hide from, the modern world.

Mickey 'Two Fists' had spent a day walking around it a few months back. Surprised to find that the streets were largely empty. No children played on the roads. No mothers met on the wide pavements, push carts parked with wailing babies, discussing the local gossip. All he had been able to see was a dozen mobility scooters trundling about, transporting their aged and obese passengers to and from the local shops, as they spent their disability benefits or state pensions. It was a living graveyard.

Reflecting on how times had changed, he encountered the occasional oddly dressed man or woman seen pottering and twitching in their therapeutic gardens, making the effort to maintain their dignity despite the voices in their heads telling them that nobody liked them. Cutting the grass obsessively with scissors to ensure that each blade was the same length, or scrubbing the crazy paved pathways with a bowl of soapy water and a dustpan brush. A life's work. These were the victims of 'care in the community'; dodging the searing, accusing alien gazes of the neighbourhood cats, who knew their secret thoughts and fears, who gathered together each night to torment them.

Once in a while, he observed that younger residents would risk exposure to the daylight, being more accustomed to nocturnal pursuits, cycling as fast as possible to transport their pharmaceutical payload to its required destination. Charlie Fletcher lived around the corner from the chippy, but Mickey didn't want his car to be seen there.

'Come on, Little Man. Let's go find yuur Muvver,' Mickey grunted as he closed the window and opened the driver's door in a single motion. He removed his keys and breathed fresh, polluted air.

The car's doors closed simultaneously, as Lewis leaped out. This was turning into the best day ever for him! Uncle Mickey had first taken him to breakfast in Wetherspoon's and let him have whatever he wanted. He went for the Full Traditional breakfast with an orange juice, but could only eat half of it and didn't bother eating the toast. Lewis expected to be told off for being wasteful, but Uncle Mickey had just grunted over a coffee and paid.

Then, he had been taken to get a hair cut, in a real barbers! The woman seemed to know Uncle Mickey and was really nice to him. She kept the door open the whole time and

Lewis got his head fully shaved. She had joked that Lewis now looked like Uncle Mickey's grandson, 'cos they had matching hair! Lewis laughed, but Mickey just grunted. The nice lady wouldn't take any money from Uncle Mickey and told Lewis to come back anytime, she would cut his hair free!

'Wot forever?' he had asked, 'Yesssss!' he hissed with a fist pump, running in circles and celebrating as if he had scored the winning goal in a Premiership football match.

The odd pair walked briskly around the corner to a tree-lined crescent, where a series of semi-detached and terraced houses had been converted into flats by a Housing Association struggling to keep pace with demand.

Many of the houses had overgrown lawns in the front yard, with bricks missing from boundary walls. The street looked run down, with rusting and unused, decades old cars, that had once been the pride and joy of their owners, on concrete blocks on driveways or on flat tyres on the streets. Instead of the gleaming, apple of their owner's eye, paint-work, they sat as reminders that mobility didn't always go upwards. Their owners had long since passed the age where they could maintain the properties, or the decaying husks of the vehicles scattered around like big game victims in a bloodthirsty safari. The poor lost and forgotten souls sat or lay, incapacitated in rooms with mildewed, flaking wallpaper and sun-bleached paint, once fashionable in a by-gone era. The mechanical whirr and hiss of compressors and pumps, that was once the trademark soundtrack of a geriatric hospital ward, could be heard mixing with the canned laughter of day-time TV. The final stimulation for the decaying minds of the aged unwanted. It overwhelmed the sound of gently tweeting and chirping birds that sat in the trees on the street.

Mickey led Lewis into a yard with grass that reached above Lewis's head, the stems swayed in the sharp Autumnal breeze. They passed a withered door, with flaking paint and a chrome door knocker below the bevelled black number twelve. Somewhere, behind the door, a small dog barked at the intrusion. The windows of the ground floor were shut with yellowing nets and sun-bleached, thick red velvet looking curtains that were pulled tightly closed.

Above, a window to a bathroom or toilet was open and the sound of laughing voices and tinkling digital music sliced through the deathly pall of the street. Mickey led around the back of the house. A back-yard contained an algae and mould covered greenhouse that hadn't grown tomatoes for many years, with the rusted remains of a mountain bike leaning against it. The door marked '12a' had been recently painted in multi-coloured psychedelic swirls and daydream patterns. There was no visible door knocker, or bell, so Mickey banged his two fists in a deafening drumbeat on the door.

'Charley....Chaaaaaarleeeeeeeey. Open this door naow, you 'ear me?' Mickey's gravelly voice couldn't be said to be shouting, but there was no mistaking the call in the upstairs flat.

Muffled voices seemed to be arguing as footsteps thumped rapidly down the stairs. The colourful door snatched open, catching on the door's safety chain abruptly, and slammed closed again. The scratch of the chain's removal was followed by a calmer effort to open the door.

A pale, drawn face appeared in the doorway. Scruffy, shoulder length brown hair was tied back at the nape of the neck, above the hood of a gaudy, bright athlete's sweatshirt bearing the word 'Plank' across the wearers chest. The toggles of the drawstrings of the hood rocked back and forth, pendulously - echoes of the brief exertion that had been expended in the rush down the stairs. The baggy recreational garment hung ironically on the slight frame of a man who rarely exercised himself beyond the monumental task of making himself a cheese toastie,or rolling a 'fat one'.

Charlie Fletcher was not a raging example of masculinity. His wiry physique and drawn, skeletal face owed much to the properties of the illicit substances that he regularly ingested in the stead of nourishing meals. He instantly recognised Mickey 'Two Fists' Butcher, but struggled to think of a reason why he might be there with a small, bald child.

'Are you just gunna stand there, you lanky streak of piss, or are you gonna invite us in' Mickey sardonically demanded from the dumbstruck Charlie.

'Oh..yeah..of course, man, I mean Mr Butcher. Come in!'

Charlie opened the door wide and welcomed them into his palace with a sweeping flourish of his arm. Mickey fixed the drug dealer with a withering glare and pushed Lewis in ahead of him.

'Come on Little Man, up you go,' he guided the boy to the foot of the stairs and indicated that he should go up them alone.

From upstairs the sounds of laughter and a simple digital musical tune continued as before. A woman's voice called down for Charlie to hurry up as he was missing his turn. Mickey watched the boy go up before turning around to confront Charlie. He pushed the diminutive figure of Charlie against the door that had just been closed.

'Alright Charlie, you waste of space, is she 'ere?' he demanded.

Charlie visibly shook, his fingers looked like twigs as they pushed against the grip of the much larger man.

'Is oo 'ere? Oo you lookin' for? I ain't done nuffin' Mr Butcher, you know me. It's only to friends. Small amounts like. Nuffin' that affects your business, sir.'

'Maggie. Maggie Tracey. I know she comes to you. Is the stoopid bitch 'ere?' Mickey asked.

22

There was a room that lead straight on from the landing at the top of the stairs. Lewis looked into it tentatively and tried to take in what he saw.

In the corner, was a sixty inch LED TV illuminating a room that resembled a Bedouin camp. The centre of the room was dominated by a large hookah pipe, with a smouldering brass bowl above an enormous urn of smoky water. A snake-like pipe and mouthpiece lay curled around it, waiting to bear the next victim into the stupor of the lotus-eater. Beside this was a low, dark oak coffee table, that was strewn with tobacco, cigarette papers, over-flowing ashtrays and other paraphernalia. A single wireless game controller stood in stark contrast to the esoteric ripped, curved wooden and metal items. A familiar piece of moulded plastic that Lewis could comprehend. Beanbags and a single mattress surrounded the table providing seating around the walls.

Loose, variously coloured fabric sheets hung above them obscuring the ceiling, bunched into the centre like a circus big-top.

Acrid, bittersharp herbal smoke swirled and curled around the space. Astral clouds of it rippled and collided around the room in competing galactic tides as the dark occupants of the room jerked, swayed and gesticulated in the murk.

Three people could be seen in silhouette in the room, reclining on beanbags and had their backs to Lewis. They were concentrating on the huge TV, an electronic window providing an ever-changing vista of a surreal virtual world. Each flicked their hands, which were holding game controllers, hoping that their physical movements would be translated into the actions of their characters in the game. It seemed to be a crazy race between a giant gorilla, a crocodile or a dinosaur and a strange turtle. Each character had their own Go Kart and they were racing around an increasingly incomprehensible race track.

One, a young woman, flinched as her kart was spun off by a precision targeted coconut. She squealed as the kart dropped off the road, falling into cyber oblivion, only for it to reappear inches above the track as it was digitally reincarnated, ready to continue the eternal race.

He looked back down the stairs to see Uncle Mickey holding Charlie up by the scruff of his neck with Charlie remonstrating his innocence - hands, up by his ears in surrender and supplication. He couldn't make out what was being said, but it sounded like it had something to do with his Mum, who seemed to come to this place regularly.

He realised that this was 'Charlie's'. The place his Mum had told him about when she was partying with friends. Lewis watched the trio in the room playing on the game and wondered if his Mum had ever played it too. He simmered at the the thought.

'She woz 'ere a day ago, 'bout this time. Said she needed the usual and a little sumfing for a client. An olda bloke who struggled with his...' Charlie closed his fist and raised his forearm as a reference that the virility of the subject might be in question. 'I gave a few pills to 'elp 'er owt. That's all I know,' he nodded vigorously as a declaration of his honesty.

'If I find out you're lying to me, you wanker, I will end you,' Mickey said in his best Vinnie Jones way. His mean little eyes became slits to emphasize the various ways that he could could inflict harm on the drug dealing wastrel.

Charlie went completely still and took a deep breath, 'Wait...,' The lids of his eyes twitched, his voice flattened into a monotonous drawl, 'wait...'ang on, she did say where she was goin'.' Charlie seemed to enter a transcendental state.

'Wait..she said she woz goin' to the school to meet someone about her son. Sumfing 'bout 'concerns'.'

Charlie looked over Mickey's right shoulder, forming an imaginary holographic repeat of the scene just a day before, straining his addled memory to recall his last conversation with Maggie. He remembered her eyes, the almond shaped eyes with deep brown, chocolatey irises that made him melt every time he looked into them. In contrast, his mind's eye followed the path of her sharp, carefully tweezed and plucked eye-brows. The curve of her cheek as it arced into her jaw.

'The class teacher. Mister...mister...' he struggled.

'Mister Magoo? Mister fuckin' Bump? 'Oo?' Mickey was not renowned for his patience and it was being stretched today. He was beginning to struggle, as the simple task of finding Maggie, was turning into a huge fucking effort.

'Meester...Meester   Crapper.   No...wait..Mist..er Carpetman...Mister Carpenter! That's it. Mister Carpenter, her kid's teacher.' Charlie had finally trawled the name out, he blinked rapidly and smiled proudly.

'Mister Carpenter. His teacher,' Mickey repeated and cast a glance up the stairs to where Lewis stood transfixed by the scene in front of him.

'Right, look after the kid and clean 'im up. Smells like he shit hisself. I need to find Maggie. If she has shacked up with some noncey teacher...' He left the sentence hanging. With a last withering look at Charlie, he opened the door with sarcastic ease and left.

23

Wiping clean the previous days declarations and instructions to staff, with a single decisive sweep of her left arm ('Wax off! Daniel San' a memory flashed across her consciousness), Aileen stood facing the blank, white noticeboard. Board rubber in one hand, black marker pen in the other.

Her back was to the gathered staff, who had managed to ignore her unusual appearance in the room during a lunch break. She stood poised to write the update on the board regarding the new school lock down procedures, as well as a notice to the school of a drill; she hesitated.

The voices around the room clattered together like a puzzle in her head. There was happiness, consternation and an intimacy of collegiate friendship. A shared experience, a common purpose that drew them together.

How long had it been since she had felt part of that? She wondered if she ever really had. Her attempt to reconnect to the devotions of her past self using the rosary had left her feeling disorientated.   Dislocated. Every thought and action seemed dream-like, like walking sub-merged through crystal-blue water on a sunny day. Hazy, warm and sluggish. She was also acutely and minutely focused on the tiny details of her movement and the sounds and smells of the environment around her, feeling every fibre of the sweater rubbing against each nerve ending of her skin. Hearing every voice, every intonation and inflection. Words jumbling and tumbling from each corner of the space surrounding and enveloping her. She could hear staff gather at the free food, the left overs from the Governors' meeting. Aileen felt an unusual pang of guilt for leaving the tainted offerings on the table.

Marvelling at her own sense of responsibility for these people still, she felt she could stop, now. Pull back from the edge. These were people who, even though she detested and had little or no respect for, had supported and worked with her in the struggle of these last years.

'No idea why those people attacked schools...I spent hours marking..waste of time...Kayleigh slapped him, again..Safeguarding...Maths...Henry's Mum shouted at the Marks brother's Dad in the playground this morning...then Suki actually farted really loudly and it all kicked off...those boys should not be allowed to play football...you don't think it could happen here do you?'

The voices of the men and women played on different channels in Aileen's mind and she pictured each pathway as a different coloured light, a complex E.C.G. of the school pulsing in harmonious and conspicuous health.

'...Oh, what a classic...Mm..delish...mmm...creamy, with a hint of garlic...try that!' She singled Aaron Parminster's voice out. She thought his accent was a parody of those 1960s buddy movies, the ones with young women and men going, perhaps on a summer holiday, his voice rising uniquely on the last syllable. He was a naïve innocent and she felt a twinge of guilt for the first time.

Aileen turned towards the room's centre. Still, the impulse to stop them from their unintentional abominations was clouded. Her momentum halted. With a sweeping gaze she took the scene in. A small knot of the school's staff were surrounding the unclean feast; appreciative glances were cast her way. Too late.

In the corner sat a very sick Charles Syndale. Suzy Tallister sat with him. A hand rubbing his back in sympathy as she whispered consoling platitudes in his ear. Aileen let her arms relax and hands hang loose, the board marker and rubber held in a relaxed grip. She froze. Suzy's eyes were yellowed with a single vertical black slash, like that of a hunting reptile. The steady hypnotic stare focused her prey on the gentle swaying of her head. It would be unprepared for the sudden, deadly strike.

She blinked and looked back to the group at the table. Aaron Parminster grinned his approval to her, his mouth full and cheeks stuffed. The mouth opened and closed, revealing the churned up vol-au-vent he was consuming. In her dream-like, sensitive state, his teeth gnashed and ground the minced meat of Maggie Tracey's body as loudly as a clash of cymbals and timpani drums; the percussion of a satanic orchestra. His eyes were gashes in his face, inward navels that sucked the light from the room.

Aileen shifted her eyes back to the food on the table and flicked to each person eating it. They each had navels in the place their eyes should have been, some with inwards gashes that blurred and distorted the room around them. Vortexes twisting time and space into the wormholes that had replaced their eyes, taking matter and energy from this universe and taking it – somewhere else. Others had outward, bulging and pulsing navels. Straining to contain the bile and filth that their monstrous lives had built up; epidermal dams struggling to contain a flood of the diseased corruption bursting to erupt.

Far from any of the others stood Robert Carpenter. He had avoided the canapés as he had avoided the poisoned milk. The crisp snap of the apple he had half eaten filled her hyper sensitive ears as their eyes met again in a thunderclap as the next fresh green bite was sheared away.

Aileen felt the spectre of Maggie Tracey standing at her shoulder, betraying her, as he inspected the list of violations written on her face, devouring her confidence and authority with each clench of his jaw. She watched as he took another bite. She wondered how he could stand to be surrounded by such foul disease.

She realised with a sense of relief, that his eyes scanned the room, too. His glance paused on Charles and those at the table of canapes. He didn't know. He couldn't see the others' filth. He couldn't see her guilt. Didn't know her true intention. The phantom she sensed behind her was invisible to him. He would have stopped them eating if he knew; he would have warned Charles and taken him to hospital. He would have acted to restrain her and elicit a confession of her sins and transgressions against the doctrines of faith, as Father Murphy O'Riley used to.

Her hallucination had renewed her resolve and returned her impetus. All sense of empathy, or maternal sympathy, for the staff that surrounded her had vanished. They were inhuman monsters that deserved all that was coming to them. She returned to writing her notices on the whiteboard.

Robert Carpenter, though, presented a problem. He was the only person in the room that was aware. His awareness had helped him to avoid her traps. He had eyes that could see, although they had not been opened for him. His awareness provided Aileen with an unforeseen challenge.

It could be solved easily, she reflected. He could be written a confidential letter that she could leave in his pigeon-hole requiring him to attend a meeting with Aileen at the time of her choosing. She could twist him up like a pretzel using the stress of an inquisition into his capability in discharging his professional duties. Safeguarding was always a good one to turn the screw. He would be too proud to bring anyone with him to the meeting. His planning, teaching and feedback strategies were sound, and he knew she knew it. She could exterminate him quickly using a skipping rope as a ligature, perhaps, or bludgeon him with a rounders bat. Then he could be disposed of in a similar manner to Maggie Tracey. Although, she still had not fully disposed of the dead parent's body yet and another would be an added burden considering how much time and effort her new project would take. He also had an uncanny knack of seeing the pitfall and avoiding it. Could she risk being completely uncovered by him? Physically, he was a more formidable opponent.

Robert Carpenter gained a second reprieve.

Her mission completed, her momentum restored, she returned to her office to e-mail out the new lock down protocol to her demonic staff, ensuring that they would know what actions to take when they heard the new alarm. She had selected one of the automated fire alarm settings, one with five, one second blasts of the bell separated by intervals of two seconds of silence, to alert everyone that an intruder was on site and begin a school wide lock down.

Dealing with Robert would have to wait.

24

Robert had arrived in the staffroom quite late, there was little chance of him escaping without interacting with some of his peers. A group of his colleagues had already surrounded a table.

Free food on a platter sat attracting them like bees swarming to a flower, or he thought more appropriately, like flies to shit.

He had sneaked behind them and reached the coffee machine without being noticed. Charles and Suzy sat in the corner, on the uncomfortable, armless chairs together, again. It was getting a bit obvious and Robert noticed that a couple of the other older female staff looked on disapprovingly.

Charles looked ill. His hair looked greasy and he had a blotchy pallor. He stared fixedly on the floor in front of him, his arms around his belly. He was doing his best to accept the sympathy of Suzy, but to Robert, he clearly looked awkward at the public display of intimacy.

Eating his fresh, Golden Delicious apple, he wandered over to the coffee pot and considered whether it was time to put the nonsense of yesterday out of his mind and drink a much needed brew. The room bustled with its usual hubbub of pointless short conversations and friendless, but polite salutations as the staff did their utmost to maintain decorum, despite many of them having little or no respect for each other. In some cases plastic, fixed smiles masked scorn, derision and often jealousy. Real or imagined slights and insults were not easily forgotten in this world.

With this in mind, as he absent mindedly munched on the juicy fruit, he heard Aaron's voice delivering his culinary critique in his best Greg Wallace imitation.

'...Oh, what a classic...Mm..delish...mmm...creamy, with a hint of garlic...try that!' Robert reflected how gormless and irritating Aaron was. He always, without fail, emphasised the last syllable, accentuating every annoying sentence of his puerile life like a moronic gameshow host.

Robert looked over to the group to ensure that he had not been spotted by Aaron. He could well do without a facile five minutes. He was lucky today, as Aaron had his back turned to him. Over the shoulder of Mr Parminster, beyond the group harvesting the crop of free lunch time treats, stood Aileen Byrne. A board rubber and marker pen hung loosely in her hands at the end of each slack arm. He noticed that the colourful scarf that had been tied in her hair earlier had been removed. Her face looked drawn and pale, framed by the raven black hair.

He watched as she quickly scanned the room with a regal nonchalance; a queen regarding her subjects benignly.

The beneficence vanished as she fixed her gaze on Aaron, her eyes flicked in panic between the contents on the table and his face. Robert watched, transfixed as the Head Teacher's face animatedly transformed, portraying her innermost thoughts, visibly for all to see like a lighthouse broadcasting a warning of a dangerous tide and a rocky shore. Her eyebrows drew together, her lips pressed tightly into a single tiny fault line, the furrows on her face advertising the canyons of her anguish and regret. There was something else, too. A sense of horror and revulsion at the sight of the staff.

His surprise made him bite into his apple much deeper than he intended. His teeth sliced through to the sour core, his mouth filled with the bitter taste of the broken pips. Again he experienced the unreal sensation of sharing something like a telepathic bond with the Head Teacher, as their eyes met once more. He felt the hair on his neck and arms stand on end. Her eyes and face twisted and contorted as they attempted to keep pace with the fleeting emotions and thoughts she experienced. He almost choked, chewing the fruit carefully and deliberately, ensuring that he did not cough the contents of his mouth over the staff nearby.

He couldn't tear his eyes away. He watched as Aileen Byrne's face adopted the guilty expression of a naughty puppy dog. Caught-in-the act. Caught in the act of what though? He wondered.

He let his eyes scan the room, flicking back and forth to her face to discern any changes, taking another bite of his apple to replace the sourness left over from the bite before. Aileen's face betrayed her twice. Once, when Robert looked over to Charles. She noticed and followed his glance. When their eyes met again Aileen seemed to regard him with anger. As if Charles's current illness was his responsibility.

The next time she betrayed a change of emotion was when he looked over to the table of assembled staff eating free food. The look of revulsion returned. Each eyed the other. Robert took another tentative bite of his apple as Aileen turned back to her task.

'This is not happening,' Robert, his voice distorted by a mouth full of chewed apple, murmured to himself nervously. Juice spurted uncontrollably from his lips onto the worktop, next to the coffee percolator. He wiped it quickly with the cuff of his black pullover.

For the second time in two days, Robert had felt his heart beat a little faster. This time he could not be imagining it. There was something out of place. There was a malignancy about the Head Teacher; she was hiding something. Or not hiding something. Was she trying to tell him something? He struggled to articulate his feelings in response to the presence of her.

He walked over to Aaron, putting a hand on his shoulder as he looked over it, down onto the table. There were half a dozen canapés left.

'Hi Rob,' Aaron said, as he twisted his neck around, 'ave one of these beauties! Governors left them for us and you'll never guess who made them?'

'Miss Byrne,' Robert replied impassively and picked up the last remaining vol-au-vents. He lifted it to his nose and sniffed it carefully.

'Ha! The first bite is always with the nose, eh! Rob?' Aaron watched as Rob shook his head and lowered the bite sized canapé back down and replaced it on the platter to the horror of the group.

'I wouldn't eat that if I were you,' Rob warned the others as they looked at each to communicate their disgust at his uncouth and mysterious behaviour. Robert looked at the door as the Head stalked out of the room without a backward glance.

'Well, I'm certainly not going to eat that one!' Aaron chirped up, to the amusement of those gathered for the feast.

25

Charlie leant against the door as it closed behind Mickey's huge frame. His forehead and palms pressed against the wood of the door as if he was preparing to exercise his spindly arms with vertical press ups.

Maggie was in trouble. If Maggie was in trouble and Mickey Butcher had visited him, then it was big trouble and he was likely to be in big trouble, too.

He breathed steadily, to calm his nerves after the physical confrontation with the town's most notorious gangster. He could still taste the dry fear in his mouth and the light fluttering of a whirlpool in his belly, a reaction to the mortal terror he felt in the large hands of the dangerous mobster. His legs, no stronger or more robust than the tentacles of a jellyfish still struggled to maintain his weight.

The day had started so normally. He had gotten up after a couple of hours of sleep and smoked the blint of an epic spliff that he had rolled a few hours before. He had had a great week. Shifting the last of the grass that he had managed to get from the Dutch student, who brought a couple of ounces back every month from his visits home. He had also managed to get hold of some premium Class A stuff which he had managed to punt on at a bit of a profit and used his connections to get some pharma gear for Maggie. Charlie had spent the last night enjoying his personal supply with a few of his best customers. He was going to take a few days off, to straighten up a bit and get some sleep. Maybe even visit his Mum to get some washing done and actually eat something. Her Sunday Roasts were magic.

He made the monumental effort of straightening his arms and pushing his head away from the door. The first and last push up of the day. Instead of a cool relaxing couple of chilled out days before getting ready for another hectic weekend, he was totally stressed out and in more shit than he could cope with. He needed to warn Maggie and get her to sort it, fast. He needed another bong hit to calm down. Pulling his phone from the pocket of his hoodie, he turned and began walking up the stairs, scrolling to find her number. He managed to compose a brief text message as he climbed: *Mickey woz ere 4 u. ? r u. Call me.*

He paused and looked up, before sending it as he reached the top of the stairs, alerted by the proximity of the stench of body odour, urine and faeces. The boy stood on the edge of the landing, three steps up from Charlie. His bald head was a clean pink colour, the rest of his face was discoloured by various stains of dirt that had been smudged and cleaned off badly, with smears of his last meal around his mouth.

'Where's Oncle Mickey gone? Oo are you? Where's my Mum?' Lewis asked, as he backed towards a wall, fists clenched and shoulders hunched, ready to fight his way out of this stranger's home.

'It's alright, kid, Lewis is it?' Charlie noticed the similarities between the boy and his Mum. They had the same jaw line and high cheek bones. The boy had also inherited Maggie's almond shaped eyes, but instead of dark brown, he had lighter hazel eyes with streaks of green.

'My name is Charlie. I'm a friend of your Mum, a good friend. She comes to see me a lot and we go way back. We went to school together. She woz a coupla years ahead of me,' he smiled, 'So you don't need to worry.' He looked into the darkened room and called to the figures who remained seated, glued to the game.

'Sorry guys, the sesh is over for now.' He smiled down at Lewis, 'I'll look after ya 'til your mum comes and picks you up,' he pressed the green 'send' button and rubbed the boy's bald head as a friendly gesture.

26

Lewis had heard the door close behind him downstairs. Mickey had left without him. Had left him here with strangers.

He looked back into the darkened, smelly, hazy room where the three silhouettes still ignored him, entranced by the scrolling graphics on the TV and the simple, mesmerising, repetitive digital music. He felt a little bit dizzy and sick, the taste of the sausages he had just eaten kept repeating.

He backed away from the threshold, back onto the landing and turned, just as the skinny man, Charlie, was reaching the top of the stairs. He was surrounded by people that he didn't know, unsure of where he was in relation to his own flat, so he got ready to fight, just like in Fortnite.

His Mum's warnings about men like Mickey rang in his ears, that they were 'bad news' and 'not to be trusted'. Mickey had just ditched him here, without saying goodbye or anything. She had also told him not to do anything any of them said. Yet here he was with someone who was 'bad news': alone. His Mum had abandoned him, too.

When the skinny man rubbed him on the head it was too much. Lewis saw red. He jabbed his right hand into Charlie's thigh and swung a big left hook, aiming between the taller man's legs. The hook connected and the man doubled over, his phone clattered as it was dropped and he crumpled on top of it onto the floor. Lewis stood over him, waiting for him to start to get up so that he could kick him and keep him on the ground, ducking and weaving, just he did when he got into play fights with Will and Toby. Except, they got up quicker. Lewis decided that adults, with the exception of Mickey, were all pussies.

Charlie was completely taken by surprise as the tiny child stepped forward under his arm and hit him first in the leg and then caught him with a big haymaker hook in the crown jewels. The kid was like a lightning bolt and he didn't have any time to adjust his stance to protect himself.

His breath whooshed out as the excruciating pain between his legs first contracted, causing his limbs and torso to fold over to protect the area, then exploded through his body as he fell in slow motion onto the floor, crossing through the doorway into the lounge, where his three guests turned in frozen, stoned astonishment. A silence followed, broken only by the tinkling digital music cascading through arpeggios as each player's avatar fell from the track.

'You alright, Charlie?' a shadowy figure in the depths of the room asked pointlessly before sputtering out a disjointed croaking, dry throated laugh.

'No Zac, 'e is not alright as a ten year old has just hit him in the nuts,' replied the other male voice, before it too joined in the duet of giggling and laughter that erupted.

Only the young woman seemed capable of action, as she stood and moved over to the prone body of Charlie, which had begun to writhe and groan. She hobbled on her unsteady, numb and blood deprived legs, fizzing with the tiny sensations of a million acupuncture needles continuously stabbing her as the circulation returned. She first rolled Charlie over to make sure that no serious injury had occurred to him, then she stepped over him to soothe the frightened looking child.

'Ben, will you stop laughing and get Charlie an ice pack, or some frozen peas or something from the freezer. Zac, will you turn that game off. Charlie's hurt and there's a kid 'ere,' she gave instructions to the two teenage boys who accepted her authority.

'You alright, luv? I'm Alysha, what's your name?' she asked, she had pronounced her name Aleeeshaar; it sounded familiar to Lewis.

'Lewis,' he replied. 'There's a girl called Alysha in my class,' he uncurled his fingers and opened his hands, relaxing his shoulders as he talked to the young woman in front of him. He instantly felt that he could trust her, his Mum had not told not to trust other women, especially as the others in the room had done as she told them.

Ben returned, still giggling, from the kitchen with a bag of peas, that had been in the freezer for more than a year, wrapped in a tea towel and passed it to the grateful Charlie, who gently cushioned the package between his legs.

Charlie had been terrified of the pension aged gangster earlier, now he had been beaten up, in his own flat, by a tiny, dirty, smelly child. He sat up and bottom shuffled himself away from the boy and onto the mattress in the lounge. After rummaging in his pocket, he extracted a bag containing something green, and threw it at the laughing Zac.

'Roll one up, Zac,' Charlie curtly instructed before returning his attention to Lewis.

'Why the fuck did you do that? You little shit! You wait 'til your Mum comes...' he winced as the agony transformed into a dull resonating ache that transmitted the pain like an emergency broadcast signal to the rest of his body. Charlie failed to see the funny side and wanted to batter the child, only he still couldn't move, so he vented his anger verbally.

'Charlie! He's just a scared kid,' Alysha interrupted, instantly defending the young boy. Even though she had not moved earlier, when the boy stood in the room, she had noticed his presence and continued to play the game with the lads. She had overheard some of the heated discussion downstairs and heard Maggie's name mentioned. If the boy was Maggie's, then she would look after him until she came back to get him.

'...back, you little bastard!' The ice-cold peas were finally numbing the area and Charlie began to fell a little better, but thought better than to move.

'That kid stinks, man,' Ben who was not the most sympathetic individual at the best of times ignored the increasing distress on Lewis's face, 'Did you shit yourself?'

Lewis had had enough and burst into tears, ' I..w.want..m.my Mum.'

Alysha put her arms around him, turning her head away as she did, raising her eyebrows in response to the smell of neglect. She looked at Ben with more disgust and revulsion than she felt for the child.

'You're a total twat, Ben. Why don't you just get lost?' She turned to Charlie, 'Tell 'im to go, I'll help sort the kid out, just tell him to go.' She jerked her head at the still smirking Ben, who looked between the occupants of the room, like a nodding dog in the back windscreen of an insured car, with addled idiocy.

Zac had finished his DT project and lit the enhanced cigarette up, taking a long, loud puff, before nodding his head in the direction of Charlie as he reached up to pass the grass joint to Ben.

Ben examined the burning cylinder and blew gently on the glowing end, causing an acceleration in the ignition of the substances rolled inside. He conspicuously took a long, hard and expansive drag on the spliff and held his breath. His face contorted by the strain of not expelling his full lungs of heated smoke. He passed the remains of the reefer to Charlie, who took it and looked at the much diminished length before taking a long pull on it himself.

Ben saluted the others and took his silent leave from the room, exhaling a large cloud of smoke as he travelled down the stairs. Lewis had once seen an old train, from olden days, that spewed smoke from a large chimney on the top of a tube thing at the front it, go through a tunnel on a telly programme when he and his Mum had watched something called the One Show. Ben reminded him of that.

The memory distracted him from crying and missing his Mum. He took a moment to look at the three remaining grown ups around him. Toby had told him about a book that he had read about a boy who had to train dragons. Lewis wondered if they were dragons or something, because they all breathed smoke. He couldn't wait to tell Will and Toby. Maybe they could train these grown ups and go on adventures.

'Thanks Zac, I'll call you as soon as I get clear of this and get my next package, OK?' Charlie dismissed the still seated Zac.

Zac nodded his understanding, however the effect of the drug had briefly incapacitated him. It took a while for the eighteen year old's brain to process and actuate his limbs. The instructions to stand and walk out of the room got delayed like commuters lined up on a platform, waiting for a Southern train to arrive to take them to work. He sat and giggled for a moment or two, before looking surprised and disorientated.

He stood, 'Yeah, man. Like, ah...whatever. Thanks for the...' his sentence trailed off as he waved his arms around the room.

'Yup,' he tapped his pockets down to make sure he had everything he needed, without any thought of what he might find in the pockets, or what he might identify as missing, 'Yup,' he repeated. Then, he ran a hand through his short brown hair and with heavy footsteps, he left the room and staggered down the stairs. The three watched him go silently.

Charlie imagined David Attenborough's slow, naturalists commentary describing Zac's efforts to navigate the complexity of a stairway and door. He reflected that this was bang on gear and wondered if his Dutch supplier would consider bringing more of it across the channel next time. The door closed behind Zac with a soft click.

'Alysha,' Charlie brought the young woman's attention back to the pressing issues of the morning. 'Mickey Butcher woz just 'ere. 'E brought the kid. It's Maggie's boy,' he began to explain between long pauses as he dragged on the medicinal spliff. He held his breath each time and exhaled slowly through his nose, feeling the pain ebb away in his testicles. Charlie began to buzz and felt his head float on his neck. The pain in his body became dissociated from his consciousness. He stood up haphazardly, careful not to burn the mattress with the burning end of the joint which he held out to the young woman who still cradled the boy in her arms.

'She's gone AWOL, so 'e's not 'appy,' she took the burning offering with reverence and gratitude, and nudged Lewis over towards Charlie.

'You need to say sorry, Lewis,' she advised as she took her first drag.

'Sorry,' Lewis offered, with head bowed, he stood first in front of the grown man that he had just kicked the arse of, then he moved next to him, his back to the same wall beside Charlie.

He noticed that the two grown ups seemed to be slowing down. The words and sentences taking longer for them to complete. It was as if the weird smelling cigarette that they were smoking was making them really old or something.

'He needs a shower Charlie, and some new clothes.' Alysha prescribed the simplest solution to the short term problem of Lewis's hygiene that she could think of.

'Mate, I am not goin' to Tesco's to get 'im some new stuff. I am totally wasted. And my nuts still hurt,' Charlie looked down at Lewis's head, catching his hand above the child before he made the same mistake of touching him again.

'Alright, you get him cleaned up, then. Gimme fifty quid and I'll go into town and get him new clothes,' even in her inebriated state, Alysha could see that Charlie had been blind-sided by the appearance of Mickey Butcher and Maggie's boy at his flat, and saw an opportunity to make a few quid back from her dealer. She would give it back to him later, in exchange for a couple of bags.

27

Robert walked through the corridors of the school without direction, needing time to think, somewhere where no-one would go.

A destination finally in mind, he headed for the Art Cupboard – nicknamed the 'Mouldy Cupboard' by the staff some years before, on account of the small room's mouldy, ratty smell – it once would have been a space for the caretaker to house his carpentry and maintenance equipment. He hoped that no classes were preparing for an Art lesson today.

Finding the door closed, he looked around furtively to make sure would no-one see him. Entering without being seen, leaving the light off, he crept behind a rack of variously coloured rolls of paper used as backing for the display of children's work and crouched down to think. He could feel the thumping of his heart on his ribs and the hair on the back of his neck was wet. Sweat was dripping onto his shirt collar, the material had begun chafing his skin.

There was something about Charles's sudden illness that made Robert uncomfortable. The strange interview with Aileen yesterday afternoon had left Robert feeling ill at ease. Had he too quickly dismissed it as a paranoid reaction to the terrorist attacks in London? It was something to do with Lewis Tracey, he thought. Was there a breach in the safeguarding? He recalled what he thought was a momentary look of insanity on her face. What was the Head Teacher up to? Why was he invited into her office the day before? Was Aileen Byrne going crazy? Was she asking for help or warning him off? Was he losing his mind?

He began to hyperventilate as his frenzied thoughts ran out of control. His panic escalated to mortal terror, of the Head Teacher, or of his own paranoia, he wasn't sure. His eyes closed and he began to feel his chest contract. A pain in his sternum made his breathing fast and shallow. His pulse raced. He felt as if his spine had been attached to a wire that accelerated his essence, up through the ceiling and into the air, through endless blue skies and fluffy, cumulus clouds. Endlessly accelerating.

A dark haze encroached the periphery of his vision. The sensation of racing upwards overcame the awareness of his surroundings as he was swallowed by undulating waves of grey and black oblivion, drubbing into his consciousness with the wet, dull beat of his blood rushing around his veins.

He woke amongst the beads of polystyrene and discarded staples on the cold floor of the Art cupboard, unsure of how much time had passed.

Dazed and unsteady, he rose to his feet, brushing himself down, establishing his link to reality. He breathed in slowly and deeply through his nose and counted to three, before exhaling silently through his 'o' shaped mouth. He repeated this over and again until the dizziness ended and his fevered mind calmed.

'This can't be happening,' again Robert attempted to convince himself that he had imagined the entire encounter and the subsequent panic attack.

'Oh my god, Robert. You've totally lost the plot.' He imagined how Elle would react if he confided his suspicions about the Head Teacher and recounted this lunchtime's events. He pictured her face with an incredulous look as it turned away, mockingly, to pour him another glass of wine.

In his mind, he ran through the possible responses she might make to him, to regain a sense of predictable normality.

'Get a grip, loser,' he heard her low sensual voice demand. 'Are you like, delusional?' she might ask derisively with a haughty chuckle.

'Psycho,' he decided, would probably be her most likely statement, 'you're a teacher in a primary school for the rest of your life. Accept it and get with the programme,' she would conclude, definitively drawing a line under the imagined conversation.

Looking at his watch, he made sure that he hadn't been passed out for so long that he had missed the beginning of the afternoon session. It wasn't quite One O'clock yet. He had only been in the room, unconscious, for minutes. No one would be missing him, yet.

He rubbed the palms of his hands on his cheeks, feeling the emergence of stubble breaking the smooth surface of the skin. He needed a plan. A way of confirming his suspicions, or at least confirming his delusional state.

'Go back to the beginning, Robert. When did this start?' He whispered, urging controlled thought.

He pictured Benedict Cumberbatch, dressed in tweed, and forced himself to be logical.

Eyes closed, he pictured a timeline, throwing thoughts and observations up against it like magnets to a fridge door. Charles's face, Benedict Cumberbatch, his meeting with Aileen Byrne, Elle being ill after ice-cream in Cornwall, coffee, canapés, a question from his sub-conscious wondering if picturing Benedict Cumberbatch demonstrated a homo-erotic fascination, Aaron, milk.

It had all begun with the coffee in her office and his refusal to use the milk carton. He remembered the anger in her eyes when he told her about Elle's dairy intolerance as he had refused the milk in the cartons that she had offered. They had little green stickers, and she hadn't used them.

The look in her eyes had been similar to the look when he had glanced at the sickly Charles Syndale in the Staffroom, minutes earlier. He needed a closer look at the milk cartons that she kept segregated in her office.

Robert did his best not to picture Martin Freedman's disdainful and questioning face when confronted with the outlandish theory presented in his mind's eye, but failed, and wondered how he was going to contrive a visit to the Head's office to search for incriminating lactose based evidence. The game was very certainly, afoot.

28

Robert returned through the corridors, his head hung in rueful embarrassment at the episode in the Art cupboard, towards the classroom where he spent his life's energy on other people's children. Elle's voice of reason whispering calming and soothing, rational reassurances in his head.

It would be his secret. He didn't need to tell Elle, or anyone else of his suspicion, or his collapse. As he walked past the main hall, the supervisors were tidying away the last of the lunch tables and mopping the floors. Looking up briefly , he saw that the door to Aileen's office was open. Without breaking his stride, he made his decision.

As he approached the door, an excuse for his intrusion presented itself in a timely coincidence. Lewis Tracey, the son of the parent that Aileen had discussed meeting due to Safeguarding concerns the day before, had not arrived at school today. This, he thought, would be a relevant pretence for arriving at her door.

He stood tentatively at the threshold, peeking in like an errant schoolchild, who had been sent there to be disciplined. The room was empty. The Head Teacher must have been called away by a supervisor to deal with an incident. Bet it had something to do with Year 6 boys and football, he thought.

Glancing around the room, he took it in. He had always thought it looked sparse, tidy, organised and professional. Now his eyes tuned into the barrenness, iciness and bare, emotionless malevolence of the room, wondering for the first time what the children who were sent there, on rare occasions, thought of it.

To his right, just inside the door stood the coffee making utensils on a tray by a small sink, including the UHT milk cartons with red and green stickers. With a quick look in each direction down the corridor, to ensure that the coast was clear, he darted into the room and grabbed a UHT carton with each hand. Red sticker in his left, green sticker in his right. He stood staring at the two cartons in his hands for a moment, then thrust them in his trouser pockets and almost ran out of the office, down the corridor to the Year 4 classroom.

Only his inner teacher voice objected to this, self censoring his actions: 'Walk, don't run!' Instead, he walked suspiciously, looking over his shoulder every few steps, back to class, remembering his attempts at criminality in his youth.

He had never been a good thief. Once, he had stolen a book, Jack Kerouac *On the road*, from a branch of Waterstone's as a Christmas present for a friend when he was a teenager. His weekend job paid a pittance and he considered the act as a modern day Robin Hood might, redistributing cultural wealth from the rich corporate bodies that had sequestered them in the inaccessible capitalist ivory towers of consumerist nirvana, to the poor, the needy and the worthy.

He stuffed the book, in blind panic, haphazardly, into an inside pocket of an oversized camouflaged army jacket that was fashionable at the time, and ran for the door.

Later, as he perused novelty sock gift packs, he discovered he was being followed by a man in a suit with an earpiece, as he skulked around Debenhams.

Ducking out of the department store rapidly, he followed a group of lively Uni students into a pub, ironically called 'The Straight and Narrow' and walked directly into the Gents toilet, depositing the stolen merchandise out of the window. Out of sight. Sadly, also out of reach. He couldn't recover it later, as he saw the book had fallen down past the window ledge, between stacks of empty metal barrels that had been brought up from the cellar for collection by the brewery.

Ruefully, he bought a pint of ale at the bar with his limited cash reserve, seeing the pursuing security officer, charged with recovering the stolen item at the window, he raised his glass in salute. Thus ending his career as an agent of free redistribution.

The following week, he bought a copy of the book from a competing local book store, justifying himself by supporting a local independent business.

Robert sweated his way through the rest of the afternoon. Half moons saturated the under arms of his shirt and would have been clearly visible, were it not for the dark pullover that disguised his anxiety. The illicit milk cartons had been placed on the top shelf of his 'Teacher cupboard'. A tiny space that was used by teachers all over the country to keep the illusion of control and organisation in a classroom.

The mess caused by too many tasks and not enough time, too much paperwork and not enough folders, too many new initiatives and not enough book shelf space, was contained in a six foot by two foot cupboard at the back of the room, through a door hidden from sight by a range of changing posters and displays.

He hoped that when the Head Teacher discovered the theft and put two and two together, she would not find the evidence she needed to uncover him as a thief and a criminal to the rest of the staff. The imagined shame hung heavily on his shoulders and he could barely cope with being in a classroom that afternoon. He watched each slow, mechanical movement of the clock on the wall. It seemed to take forever for the afternoon to end.

Pacing the room, trying not to walk in a repeating circuit, he occupied his mind by trying to weave through the maze of tables and seated children like a Pac-man. His path obstructed by ghosts of teachers past, pointing accusing fingers at their unworthy successor, blocking his progress, requiring him to in an almost random manner. Every time he passed by the door, an urgent impulse ordered him to leave. To run. To not look back.

Avoiding a path that led passed the door was the biggest challenge of the afternoon, as he had set the children of the class a science test that would take the whole session, until home time.

They had groaned. He knew he was going to 'file' the test papers straight in the shredder so there would be no evidence and he wouldn't need to mark them. Their grades were already decided, the mark he would feed back to them, would be based on their maths work for the term.

He had to restrain a cheer himself, when the bell rang to dismiss the school for the day.

Once the children had collected their coats, bags and sundry lunch time containers, he escorted the the class onto the playground for collection by a parent or any responsible adult he could find that would take them.

29

Mickey had spent the afternoon visiting a couple of his important business interests, a snooker hall and a pub with a late night license, to ensure that all was well and that the staff were ready for the night ahead.

Having satisfied himself, he switched on one of his 'burner' phones that he kept in a box in the boot of his car and called Shelly – the Madam responsible for running the town's girls. He wanted to check in and find out if Maggie had been in contact.

'Mickey, darlin', I ain't 'eard from 'er for a coupla days. You should go and find that twat she shacks up wiv. Charlie Washisname. 'Er dealer,' she advised him. She additionally confided, 'It's 'is kid y'know. She don't want 'im to know on account of 'im bein' a prat.'

Mickey closed the connection, removed the battery and crunched the Sim under the heel of his shoe. Twisting it as he ground. He groaned as he ran a hand over the smooth curve of his bald head.

'Not my problem, luv,' he muttered to the absent Maggie.

He returned to the driver's side of his car and sat heavily in the seat. The keyring hung loosely from his sizeable index finger. The prospect that Charlie Fletcher was a liar had already occurred to him so he had phoned one of his lads, a bouncer at a club to sit outside Charlie's flat. Just to make sure he didn't try to meet up with Maggie, and do a runner with the her and the boy. He needed to find Maggie urgently, teach her a lesson, get the kid back to her and get her back on the game earning money to keep her son in clean y-fronts.

The car purred into life as the grizzled old gangster turned the key in the ignition and pulled the door closed, cutting off the sound of his chainsaw laughter, as he thought of the skinny little wretch who opened the door to him that morning. He couldn't help but like the kid. Reminded him of his boyhood in London.

Deciding to trust Charlie's version of events for now, he drove around town lazily, enjoying the creak of the leather seats as he made left, then right turns, timing his drive to arrive outside the kid's school, just minutes before the end of the school day.

To obscure the dull drone of the traffic, he turned the radio on, hoping that he might get a Meatloaf or 10CC tune to sing along to. He enjoyed the privacy and anonymity that singing in the car offered and often drove on motorways, not having a destination in mind, just wanting the sensation of 'going forward'. The pleasure of the big car's power and stability making him feel safe. He took these opportunities to join in with his own personal, secret karaoke sessions, as he had a surprisingly tuneful voice for a big man. However, it was Three O'Clock and the news reader was on.

'...yesterday's tragic events in London are still baffling Police,' the voice explained and Mickey snorted, no surprise there then.

'In other news, an investigation has been ordered by the Care and Quality Commission in Devon, as it appears that a number of Staff Nurses in various hospitals across the county have acted independently to euthanise elderly patients in their care. A leading doctor, speaking to journalists...' the voice was cut off as Mickey had heard enough, pressing the button to switch from radio to CD. The news was replaced by a pounding of atmospheric, repeated drumbeats and the sole voice of a middle-aged man.

'..I can hear it cooooming in the air tonight...oh Lord. I've been waiting for this moment...for all my life...'

Content, he stretched his arms out straight on the steering wheel, pushing his body back into the comfort of the leather seat and cheerfully joined in.

30

Mickey had expected to find the pavements full of mothers and grandparents waiting to collect their loved and cherished young offspring. He was surprised when school run traffic had obstructed him half a mile away from the school.

When he finally got close to the school gates, he found he could barely manoeuvre his car through the throng of people carriers and shiny SUVs, let alone find somewhere to park. A teenager in secondary school uniform sullenly wandered across the road, leaving the safety of the pavement without any care or attention and flipped him the finger, without even looking, as Mickey beeped his horn to warn the kid of the car's presence.

'Jesus 'Aitch Christ!' Mickey complained and slipped the Jag into second gear, leant on the horn and pressed his foot hard on the accelerator pedal.

A fist shook, the disgusted face of a young mother pushing a pram with the next two kids lined up for school in front of her flashed past, arses jumped and moved out of Mickey's way as the car lurched and careened its way to an empty space by the pavement outside the school. He ignored the implication of the yellow zig-zagging lines.

Getting out of the car, gingerly, aware that the eyes of the gathered parent body of the school were on him, he shrugged his expensive jacket squarely onto his considerable shoulders. Behind him car horns continued to blare in protest of his unorthodox traffic avoiding tactics.

A ten year old zoomed passed on his bike shouting: 'Oi, you old knobhead! Get outta tha way!' Then cycled off laughing.

Mickey stood proud, ignoring the little shite. Swaggering up the pavement towards the pedestrian gate like he owned the place, the adults unsurprisingly shrank away, leaving him a clear path to the playground.

Once through the horde of gossiping mothers, disapproving grandparents and morose teenagers collecting their younger siblings, he entered the school grounds.

Adults of all shapes and sizes still scattered the playground, collecting children, checking bags to make sure homework had been picked up, empty packed lunch boxes were in-hand. Ready to be recharged overnight with a mix of processed foods that were passed off as part of a child's 'five-a-day', and smelly PE uniforms were being returned home for washing.

It didn't take long to spot the difference between the teachers, who stood with tired smiles, as they discharged their burdens for the day, and the impatient, unhappy, screeching mothers whose peace and quiet was about to be ruined as the child care of school ended. Until the next morning, when they could with a sense of relief, return their darlings into the care of the staff, and their interrupted adult lives were restored to some semblance of normality.

He walked over to an older woman, with short cropped, dyed red hair and her arms crossed across her ample chest, a no-nonsense look on her face.

'Scuse me luv, could you point out Mister Carpenter for me, please? I need to speak to him urgently about my little nephew, Lewis.'

The waiting mother of three looked Mickey up and down. She didn't care who he was, or who he thought he was. His clothes did not impress her at all, but she knew the look in his eye meant he was trouble and he was probably not someone to upset. Without moving her eyes off him, she lifted her left arm up and pointed to the space between Aaron Parminster and Suzy Tallister, where Robert Carpenter stood with two children remaining to be collected.

The teacher she had pointed at waited like a racehorse in the starting gates, fidgeting back and forth, taking one step left, then one step right. Repeating this over and over again. Occasionally, Mickey saw that he smiled at a parent, hands thrust in his pockets, avoiding eye contact with as many people as possible.

'Do you mean the baby-man on the right?' he asked, meaning Aaron Parminster.

'Ha! Naa – that's Mister Parminster,' the woman laughed, warming to the stranger. 'You want the tall one in black. That's Carpenter.'

'Ta luv,' he nodded as he walked in the direction she had indicated.

He watched the agitated teacher as he approached and took an instant dislike to the man. He had a preconception that all men who worked with children were nonces and paedos. The rationale was that no-one in his right mind would want that job, unless you liked being close to little children. Hence they were all nonces and paedos.

In all of his experience, he had never met a teacher who had managed to change his opinion, and during his time as a pimp, he had met a fair few teachers. This one couldn't even look at him as he walked up.

'Mister Carpenter,' the gravelly voice intoned, 'I was hoping you may be of assistance.'

Mickey smiled as the teacher turned and smiled at him, with a nod of his head to indicate his helpfulness.

'I'm here to collect my grandson, Lewis Tracey.' Mickey saw the smile vanish from the teacher's face. He regarded him calmly as the man in black in front of him cast looks in all directions around him. He decided that this noncey faggot of a teacher knew something.

'I..I'm sorry,' the teacher had stuttered stepping forward towards Mickey, putting himself between Mickey and the two boys looking up at the two adults blankly.

'I can't help you there. Who did you say you were? Are you a relation of Lewis's?' he inquired, again as he looked around the quickly emptying playground for something or someone.

Was she here already? Mickey wondered and looked around the playground himself. He couldn't see her. He looked back to the teacher and sized him up. He thought that he definitely knew something, Charlie was right. He hadn't lied. That was good.

'Sorry, *Mister* Carpenter,' Mickey emphasised the 'Mister' in mockery of the deference that he was meant to display. 'I must've made a mistake.'

Nodding as he turned and returned, slowly across the empty playground, back to the gate and out to his car, which sat in solitary splendour, parked on the now empty street.

He sighed as he turned the key in the ignition and drove slowly away from the school. You didn't mess with one of his girls without a consequence. Now all he had to do was think of a way to get the noncey faggot to tell him where Maggie was and teach the teacher a lesson he wouldn't forget.

31

Robert had been informed that Toby's mum would be late by the office secretary as he was escorting the class out at the end of the day. The note she passed him advised him that both Toby and Will were to wait with him until she arrived.

He had screwed the message up in his hand and had called out to the two boys to wait at his side once the class had arrived in the playground.

In ones, twos and threes, the children of the class were collected. Time marched on. The longer he was in school, the more likely he was to be confronted by the Head Teacher, who was bound to notice the missing UHT cartons. She would know it had to be him. She would be waiting in the classroom to confront him, when he was alone and no-one would hear or see.

As the minutes dragged by, he became increasingly agitated, pacing like a caged lion. The year three and five classes were almost discharged and he could see teachers from Key Stage 1 already returning to their classrooms, escaping any further interactions with the parents. A step closer to going home to wine, and families and peace.

Outside on the road, Robert could hear a commotion as cars beeped their horns and raised voices could be heard. Robert, Aaron and Suzy shared knowing looks and shrugs. Parents really were becoming total scum, they had no patience, no manners or politeness and certainly no respect for the sanctity of the school.

He didn't notice the man mountain who entered the playground, slowly, with a swagger, like he was entering a prize boxing arena. Or as he began to wander over to him. Too distracted by the childish banter between Toby and Will, he just wanted them to shut up and go home, so he could get out of there himself. The first he knew of the stranger was when he heard a voice that sounded a bit like a Rod Stewart tribute act from the East End say his name. The gravelly voiced, bald bruiser went on to ask if he could help.

Robert thought the bloke looked a bit like an up-market Arthur Daley, except that he didn't wear a pork-pie hat. He was however, from the seedy side of town. Smiling his best smile to parents, compliant, helpful and willing. He tried to place the man. He was sure he hadn't seen him before. Was he going to try to take Toby and Will?

When the stranger mentioned the absent Lewis Tracey, his training and professionalism kicked in. He stepped forward, placing himself between the boys and the stranger. and looked around hoping to see Charles or any senior member of staff who could notice this intruder to the playground. But all he managed to get was a cretinous wave from Aaron as he turned and walked back towards the school, oblivious to the plea for help on Robert's face.

'I can't help you there. Who did you say you were? Are you a relation of Lewis's?' Robert tried his best to keep his composure and professional demeanour in the face of a clear case of 'stranger danger' and began to memorise identifying features. The tattoo of a fist on the left of his neck, except he was facing him, so it would be the right side. The black leather jacket with woollen lining. Single breasted, blue pin-striped suit with black brogues. The man was tall, almost as tall as he was wide, Robert thought, so certainly six foot in both dimensions.

The stranger didn't move a muscle and seemed to be sizing Robert up before finally saying, 'Sorry, Mister Carpenter,' in the most gangster voice that Robert had ever heard, 'I must've made a mistake.'

The stranger then turned slowly, and without a single glance over his shoulder, walked back up the playground, where he exited through the pedestrian gate.

'Awwwww...' a small voice from behind Robert snapped him back to the here and now.

'He is gonna mash you up, sir!' Will, observant as ever, commented as both boys stood giggling. Toby mimed beating an invisible boy to the ground and kicking him, repeatedly.

'That's what he is gonna do to you, Mister Carpenter!' Will was now in full flow and enjoying the discomfort of the teacher who had just made him sit a test about Light and Sound, a subject he hated.

'Wait outside the school office, both of you. You will be collected from there today,' Robert instructed the boys with a curt command, regaining his authority over the eight year old boys. He followed, escorting them to make sure his charges arrived at their destination safely.

32

Aileen had sat quietly in her office all afternoon, waiting patiently for the school day to end.

She had been severely shaken. Memories of her youth in Ireland intermingled, guiltily, with images of the violence of the last twenty-four hours. The wild hallucinations and emotional turmoil in the Staff Room at lunch time were being erased from her memory.

She altered her recollections of the timeline of the day in order to remember only the positive things that had happened and absently wondered if it was possible for some of them to have been the memories of the same person, of her life. Or whether, like a Hollywood movie, they were someone else's shattered, harvested experiences that had been implanted into her using 5G mobile phone masts. Some sort of conspiracy.

The cool, calm and collected veneer that she presented to the world was slipping regularly, as the enormity of her ambition began to overwhelm her. Someone would see through her, she thought. Work their way through the clues, the trail that she knew she had to be leaving behind, despite her best efforts, in her haste. Someone would catch her before she finished. A hero would save the day. Before her confession could absolve her from her sins.

She had mechanically worked her way through the tasks that challenge and face a Head Teacher as if programmed. An automaton of Hephaestus: built to serve. She fielded questions that she was forced to respond to from staff and children alike with preprogrammed responses like a robot from a Èapek play. Punch cards swapped in her mind in order to provide the correct language to placate and satisfy those demanding a piece of her precious life, feeling the time and effort required shred a little more of her away. Each question, a claw tearing flesh. Each false smile and soothing tone hiding the scream of terror and pain she felt as she perpetrated her part of the lie that bound their eyes and ears.

She distracted herself by doing what she did best. Planning and timetabling. If she left school by four this evening, then she could swing by a local DIY store and to collect a new galvanised garden incinerator and some logs to burn. Then, after carefully and conspicuously burning some garden and household waste for the neighbours to witness, and developing a hot bed of high temperature embers, she could begin the night's work of adding various parts of the body to the fire. A few greaseproof paper wrapped items at a time, with plenty more wood and waste. She could spend the dark hours, when everyone else slept, getting rid of the material evidence. Turning a body into a few biscuit tins of ash.

She had already figured out how to dispose of the clothes, and had thought through her own wardrobe and picked out items that she could donate to the various charity shops around the town.

In one bag, she could put some of her evening wear, that she used to use regularly, especially when she was a soloist in the local women's choir, but she just didn't need any more. She could smuggle Maggie's shirt into a black bin bag in with some dresses. The bomber jacket could go with some of her old coats and jumpers, the jeans and shoes could go with her shoes and skirts.

If she left the bags outside the doors of the charity shops, just before they opened, then the staff would deposit the bags in the storerooms for sorting later. By the time anyone looked through the bags, her good quality items would distract them from noticing the dead woman's clothes. The phone would be wiped clean and recycled through one of those postal services with some old CDs and DVDs. Maggie Tracey would just vanish.

Having decided on a course of action that she thought to be sensible, Aileen began to feel better again. In control. Progressing. A phase of the plan had been put into action. A child had been protected. Not in the bureaucratic and political sense. But she had guarded a child's future in a concrete and personal sense.

After her years of experience, she thought it was the only way to really keep a child safe. Exterminating the dangerous adult responsible for the risk, eradicating the infestation of cynical adult falsehood. No more risk assessments or meetings with hand wringing administrators. The job was done.

Providing the mindless, thoughtless sheep-like cattle that she worked with the opportunity to truly become the cannibals that they were, was a bonus. She thought back to the number of staff she had managed, watching them endlessly climbing over each other, sniping, biting, spitting, slipping and undermining each other in order to gain her favour. All in order for them to escape the classroom, in order to be the one making demands of others' lives, instead of the one making the ever increasing demanded sacrifices, just to survive the cut throat industry, just to 'make a living'. Now she hoped, some of those might finally be choking, on the pound of flesh, Maggie's pound of flesh, that they all demanded. She was satisfied.

From outside the cloistered office, the commotion of little footsteps, coats and bags being collected and the shouted instructions from tired adults indicated the end of the school day. Staff would begin to read the instructions for the planned practice of the lock down procedure the following morning that she had emailed out.

Aileen clicked her mouse button to reawaken her laptop and checked that the presentation that she would be using to explain the new alarm to the children in the assembly was correct and saved, then checked her 'Sent' folder on her e-mail software to make sure that all staff had received the new, hastily written lock down policy and instructions, as well as a message to go home as early as possible at the end of the day. The sooner they were all gone, the sooner she could lock the school up and head home, via the DIY store.

A hesitant, gentle rap on the door to her office disturbed her train of thought, followed by a a more urgent, loud knock that gained her attention. In the window of the door, the profile of Robert Carpenter's face appeared as he ducked down, turning to look into the room.

33

'Come in, Robert,' Aileen called, closing the lid of the laptop down, carefully.

The door opened and Robert walked in uncertainly. She stood and moved over to the meeting table. He glanced over to the sink, inspecting the cups and the cafetière that needed washing up, and sat down, without being invited to, in the 'just business' chair by the door. An impertinence, she thought as she placed her hands on the back rest of her chair at the head of the table. He would not have done that yesterday.

'How can I help you,' she pulled the chair out briskly and folded herself down, a cat stalking, 'Robert?' Aileen wanted this intrusion dealt with quickly. There was no time for Robert now, there was too much to do.

She interlaced the fingers of her hands on the table, a gesture that placed a barrier between them. She wanted to feel strong and in control. To intimidate him. She waited as calmly as she could, thoughts of the day pushed aside as he squirmed and twisted in his chair, unable to look at her, unable to speak. He cleared his throat and looked up.

Robert had not wanted to go Aileen. He had asked after Charles, hoping it might be an issue that he could follow up, but the secretary had informed him that Charles had left early that afternoon due to illness. That only left him two options. The first was not to report the stranger on the site at all, to ignore the incident and go home and examine the UHT milk cartons and face the affectionate derision of his wife.

This would be a professional failure on his part and he knew that both Toby and Will were likely to talk endlessly to anyone and everyone about the threatening man on the playground. The second option was to follow standard protocol and inform the Head Teacher that a stranger had been on site. This scared him irrationally. What did he think would happen to him in the Head Teacher's office? That she would attack him for stealing two cartons of UHT milk? Robert had steeled himself for the second one-to-one meeting in two days and had gone reluctantly to her office.

'Lewis Tracey, was absent today,' he began as their eyes met again, 'and I have just been approached by a man, a rather large and threatening looking man; a man who I have never seen on school premises before, who wanted to collect him.'

Sweat darkened his hair, a crown that circled his head, just above the hair line. The toll of the day's anxiety made small veins in his nose and cheeks visible. The strain had made him age since the day before. Having begun to discuss the incident in the playground, on a familiar professional grounding, Robert felt more comfortable and more confident. There could be no question that he had acted correctly, that he was following best practise and fulfilling his professional duty to safeguard the children of the school from any and all threats. He watched

Aileen's face, searching for the momentary lapses that had become evident since the bombings in London, the previous day.

Aileen turned and picked up a pen and a sheet of paper from her desk. To Robert, she seemed emotionless. The qualities that he had always respected as professional: her forthrightness, her direct economy and brevity; now, seemed factory processed and lacking authenticity. However, there was no sign of the panic, the anger or the insane revulsion, that he was convinced that he had seen earlier. He went on and recounted the event from memory and described the stranger's appearance as well as he could remember.

Aileen listened carefully and made detailed notes, despite not wanting to spend any time on the issue. Her duty had been so ingrained that she acted almost without will, accepting that the reported incident by any member of staff would take priority over any other event in her day.

As she listened, he seemed to warm and relax as he recalled the encounter. Her mind ran raced at the oversight that his report of a stranger had brought to her attention. How had she not considered the boy all day? What had she expected to happen? She had murdered his mother the afternoon before. Who was this stranger? Aileen had thought that Maggie was alone and without any notable family to look for her. Was he the grandfather that he claimed to be? Where was the boy? What was she going to do?

Robert had stopped talking and was looking at the table top intently. She placed the pen down on the paper, lining the edges of the plastic pen shaft parallel to the paper and laced the fingers of her hands together again. Looking up at Robert, she smiled.

'Thank you, Robert,' she began, nodding in his direction.

She noted the crumpled, slightly grey collar of his shirt and the ashen pallor of his face. The encounter had clearly shaken him up. There was something a little gaunt and haggard about the appearance of the late afternoon shadow on his jaw. The salt and pepper stubble that she usually considered part of his sickening machismo, today made him seem – old, tired. Washed out. In his emotionally strained and professionally exhausted state, his grey and ashen face showed her that he was weak.

Aileen was exulted. Patience, it had seemed, had finally paid off and Robert Carpenter was in pain at last. She could now sit there and make him dance on the point of a pin. However, the Schadenfreude she felt and had hungered for, for so long, was empty, and seemed somehow beneath her. She didn't need to punish or inflict any pain on him directly. It was clear to see that the life he had made had led him, on his own path, to his own agony and pain. As had hers. She found herself seeing something earnest and genuine in the way he sought to put the children's safety before his own. There had been a toll on him. She reminded herself that he seemed aware, but not awake.

34

'You've done the right thing bringing this to my attention immediately.' Sitting back in her chair, she breathed out through her nose in a long exhalation.

'The bruises on Lewis's shoulder were caused by the mother,' Aileen sighed as she began, by means of introduction.

'How did the meeting go, yesterday?' Robert enquired, his eyes still on the empty desk top before him.

'How do you think meetings like that go?' Aileen's voice lowered and softened as she recalled Maggie's face, speared, bucking and twitching in the seat, as her nervous system became overloaded with the sudden trauma of the brain damage Aileen had caused.

She continued smiling, 'Confronting parents with their responsibility rarely goes as planned. However, I think this time I might have got through.'

She paused, her eyes narrowing in reflection as she picked up the pen from the table. 'I think I made my point clearly.' She watched as Robert nodded his head, without raising his face. 'Are you alright, Robert? You seem, a little unwell.'

Robert's stomach chose the moment to release the tension of the afternoon, releasing gas in an uncontrollable and involuntary, echoing belch. He raised one hand to his mouth, to cover the eruption, and the other as an open hand in apology to the Head Teacher. The taut atmosphere that had followed him through school all afternoon, perhaps even from the previous day, dissolved, as he looked up to see Aileen's look of mock horror at his vulgarity.

'I'm...so...sorry!' was all that he could think to say. All thought of his suspicions cast aside in order to remedy his outrageous lack of physical control.

'Ah..all I've eaten today is an apple, and it..I guess... it must be the acid or something,' he quickly tried to justify himself, although all he could think of was the time honoured explanation that shouted through his mind, drowning out any chance of making a polite and rational comment: '*Pardon me, it was not me. It was my food it, was so rude. It just popped up to say "Hello", and now it's gone back down below.*'

In embarrassment and shame, Robert chose to be silent. Instead, he shrugged his shoulders and winced at Aileen by way of apology.

'I haven't eaten at all since breakfast,' Aileen offered in acknowledgement of Robert's embarrassment as she rubbed her eyes with her knuckles. 'There just never seems to be time any more. To be honest I struggle to go to a supermarket, nowadays.' She shook her head, 'Thank god for Ocado and Amazon.'

Aileen sighed again, making a long 'Oh' sound. The all consuming stress of the previous days was temporarily forgotten.

This was the most inconsequential human conversation that she had had for a long time. She was enjoying it.

'Come on, what was the last thing that you bought in a shop? Other than mints,' she wracked her brain trying to think of any pointless purchases in the near past and struggled.

'Erm...I think I bought Elle, my wife, a tooth brush that had a glowing, no a flashing brush head.' Robert recalled dully, 'She was going to her sister's for the weekend and I bought it as, you know, a jokey gift.'

The vacuous comment rang in his ears as he blurted it out. Again, he told himself to stop talking.

'How're you feeling, Robert?' she asked again.

Her gently husky voice had softened with a little humour, making Robert wonder if she were genuinely concerned for his well-being. 'You're not coming down with the same thing as Charles are you? I sent him home earlier,' she continued, 'he looked awful.'

It was her turn to cast her eyes down to the table top, she could not look at him as she said it aloud. She needed to pretend not to know why Charles was ill, but still, even lying to Robert seemed wrong. Being mendacious galled her.

He cast a glance at her, his inquisitive eyes met the expressionless expanse of her hairline and forehead. He followed her attention down to her fingers, where she slowly rotated a disposable pen, without a lid, in a circle.

The tip of the pen touched her thumb and each of the fingertips of her left hand in succession, circled clockwise. The pen nib circling like a comet around a five planet solar system. Five tiny arrhythmic tapping sounds, that he imagined might be the same as a tiny caged bird's heart beat. She made no other noise, watching her own actions intently. It seemed that after she had spoken, she had forgotten his presence, until she spoke again in the same gentle, husky, intimate voice.

'I sit here,' the pen circled around, 'and sometimes it just feels like the walls close in on me.' She did not look up, just tilted her head to one side as she addressed him. Aileen sighed deeply. The pen circled.

'I have made, I don't know, a thousand decisions and choices this week alone. Decisions and choices that change the course of people's lives.'

She shook her head slowly before returning her attention to the circling pen nib, tilting her head on the opposite side. Letting the sensation of the tip of the pen lull her, open her and inform her of the circle that she had travelled. The circle that she was trapped into travelling through and would travel into.

'Sometimes they don't even know. You didn't even know did you?' She still did not look up at Robert, and he sat silently, transfixed.

He didn't know what was happening, but he knew that he couldn't break the spell of the moment. He had perceived that she had been trying to tell him something, over the past days, in looks that were coded by an unknown and perhaps unhinged cypher, but now she was really telling him something directly. He had to listen.

'How're you feeling?' Aileen repeated the question; the tiny beat of the pen on her fingers continued to accompany her lightly accented voice hypnotically.

'I've had better days, to be honest.' Robert heard his voice from a thousand miles away reply. 'All the news about London, yesterday. Dealing with parents, and people who pretend to be parents. The kids. They have to grow up so fast, now. What we have to put them through, every year. It's not felt right for a while, I guess,' he let his guard down.

'It's not what I got into teaching for, if you know what I mean,' the rational Robert who lived in his brain had given up trying to mentally close the connection between his mouth and his rambling, inadequacy. Again, he told himself to listen.

The pen continued its circuitous journey, the sound filled the office with its almost imperceptible beat. He heard Aileen let out another stunted sigh as a blast of air was forced out of her nose. He could almost hear her smile, too.

'What did you get into teaching for?' Aileen paused, just long enough for the rhetorical question to trouble him. She knew that his reasons had not been too dissimilar to hers.

'Let me guess, Robert,' she began, her sympathetic tone continued without any hint of teasing or sarcasm. 'You wanted to change the world. Make it a better place, just like I did.'

Her eyes glanced up to his for the first time since the conversation had taken a more personal turn. Just for a moment, just to let him know that she wasn't laughing at, or mocking him. Before her attention once more returned to her hands. The repeated tapping on her fingertips were making them tingle and she could see small dots appearing where the ink was being deposited in tiny amounts. She closed her eyes, letting the sensation flood her whole mind.

'Is it?' Aileen's voice was almost hushed. 'Is it, Robert?' an unmistakable sense of melancholy, loss and regret weighed her head and shoulders down. She seemed to shrink in front of Robert as he sat there.

'A better place? Are you winning?' she paused, before whispering, 'Are we winning?'

Robert opened his hand on the table top. Spreading his fingers wide and feeling the cool of the surface. His skin felt hot, burning. His head was swimming after the afternoon he had had. He had not expected the meeting with the Head Teacher to be so emotional. The animosity, anger and even insanity he had been sure he had detected earlier, had been replaced in her eyes with an overwhelming vulnerability. She had asked him the simplest question, that he had asked himself often; his earnest answer came immediately.

'No, I don't think we're winning,' he confided, remembering the recent incident with Lewis's possible grandparent in the school playground and the way two eight year old boys had teased him about the possibility of being publicly beaten up.

'I know that I'm trying. There are days when I think that I'm making a difference.'

The cyclonic cadence intensified as Aileen's right hand twitched the pen from tip to tip with greater pace. It seemed that there was an added emphasis at the beginning, or the end, Robert was unsure which, of the beat.

'You think you're making a difference?' Aileen returned to her monotonous, menacing, mechanical questioning, although her voice remained low and husky. An echo of the sympathy that she had shown moments before. 'You're trying to make the world a better place? Is that it?'

'We're all trying to make the world a better place, aren't we?' Robert pleaded. 'Even the inventor of single use plastics was trying to make the world a better place. The trouble is that there are so many of us trying, and so many of us who are wrong, that the mistakes and wrong turns are leading us all in the wrong direction. Probably the wrong directions. It's been happening for so long. I'm not sure that we can win, not any more,' the debater in Robert took over, he was determined to make his point. Elle had grown tired of hearing his rants and tirades against the increasingly alienating system within which he worked.

'Look, you know better than I do what has happened over the last ten years,' Robert became animated, he had an audience. 'Every institution: the church, the police, the government, they have all withdrawn from the people. Or the people have withdrawn from them,' his index finger fell onto the table as blows from a judge's gavel to emphasise his points. 'All that's been left are schools, and probably doctors - GPs. We are the last line of a civilised democracy, the last place left that can influence and socialise individuals in the wider society, creating boundaries and setting out what 'acceptable' behaviour is,' he checked himself and paused, aware of who he was addressing, but Aileen seemed content to let Robert continue. 'Well, apart from Love Island, Social Media and news broadcasters,' he qualified. 'We have to sell civilisation to children. Urgently. Because, if we don't, the alternative - what the world will become - well...it's unthinkable.'

Robert took a moment to pause, looking through the window, out over the emptying car park. The staff were in a hurry to take their leave.

The sky was a clear eggshell blue. A watercolour artists dream, thin and wispy, almost white in places, as the unseen sun set behind the school building. It reminded him of his panic attack in the Mouldy Cupboard, just hours earlier. He considered the point he had just made. He had never managed to express his uneasiness with the disorder he saw quite so succinctly. There it was though.

'I don't consider myself a salesperson. Or you, or any other member of staff. I don't like that idea,' Aileen spoke slowly. The pen had ceased its elliptical journey through the vacant space between her fingertips. She replaced it onto the table once more, paying careful attention to ensure that the length of the pen was parallel to the paper's edge.

With a brisk change of pace, Aileen sucked in a deep breath of air through her mouth and looked at the time on her watch. It was already Four thirty, she had to get a move on.

'Thank you, Robert, for bringing this to my attention,' she indicated the report on the stranger and continued: 'There's a good a chance that Charles will not be in tomorrow. I need someone to help me with the school's lock down procedure. I'd like that person to be you. You're certainly senior enough. Is that acceptable?' she stood, picking up her handbag and coat as she moved towards the door, ushering a stunned, but nodding Robert out.

'Great. I'll fill you in tomorrow morning.' Aileen closed and locked the door without looking at Robert again. 'Get some rest,' she ordered him as she walked towards the exit and the car park without looking back.

Robert stood unsure what had just happened. He seemed to have spent a large part of the last two days at a loss. The day's events had left him drained and exhausted. He returned slowly to his classroom to collect his coat and bag, and followed Aileen and the other staff, who had already left, out of the school for the evening. On the top shelf of the classroom's cupboard, two UHT milk cartons sat forgotten. One had a red sticker, the other green.

35

With haste, Aileen had driven to the 'Out of Town' DIY store and purchased a hundred and twenty-five litre galvanised incinerator and three bags of heat logs, with cash. She didn't want a digital transaction trail, hoping that three bags would be enough.

She wasted no time, when she got home, putting the little aluminium legs on the bottom of the fancy named bin with holes in it, to lift it up off the ground. Not caring that the heat would scorch some of the ground when its contents were lit. She merely placed the incinerator on three broken bricks that had fallen from the old, unmaintained wall at the end of the garden, onto a patch of grass behind her garage. After looking around from the perspective of the metal bin, she satisfied herself that it was situated in the least overlooked position. Close to the kitchen door, where she could bring out the waste that she needed to burn.

The last of the light began to fade; the sunset was beautiful. The washed out autumnal blue sky had been turned into a canopy of gold as the sun had dipped below the horizon. A thin line, a vapour trail from a passing passenger jet liner, had been transformed into a red ribbon that gift wrapped the sky above the silhouetted houses of the street. Despite the urgency that she felt, Aileen paused to let the scene imprint in her memory. She hoped that it would be a daguerrotype that left a silvered image on her soul. In that moment, she wanted to smoke a cigarette. She had never even smoked one in her entire life. All good Femme Fatales smoked though, surely, she reflected.

She layered the incinerator, placing paper and dry leaves at the bottom, followed by small sticks of wood that she made into a lattice to support the weight of the heat logs, with more paper and leaves on the top. Aileen looked around her neighbour's gardens briefly to make sure that the day's washing had been taken down off the lines. The last thing she wanted was a busybody knocking on her door, complaining about the smoke. Satisfied, she lit the bonfire and left it to burn and returned to the kitchen to put a pizza in the oven.

Inside, she began collecting clothes from the various rooms of her house where she stored them. The boredom of insomnia had driven her to unforeseen depths of categorisation. She had originally arranged clothing alphabetically: clothes beginning with letter A through to M were stored in draws and rails in the master bedroom, whilst those beginning with N through to Z were stored in the spare room. This had caused her no end of problems though. Were they knickers or pants? Blouse or shirt? Was it a turtle-neck sweater or a jumper?

In the end, she had zoned clothes by purpose. Casual and work in the master bedroom, posh or seasonal clothes stored in the spare room. Jackets, overcoats and waterproofs were stored under the stairs on coat hooks above a shoe rack that contained the full range of footwear that she owned.

After gathering the required items of unused clothing that she had thought of earlier, whilst eating slices of Hawaiian pizza, she placed them, with the smuggled items of the dead parent. Sucking the grease of the pizza off her fingers first, they were placed into black bin liners in the garage. Labelled by the charity shop that were to be delivered to using Post-Its, for donation later in the dark hours. Once her cremation was completed she would drive around town and leave the bags by each shop's door on the kerb.

She returned to the kitchen as she munched on the last quarter of the simple pizza, she had been famished. She took a bottle of cold Mexican beer from the fridge.

On the door of the fridge, a novelty magnetic bottle opener waited. The simple metal bar was surrounded by a plastic caricature of Maggie Thatcher: eyes stared out angrily, her open mouth surrounded the pleated metal rim that she used to flip the lid from the neck of the bottle. It had been a Secret Santa gift, some years ago. She suspected it had been the previous Year 5 teacher's idea of a joke, as she recalled the class had just been on a trip to Parliament.

Aileen put the past behind her and walked to the back door that led to the garden and opened it, taking in the twilight scene. Once, Starlings would have swooped through the sky in a magnificent aerial display, maestros thanking the glory and bounty of the day and bowing and looping through the cooling and darkening air, welcoming in awe, the grandeur of the night. Their numbers had dwindled though, now just an occasional bat flapped in the encroaching gloom. Darting between houses and trees, seeking their feast as midges sought to find their soul mate.

The incinerator burned smokelessly; the furnace inside visible through the small ventilation holes. The circles appeared to be bending elliptically as the heat haze distorted them in an optical illusion.

Aileen swigged the lager back, feeling the bubbles sparkle around her mouth, under her teeth and at the back of her throat. The tart flavour of the lager tempered by a hint of lime.

Turning the light out in the kitchen, she strode up to the end of the garden, swigging the beer as she walked. Gone were the vibrant colours of the summer flowers in the beds that surrounded the shaped lawn. Hydrangeas, petunias, zinnias and marigolds. All gone now. Just the rich brown soil and the green of the lawn and the privet hedges, some brown stalks of climbers, remained.

At the back end of the garden, she casually swept her gaze around, observing the condition of the windows that she could see. Squares and rectangles of glass were backlit yellows, blues and purples. Curtains and blinds obscured the drama unfolding within each closed compartment of family life. To Aileen, the windows looked like backdrops for Chinese shadow puppet theatres. Empty stages waiting for rod puppet emperors, dragons and gods to tell tragic and heart breaking stories of loss, grief and the afterlife in an imagined netherworld to the eager crowds of tired and hungry peasants. Glossy stories of hell to distract the poor from their humiliation. She wondered if soap opera reality was really much different to the folk traditions of antediluvian Asia.

The sky above her had turned black, only the orange glow of the lights at street level and the gilt silver disc of a gibbous moon lifted the gloom of the dark. The expanse of the night sky showed only the occasional pin-prick of ancient light. The distant stars could not compete with the luminescence of the LED street lamps.

Aileen returned to the kitchen, depositing the empty bottle in the recycling bin as she went. She first returned to the fridge, taking a second beer and proved that 'the lady was not for turning' by levering and flipping the lid off it using the same novelty opener, which she again re-placed back on to the fridge door. It's gaping mouth locked open in a formless political monologue, espousing the emptiness that, perhaps was indicative of the legacy of the real woman herself. It was clamped to the door of the fridge through the force of nature, waiting until it could fulfil its purpose again; the intense plastic, accusing eyes staring out at her.

36

She began the night's task with smaller items, a hand, a foot, both wrapped in grease proof paper. They were tossed into the glowing embers that still filled over half of the incinerator. She threw in two new heating logs on top to keep the conflagration intense.

The first moth of the night was drawn to the orange glowing flames of the fire, dashing through the garden's air, its wings alight, like a shooting star through the heavens. Aileen made her wish.

Taking a garden chair from the garage, she sat near the incinerator and settled in for the night. The smell emanating made it feel more like a BBQ, a crackling meaty, pork smell rose from the fire. She considered following the quickly vanishing beer with a hot chocolate next. The smell and the heat from the fire reminded her of the end of summer term BBQs at school, with sausages and burgers being prepared for the celebrating staff, as they readied themselves for squeezing as much life into the five or six credit card busting weeks through the late summer months. When she recalled why it smelled like that she wished she had eaten a quattre formaggio pizza instead of a ham and pineapple one as her stomach turned at the thought.

The gentle snap and crackle of the fire was timeless, linking her in a very human way to the uncounted hordes of humanity that preceded her. The mesmerising dance of the willowy orange flames had the same effect on her as it had on the those pre-industrial peoples who sat in the darkness, waiting for the light to return to the sky and their striving endeavours to progress their life, their family's life, to begin again.

Aileen had no family left. A tragic and accidental collision on a rain soaked road in Galway had taken them all, instantly, together. Leaving her alone in silent and unimaginable grief, hundreds of miles away in a heartless country, surrounded by sycophantic slaves of stability. She didn't loath the English, any more than she loathed any other nation of people, but she hated the way that just kept trundling on. Nothing got in their way. They had lost their empire, they had lost their economic ascendancy and their global influence. But they just didn't let it bother them. Their satirical national character was undentable. Well, she reflected, that was the impression that she had been given. She was not sure that it was true any more. The 'Keep Calm and Carry On' mentality was being challenged every day and the onslaught of social media had Americanised most western cultures into becoming moronic clones of Californian, asinine, fatuous and senseless consuming cattle.

Her mind wandered back to her meeting with Robert earlier that day. She considered his notion of selling children the ideas of civilisation a little distasteful. It meant that she was no more than a door-to-door saleswoman herself. Knocking on parents doors and selling them free child care. Although, now she considered it, that probably wasn't so far from the truth.

She swallowed the last of her beer and returned to the house; taking a couple of limbs from the garage, she added them to the bonfire, before returning to the kitchen to froth up some warmed milk. She stirred the thickened hot milky mixture absent-mindedly, as she considered why she was offended by the idea that she had spent the better part of her adult life in corporate sales. It shouldn't really bother her now. She picked up a tartan blanket, wrapping it around her shoulders, and returned to the garden chair with her steaming mug of cocoa. The furnace was radiating heat constantly, the flames had been replaced by white hot embers in the incinerator.

Perhaps it was because Robert was right, but he hadn't gone far enough. That was why she disliked him. It was obvious that the education system would support the presiding global political and economic system of civilised organisation. Robert had not asked himself who benefited from the country's children being literate and numerate. But not too literate and numerate, she reminded herself.

The system that she had been a leader in, had been transformed from one where each individual child was encouraged to learn for the sake of learning. It had gone beyond a modicum of measurement and assessment, for meritocratic and feedback purposes only. Now, each child was a data point.

Each six week term of each child's life, from the moment they entered the education system to the moment they left, was assessed, measured, quantified, digitised, monitored, moderated, compared, projected and investigated. Progress curves were used to predict how they would perform on tests ten years in the future, and 'teaching' staff were interrogated and pressurised into ensuring that the child was performing at the required level each year of their lives.

These 'professional' teachers were now so busy covering their own backs, that they had stopped being an effective force. These new bureaucratic teachers did not critically evaluate what it was that children were being taught, or consider why they were being tested, or the method being used to test. They just tried to keep their paperwork in line with the ever changing goalposts of acceptability as presented by the 'experts' of Ofsted.

Sure, there was always a little subversion as individual teachers, like Robert, sought to implant seditious and dangerous ideas like honesty, truth and critical thinking into their day, wherever possible.

In London, mandarins and political quislings, of any persuasion: left, right or centre, it didn't matter any more, would use the data to categorise young people and determine their access, or lack thereof, to the benefits of modern civilised liberal society. This data would at some point be leaked or sold to the big global corporate technology companies who would then utilise the information to target individuals with lifestyle choices and sales techniques befitting their social and economic level.

The mug of hot chocolate warmed her cold hands. Robert had realised that he was not winning. He had not understood that he was not even fighting in the right war. Aileen let her eyes close as she felt the warmth of the fire's heat on her face. She let her train of thought carry her on.

He was aware that things were not right, that he was not really an educator, or teacher. He had failed to recognise that, worse than being a salesman, he was a gaoler. That despite his best efforts, he couldn't really free the young minds that he sought to influence, because the system that he worked in did not want free thinking, critical, questioning minds.

The system, that he was an integral part of, was a machine that processed children like products. Providing them with a narrative continuum of obedience, not to adult authority, not to fixed truths or the rule of law, but to the ever present system of reward and sanction. Schools had begun to reflect the corporate economic system of rewarding desirable consumer behaviours, just like gaining medals in a game, or collecting points on a nectar card for shopping at the same supermarket every time.

Sanctions had been watered down, and at some point became rewards in themselves. Being excluded from class or school often involved spending time, one to one, with a sympathetic and patient adult, because there weren't any other ones in the child's life. Reintegration programmes provided anti-social pupils with bonuses and rewards, such as monetised tokens, time on games systems in school or timetables that gave them more time at home for extra play.

Adults found themselves swallowing their pride and accepting that certain children could be as rude and insolent to them as they liked, there was no boundary to enforce. The children just had to understand that if they followed some societal norms, that they would be tangibly, temporarily rewarded and it would make them happy. Moreover, they would like it and want more of it.

Children were being raised, being educated systemically, to become consumers, that was for certain. But Robert still thought that the goal of education was to create artists, scientists and free thinking philosophers. Sure, she thought, a few of those were allowed. But the system that she knew she was a part of created buyers, sellers, consumers and disposers. Wasters or savers, passive or aggressive. It didn't matter. Just so long as they didn't question why. So long as they didn't want to live any other way. So long as they could 'Keep Calm and Carry On'. Accept the gratification of a small reward and want more of it.

She had spent most of her adult life perpetrating this lie, this oppression. Hiding it from herself by burying her head so deeply into the sand offered by the bureaucracy, that she didn't have to acknowledge that she was the generation that submitted freedom to tyranny. Not a monolithic 'Big Brother' or Hitler tyranny. The fascists had realised that they couldn't impose their will by force, so they put on a tie and went to work in the banks, swapping racial purity for economic sanctity.

Aileen was one of the many that allowed this distributed fascism to slowly creep into everyone's life. To make consuming dominate the human purpose. Not intentionally, not maliciously. The road to hell was paved in good intentions as her Granny used to say. This was her sin. She had been so fervent, so passionate, so easy to convince. So blind.

Robert was aware and now it was her obligation to make sure that he was awake.

37

Charlie had stumped up the fifty quid for Alysha. He kept quite a lot of cash hidden in the loft space above his bedroom. There was an access hatch to it in the ceiling. It wasn't the most original place to use to hide his stash, of money or drugs, but he hoped that its obviousness might mean that no-one actually looked there. Besides, it was easy for him to access it quickly. Additionally, he didn't have many enemies. He was on good terms with enough of the right people to discourage anyone from ripping him off. As for the 'Old Bill', he was small enough fry for them not to be interested and he provided occasional freebies to a Drug Squad D.S. so he hoped he was protected on that count too.

Alysha had been sent into town with the strict instruction to only buy stuff that was on sale for the kid. He didn't want her buying designer stuff at full price and then charging him for it. He doubted that Mickey Butcher would be interested in reimbursing him either. He knew that Maggie would laugh in his face and probably offer him a blow job. He didn't want to give her any excuse to start treating him like one of her customers. He had been utterly besotted with her since they were kids.

That left him alone in the flat with the smelly little psycho, who he needed to convince to have a shower. He wasn't even sure the boy knew how to clean himself.

He had tried calling Maggie, a couple of times, but her phone was disconnected. Either switched off, or out of charge. If she was shacked up with someone, then she was going to be in serious trouble, with Mickey and with him. However, this was a little out of character, even for her.

She had been known to vanish for days at a time and reappear with a wad of notes. Providing a 'girlfriend experience' for some lonely, inadequate loser, but she had always contacted someone to look after her kid, he thought. He had never heard of her just dropping off the map like this. Even Mickey Butcher had no idea where she was.

As he worked his way through the deduction, Charlie began to worry, hoping nothing had happened to her. The notion stressed him out, so he left Lewis watching Cbeebies and went to the loo to smoke a pipe. He sat on the toilet seat and packed the bowl with some of his 'percy', the amount of grass that he allowed himself to have for free, without it affecting how much money he made from selling the ounce.

Basically, he 'taxed' a small amount from each transaction, providing his customers with just a little less than they were paying for to make sure that he got a stash for his own personal – hence 'percy' - use.

He sucked through the pipe as he lit the herb in the bowl, the flame from his lighter bending down, following the stream of air passing through the pipe. He clamped his thumb over the bowl, once he had filled his lungs to capacity, to slow the combustion down when he wasn't inhaling. He held his breath for as long as he could and let it out, explosively. The small room was filled with a fragrant cloud of smoke.

He couldn't get his head around what had happened, and as the buzz replaced his emotions and rational thought, he stopped caring. He just needed to get the kid clean, wait for Maggie or Mickey to turn up and hand him over so that he could go back to his normal routine.

He sat and waited for the last embers to go out in the pipe, saving the rest for later. He suspected he might need it.

He checked that the shower was furnished with some shampoo and body gel and paused, looking at the branded plastic moulded containers, wondering how they had managed to get the smell of Africa, into a shower gel. The idea just blew his mind. That he could rub this stuff all over him, wash it off immediately with water and he would just, smell better. He put the container down, pondering whether it actually had some lion shit or something in it to make it smell authentic and looked at the back of the bathroom door. The kid couldn't use his towel. He had to find another one.

38

Lewis leapt at the chance to watch some TV. He wasn't sure if he liked Charlie yet, but at least he hadn't hit him back, or shouted at him for too long after he had punched him in the nuts. So, he thought, he would give him a chance.

He sat down on one of the bean bags, it was still shaped like Zac and it was still warm, too. Sitting contentedly, he watched as Peppa and George went on a day trip with Mummy and Daddy pig. He knew he was a bit old for it, but he still loved watching it. His Mum had to be in a really good mood to let him watch Cbeebies. He was left alone long enough to watch a couple of awesome episodes.

Charlie walked back into the room with a black bin liner and a towel, which he held up to Lewis.

'Right, Lewis. I'm not coming in the bathroom wiv you. But I'm gunna show you what to do. Is that OK?' he spoke slowly and carefully. He didn't want the boy to start making accusations about him being a kiddyfiddler.

Lewis just looked at him and wondered why he was acting like an old man again. The grown up was speaking slowly, with a weird cowboy like drawl, and moving really slowly, too. Lewis watched as Charlie seemed to … wobble. His head and arms just sort of wobbled a bit, like he was made of jelly. His eyes looked like they were sort of covered by cling film or something. Lewis couldn't really understand it, but there was something distant about Charlie's eyes.

'Alright,' he replied and stood up, holding out his hands for the towel and bin liner. He looked at the black plastic bag, his face squinted up in confusion.

'Wots this for? I ain't wearing that!' the boy exclaimed.

'No, no,' Charlie held his hands up to slow the Tasmanian devil in front of him so that he could explain what he wanted him to do.

'Stop, Lewis. Just... wait.' Charlie waited for the boy to pay attention. 'The black bag is for your clothes mate. You're not putting them back on.' He shook his head. 'Just, wait. When you go into the bathroom and you … you know, get ready to take a shower. Just put your … washing,' Charlie felt inspired, 'your washing in there, mate. We'll get it cleaned, yeah?'

He breathed out. This was really stressful. He turned and walked into the bathroom, hoping the child would follow, at a distance.

Charlie resumed his place on the closed toilet seat and waited as Lewis walked in, looking around as if he had never seen a shower before.

'Right, Lewis,' Charlie began as he prepared himself for the monumental task of explaining how to turn on and off the water for the shower and the difference between shampoo and shower gel. He sighed deeply and took it one step at a time.

Charlie had decided to demonstrate the mechanics of cleaning yourself in the shower, using his arm to model what to do after Lewis began asking what words meant. It was all way, way too much for him to do. So after he had successfully shown Lewis what to do, he left him there, alone. He closed the bathroom door behind him and staggered over to the mattress, collapsing dramatically onto it.

'Fuuuuuuck mmeeeeee,' he groaned to Grandpa Pig who was trying to explain to Peppa what hide and seek was. He pulled the pipe from his pocket and immediately lit the contents of the bowl up and took the deepest breath he could.

In the quiet moment, when his body didn't make a sound, Charlie held the smoke in his lungs and listened. He heard the chatter of the characters on the TV; the sound of water splashing in the bathroom, accompanied by little squeaks and squeals of joy from the boy who was scrubbing layers of filth from his body; the gentle rattle and click as keys turned in the door and the rustle of plastic bags, as they were manoeuvred into the small atrium, bumping into wall and door and legs, followed by the click of the lock as the door closed.

His breath exploded out, but with a satisfied and dopey grin, he noticed that very little smoke had escaped. He had absorbed as much of the active ingredient in the smoke as he could. He had to admit to himself, despite everything, he felt great.

Alysha walked in to find Charlie laid on his back smiling with his eyes closed. The sounds of Lewis in the bathroom told her that the boy was cleaning himself thoroughly.

'Got some clothes for 'im.' she remarked as she walked past the prone figure of Charlie, to the bathroom where she knocked on the door.

'Lewis? Lewis? Are you done yet?' she called in unconscious imitation of the voice her Mum used to use to call her to get up in the morning.

She heard a muffled, 'Yeah,' from Lewis inside the bathroom and opened the door. His face appeared around the shower curtain. She could just make him out through the steam. He was smiling.

'I've got sum new clothes for ya, hope they fit,' she held the bags of clothes out to show him and then placed them on the floor by the sink.

'Come back thru when you're ready, OK? If you need any help wiv anyfing, just shout.' She smiled at Lewis and left, returning to the contentedly stoned Charlie.

She sat down on the mattress and took the pipe out of Charlie's hand. He offered no resistance, but just smiled at Alysha.

'Ta, for doing that mate,' he muttered.

'Charlie, sort your self out. Maggie's gone missin' an you have got Mickey fuckin' Butcher breathin' down your neck. What are you gonna do with this kid?' she hooked a thumb towards the bathroom door, then as Charlie shrugged, she reached over and took the lighter from his other hand, lighting the pipe immediately.

'This is proper fucked up!' she croaked, each word expelled a little cloud of smoke until she exhaled, emptying her lungs fully.

The door to the bathroom opened slowly and Charlie sat up on his elbows, smiling at the newly washed and clothed Lewis. He was transformed from a Dickensian character from Oliver Twist into a skin-head mini-thug from *This is England*, all that was missing was a tattoo of a tear or a swastika on his face.

'Coooool dooooood,' Alysha crowed, admiring her styling. She had bought him some Nike trainers and a grey Addidas hooded top and Jogging pants combo; Lewis was grinning from ear to ear. She looked between Lewis and Charlie several times, her eyes squinted in the gloom.

'Nice one,' Charlie affirmed, smiling. 'Anyone for a cheese toastie?' he asked, looking between Alysha and Lewis for confirmation of orders. He had pulled his face into the fawning image of a waiter in a posh restaurant. Alysha and Lewis both laughed, nodding their heads together.

'He's got your eyes, Charlie,' Alysha observed. Charlie's phone began to buzz and play the opening bars of a popular nineties club hit prompting her to join in, "...better off alone?"

Charlie looked at the phone and stopped smiling.

39

The dew rose in a fine pre-dawn mist in the garden as the last embers concentrated their heat into the bottom of the incinerator.

Aileen had scooped as much of the ash and charred bones and teeth from the slightly buckled and carbonised aluminium bin as she could. The larger fragments of bone had needed to be broken up, so Aileen had wrapped them in a teacloth and bashed them gently with a claw hammer, until they had disintegrated enough to fit into one of the biscuit tins that she had collected for this purpose. She had filled four so far, so she figured that quite a lot of the ash must be from the wood and garden waste that she had added to the fire.

She had placed the biscuit tins in a cardboard archive box, that she had taken from school. There would be no suspicion at all of her carrying such a box, as they were stacked in any spare corner or space throughout the office space in the building. She simply labelled the box '*Finances 17 / 18*' to increase the box's authentic appearance and reduce any desire of anyone to open it.

On a whim, she had placed Maggie's disassembled phone on top of the biscuit tins. She would think of another easier way of disposing of the incriminating technology later. With the archive box containing the cremated remains of the dead parent, and the black bin liners lined up in the boot of her car, Aileen locked the house and set off to begin her final disposal of the evidence linking her to the murder of Maggie Tracey.

The roads were as clear as the Wednesday morning sky. Blackbirds sat watching the last of the foxes returning to their holes from their vantage point, lined up on the telephone wire; a jury casting their secret ballot, as the raven haired woman drove her hatchback SUV below them, past the grass verges and driveways of the still silent homes.

40

Robert listened to the alarm chiming beside him. He heard Elle begin to groan in protest to the electronic trilling that had invaded the last of her cosy sleep cocoon she had wrapped herself in.

It had not been a restful night for him. After a brief journey into the limbo of unconsciousness, anxious colour coded thoughts returned him to wakefulness. He had lain there, still and unmoving, staring up at the shadowed ceiling above him. Paralysed by an in-articulated fear, his leaden limbs immobile.

He had waited through the hours of darkness. Had remained completely still, though he felt as though he was tipping over backward, falling, arcing through an endless repeating path; an electron circling an unseen nucleus. Shafts of light pierced through the gloom as occasional cars passed by the house, their headlights swept across the ceiling through cracks between the curtains, ghostly flashes of neutrinos though the endless atomic chasm of the room. Accentuating his sensation of timeless motion.

The cat, Chairman Miaow, had graced him with his company for a time. The silky fur rubbed against his arms and face as the cat gently purred, trying to sooth and reassure him through his night terror. The cat curled up against Robert's neck.

The throbbing beat of the cat's presence and contentment transmitted silently through their physical contact. Lulled and relaxed by the cat, Robert had fallen asleep again, only to be woken as the cat, rested and ready to lead the night's adventures with its feline comrades, stood, stretched and leapt from the bed. Robert returned to unwelcome sensations of twisting, rolling and falling as if he were cast adrift on an angry ocean until dawn and the alarm.

'Rob, turn it off, hon,' Elle mumbled beside him, her mouth impeded by a face full of pillow, the edge of the duvet pulled tightly up to her chin in protest to the demands of a new morning. She wriggled in denial, eyes squeezed shut ensuring the eyelids presented full darkness instead of the light of the Wednesday morning to her brain.

'I'd love a coffee,' she murmured the instruction as a statement of her wishes.

Robert numbly reached his arm over and his fingers fumbled with the screen of the alarm clock, eventually finding the region of the the flashing screen that silenced it. He rose from the bed like a resurrected Mummy from a black and white film, only his pyjamas betraying the modern era. Lifting the duvet across his body in slow motion and swinging his legs over the edge of the bed so that his feet landed flat on the floor. Without responding to Elle, he left the bedroom, first pausing to relieve himself in the bathroom, then mechanically, he descended to the ground floor and performed the routine of making the morning pot of coffee.

He sat at the kitchen table and waited; evidence of his troubled night etched onto his face as the kettle boiled turbulently. It occurred to Robert that he had spent the night worrying, without once attempting to broach the subject of the worry with himself. He had given in to a formless stress, obliterating any notion of problem solving or coherent thought. Focusing solely on sensation, the regularity of his heartbeat and his breathing, the lucidity of falling, without moving a single muscle. He wondered if, in his dreamless state, he had somehow detected the motion of the planet as it spun on its celestial circuit, a spinning top for the Gods, circling a bright yellow pinpoint in the darkness.

The kettle clicked to indicate the water had reached boiling point. He got up and walked to the sink, opening the cold water tap fully. He cupped the ice-cold water between his hands and splashed it onto his face, shocking the skin of his cheeks and eyes. He cupped his hands a second time, this time splashing his face and running his cold, wet hands over his forehead and through his unkempt, morning hair.

'I am completely losing it,' he informed the tap as he placed his hands either side of the basin.

'Of course you are, dear,' Elle's voice chirped from behind him, a kiss pecked the back of Robert's neck. 'I've been waiting for a coffee for five minutes. Do you know what that means?' She was sleepy, happy and jovial.

She circled her arms around his waist and hugged him. Her head resting between his shoulders, she gave him a playful squeeze.

'I need coffee, and by the state of you, I think you do to,' she summarised as she broke the embrace and poured the boiled water into the coffee pot to brew.

She collected the items needed for an impromptu continental breakfast onto the kitchen table from the various cupboards and drawers around the room as he carried the coffee pot, slowly. Collapsing into a chair, her mouth stuffed with brioche, Elle asked, 'Nod a gud night sleep?'

She stretched and reached for the pot to plunge the filter through the black sludgy mix. Swallowing the sweet bread she continued, 'What's wrong, babe?'

Robert rubbed his eyes and wondered how to explain his week to her. He walked slowly over to the table with Elle's Soya milk and sat opposite her, a wan smile and a shrug indicated his quandary.

'Work,' he ventured. 'This week. The news.' He picked through the items on the table. 'I'm just being paranoid.' He paused and tore a chunk of brioche from the loaf. Elle smiled encouragingly and poured them both a mug of strong, black coffee. She diluted hers with Soya milk, but left his untouched.

'OK, I understand,' she began, 'it has been a weird week, but it's something more than that. You look as rough as, hon. Honestly. What's going on?'

He dipped the bread into his coffee and chewed, hoping that eating would help some strength return to his enfeebled character. He smiled at Elle wondering how she could look so good in the morning so effortlessly. She returned the smile and split her attention between sipping coffee and spreading blackcurrant jam on an uneven slice of the French breakfast bread.

'So? What's up?' she asked, whilst dribbling jam onto the table and scooping it up using her little finger, delicately adding it to an empty corner of the bread.

'The Head Teacher,' he began, then sighed and drank coffee. He couldn't tell her about the meetings, the shared looks, the way Aileen Byrne had looked like she belonged in an Arkham Asylum in the staffroom at lunch time. His panic attack in the Art cupboard. His theft of two cartons of UHT milk from her office, that he had sequestered in his classroom cupboard. The crazy, intimidating grandparent in the playground. He'd sound madder than the Head teacher had looked! He thought he probably was madder than the Head Teacher.

Elle would tell him to take the day off and see a GP. She was far too sensible and practical to entertain his flight into the fantastic.

'The Deputy is off sick and she asked me to stand in as a Senior Leader today for the lock down drill,' was all he could face telling her.

'Oh,' Elle raised her eyebrows as she chewed her breakfast, unsatisfied with the brevity of the answer. 'So?' she continued, 'why are you such a mess then?'

She sucked the remains of jam from her fingers and put her relaxed arms on the table. She fixed a look squarely at him. 'A little bit of responsibility, for a day. You can't be that stressed out by it? Can you?'

He tried his best to look seriously back at her and hold her gaze without blinking, but he only managed a few seconds.

'Wimp,' she jokingly challenged, 'no wonder the kids in your class run rings round you.' She tore a sheet of kitchen towel from a roll and began to fold it up into squares.

'They do not,' he felt stung and couldn't help but rise to her teasing. 'They behave themselves and work hard.' He thought of Will and Toby and the large grandparent of Lewis Tracey. 'They do exactly what I tell them to do.' He continued his defence.

'Good,' Elle declared, 'glad to hear it.' She smiled her winning smile at him. 'Now tell your face that and get ready for work.' The last word was punctuated by a carefully aimed knot of paper, thrown by Elle. It hit Robert on the nose.

'Thanks,' was all he managed to say as Elle burst into laughter, topping up their coffee.

'Come on, Mister 'Grumpy Pants' Carpenter. Cheer up. It's nearly the weekend. Which reminds me,' she shook the soya milk carton, it was nearly empty. 'I need to stay in London tonight,' she saw his look. 'I know, I know. I'm sorry. We have a big client soiree tonight and I need to get up to Manchester early tomorrow morning.' She stood and leaned over the table to kiss his nose better.

'Amel and Arleta are putting me up tonight. They'll make sure I don't drink too much Champagne and make a tit out of myself. OK?' Smiling, she held his face between her hands and kissed him again, dipping her pyjama top into the jam jar, the flat blade of the used knife smeared its sticky preserved fruit against her exposed belly.

'Oh, bugger,' she leapt back reflexively, examining the mess, 'I need to go for a shower.' She looked up at him and paused. 'Are you really OK?' she asked over her shoulder.

'I'll be fine,' he replied to her back as she left and stretched in preparation.

41

Charlie woke to the sound of Blackbirds singing. He was cold and his arms and legs felt stiff. Half a cheese toastie sat uneaten on a plate a few inches from his partly obscured nose. It smelled of cheddar and Worcestershire sauce.

The hood of his top had been pulled tight around his head at some point in the night. Through the open window he could feel the cold blast of a new autumnal morning. Sleep had allowed mucus to gather and harden in the corners of his eyes, making it an effort to open them. Yawning, he stretched gingerly, rubbing the discharge away from his eyes, slowly allowing them to focus on the chaos around him, as he completed his arm exercises for the day, by pushing himself into a sitting position.

Yawning again, he pulled his knees up to his chest and wrapped his arms around his shins. He could smell his body odour over the herby aroma that permeated his flat. He needed a shower, a cup of tea and a spliff. Or, he needed a cup of tea, a shower and a spliff. Patting himself down, he searched for the last of his weed, pulling a bag with a small bud and lots of dust in it out of his back pocket.

'Get your priorities straight, Charlie,' he said to himself in the empty room.

He bottom shuffled over to the low wooden table in the middle of the room and cast about for ingredients, finding some cigarette papers and about a third of a cigarette that had been ripped up and used earlier in the week.

In the ashtray he found a half smoked 'rollie', a hand made cigarette, and lit it, taking a deep first drag of the day. He coughed shallowly and weakly; the tobacco inside the rollie was old and dry and tasted awful, but it was the nicotine that he needed. Gathering the required materials, he slowly and carefully stuck the papers together in a 'v' shape. He considered what he could recall of the previous day as he worked the dust and cigarette tobacco in the papers into a short cone.

The boy, Maggie's boy, was still here. He had given the kid his bed for the night, whilst he and Alysha got properly wasted. They had stayed up into the early hours smoking and taking a line or two (there goes your profit Charlie, he thought), trying to figure a way out of the predicament that they had found themselves in. Alysha pointed out that all she had to do was walk out the door; it was Charlie's problem, not hers, as she later proved by doing just that when he closed the door on consuming any more of his gear with her.

It had been the phone call. Mickey Butcher had called him. He had spoken to Mickey Butcher twice in one day. Maggie could not be found. Not a word had been heard from her, not a hair or a sighting of her had been reported around town. Something was wrong. She was genuinely missing. Mickey had, for some utterly unknown reason, confided that he had visited Lewis's school and met the teacher to Charlie.

'E's a nonce, Charlie. There's somefink not right abowt him. Know what I mean?'

There was something about the gravelly voice's tone in the small electronic speaker of the phone that made Charlie's blood turn to ice. It was sort of like Mickey had been miniaturised to the size of a mouse and placed a couple of inches away from his ear. It was a mean Mickey Mouse! He had stifled a giggle. Somewhere in his muddled consciousness a warning sounded that there was real trouble heading his way.

He lit the open end of the cone, inhaling in short, deep puffs to spread the fire evenly. Tiny ignited particles of tobacco and marijuana fell from the receding paper; miniscule meteorites succumbing to gravity's pull scattering across the barren landscape of the pockmarked floor. Evidence of previous meteor strikes littered the cheap rug that covered the carpet under and around the table with small blackened impact craters. A moonscape that was anything but a 'Sea of Tranquillity'.

Charlie held the cone up and let the burn even out. Each shallow puff was followed by a sharp intake of air, to cool the smoke in his throat and force it further and deeper into his lungs, ensuring that his blood had the best chance of absorbing and carrying the drug around his body to his brain. He decided that a cup of tea and some toast would fortify him for the day ahead. He had kept the boy as instructed.

'Keep the boy tonight, and don't worry abowt 'im goin' to school wiv that noncey bastard. I'll send Lee, he'll be driving a black Audi, to pick you both up around Nine. Got it?' The mean Mickey Mouse demanded.

Charlie filled the kettle and put it on, placing two rounds of bread in the toaster in the same fluid motion around the kitchen. He remembered being obscenely stoned last night. The words felt like they were coming from someone else.

'I'm not great in the morning, Mickey. Can we make it more like Eleven?' Charlie couldn't help giggling at the memory and he blew smoke into the sink.

'Can we make it more like Eleven? The Mickey Mouse voice in the phone repeated. 'Yeah, Charlie, you fuckin' twat, we can make it more like Eleven. You...' the line had gone dead.

Charlie recalled the fits of the giggles that had torn through the three of them. He squeezed the teabag out and tipped a little milk into the mug. Proper builder's tea, he thought proudly. Although he had never been near a building site, or lifted his fingers to complete even an hour of honest work in his life. He munched on his toast and sipped his tea between blasts and became content. He still had hours to sober up, get showered, feed the kid and be ready for his meeting with Mickey Butcher. He decided that he was going to hand the kid back and get out of there. He had done his bit for Maggie. She and Lewis were on their own. A moment of clarity reminded him that Mickey was no tiny mouse, but he was mean. He was really fucking seriously mean.

42

Aileen had completed her morning black sack drop-off duties as assiduously and quickly as a zero hours contract driver for an online retailer. Paid per item.

She did, however, need to stop for fuel. The nearest station to her being attached to a large supermarket in the middle of the town. Struck by an epiphany, she purchased a Zippo lighter and a bright green five litre petrol can, which she also filled to the brim. She placed both beside the cardboard box in her boot.

She sat in the car park of the supermarket and watched gulls circling around the overflowing bins dotted around. Pecking at fast food rubbish bags, hoping for a loose French fry or scrap of burger bun. She wondered absently if the birds had developed a taste for the burger sauce. Did they caw at each other discussing the merits of Mayo versus BBQ? She turned on the radio and tuned in to the Today Programme. Martha Kearney was introducing the news read by Mishal Husain, which suited her fine.

The news report sounded like it was a hoax, or a script from a Science Fiction movie. The smooth, dulcet tones of the Radio 4 newsreader relaying the horror engulfing the nation with the gentle manner of a late night jazz singer. After the seemingly co-ordinated attacks on Monday, where no connections between suspects had yet been made and no arrests had taken place, there had been a series of inexplicable events around the country.

Nurses in the South West had euthanised geriatric patients in their care, then vanished without a trace. A nurse's uniform had been found on Woolacombe beach, but no body had been recovered. In Liverpool, overnight, a number of warehouses, shops and office buildings had been burnt down in suspected arson attacks. CCTV footage seemed to indicate that men in Fire Service uniforms had thrown petrol bombs into the empty buildings. No Fire crews had responded to the 999 calls to put the fires out. A number of suspects were missing. In Lincolnshire, the townsfolk of Sleaford and North Hykeham had been warned to remain indoors with their windows shut. At least one lorry containing industrial chemicals from a local agricultural processing plant had been driven around with the spout open, spilling the toxic payload on streets and gardens as it passed. Increasing the mystery of this event and the likelihood that the spill had been intentional, the burned out cab of one lorry had been located, but forensic analysis was yet to be released.

In response, the government had increased the terror threat level to Critical and began to make statements about ISIS infiltrators and Russian Intelligence Agents using biological and chemical weapons. The public were to be on high alert and report anything that might be considered unusual behaviour.

Aileen sat looking through the windscreen at the empty car park, tears streaming down her face. The sun had risen and the low golden light reflected off windows of nearby shops and houses. To Aileen it looked like the town was ablaze, every window harbouring a burning, incendiary interior. Each room behind the emblazoned glass was a combustion chamber, waiting, growing, changing. A chain reaction developing.

A genuine smile of relief set on her face. Sobs turned into gentle laughs as the loneliness and isolation was alleviated. Moisture in wispy clouds overhead caught the Sun's rays, the atmospheric prism turning them into fluffy red popcorn in the sky.

'Red sky in the mornin', Shepherds take warnin',' she spoke with a gentle, soft voice. Her accent broadening as she relaxed. She stretched her arms and pushed against the roof of the car and stretched her legs, her feet slipping under the pedals. Aileen switched from Radio 4 to Radio 2 where Katrina and the Waves informed the listening public that they were walking on sunshine. Her head felt giddy with excitement and anticipation. She knew what she had to do.

43

The morning before school passed quickly for Aileen. She had photocopied sets of instructions for staff based on a variety of different lock down scenarios. If the lock down alarm sounded and teachers were in their classrooms, then they were to instantly lock all external doors, close all windows, blinds or shutters, turn off all electrical equipment including classroom lighting and await a call on their class internal phones.

Aileen had considered using e-mail, to reduce the stress on the pupils but thought that the schools I.T. access could well be compromised in a serious lock down event. Staff were to simply state which adults were in the room, the number of children in the room from their class, and state whether any children were present from other classes.

In the event that the school site was compromised during a scheduled breaktime or lunchtime, children were to be herded into the nearest safe classroom and categorised. The school secretary would then have the job of calculating pupil numbers and ascertain whether any children were missing.

In the event of the lock down procedure being initiated by the alarm sounding: one second blasts, followed by two seconds silence on a loop; staff were to keep their charges safe and would remain until they were personally informed of the 'all clear' by a member of the senior team.

Ordinarily, that would be her or Charles. But, he was avoiding further poisoning, disappointingly for Aileen, and had called in sick as she had suspected he would. She had to deputise Robert to be a Marshall of the drill today.

With her resources photocopied and prepped, she carried her '*Finances 17 / 18*' box to the Boiler Room at the far end of the school. It used to be a separate building, but a six foot long glass corridor had been added at some point in the 1970s. The iron frames of the large panes of glass had been caked in several coats of white gloss paint. They were all peeling off now.

Aileen had to unlock two sets of security doors to gain access to the room. She wanted to place the box and the petrol can carefully, in an inconspicuous spot. There were no inspection tours planned, to check rooms that had once contained, or even still contained forms of asbestos from her site facilities contractors, but you just never knew. Council contractors tended to turn up at the most inconvenient times. The last thing she wanted was for a clipboard carrying jobsworth to report her for housing flammable materials in a dangerous location. She hid the box with the five litres of petrol and the lighter at the back of the room, near the external door that no-one had been able to open for years, as the locks and hinges had seized up, inside a big plastic chest marked *Salt and Grit* and placed the winter shovel on top of it.

With the Boiler Room safely locked back up and the key secured on the lanyard, that would remain around her neck at all times during the day, she returned to her office to send the final e-mails with copies of the new lock down map and instructions to staff regarding the day's drill and waited for Robert to arrive for his morning briefing. She felt calm, relaxed and at ease.

44

An irregular knock on the door heralded Robert's arrival. His face filled the square of toughened safety glass that provided a window into, and out of, the office, once more. He looked drawn, she noticed, lines under his eyes were darkened with the purple bruises of a sleepless night, as she beckoned for him to enter.

Robert's eyes were harrowed, hard and glassy. He hadn't let the responsibility that she had given him go to his head, as Aaron probably would have; he remained dressed in his usual dark pullover, shirt and tie combo. He acknowledged her invitation by slowly opening the door and entering. Today he waited to be seated.

Aileen wondered whether his hair had greyed overnight? He seemed to have aged in her eyes. She silently placed a foolscap folder containing the new colour coded map, lock down policy and procedures at the seat to her left and sat down.

Nodding, he walked to the allocated seat in silence, taking it with a sense of...reverence? Or perhaps, it was more submission. She couldn't decide.

'Thank you for helping out today, Robert. I know that Charles would approve of your standing in for him,' she began the meeting with a lie. 'I'm sure that you are aware of the news today. It seems that Monday was only the beginning and our endeavours are taking on a new urgency,' she paused to assess him. He looked alert and nodded his agreement, opening the folder and examining the documents inside.

'Is everything alright, Robert?' she tentatively asked.

Robert had watched the news as Elle had showered and packed her overnight bag. The reports included face shots and selfies of the nurses, as part of an appeal for information on their whereabouts; grainy CCTV footage appeared to show members of the Fire Brigade intentionally setting fire to buildings around the city of Liverpool; an on-the-scene report from Lincolnshire, by a local reporter in a gas mask, provided a muffled account of the toxic spill of countless tonnes of industrial grade chemicals onto the streets of the unwitting denizens in the area.

Finally, there were continuing reports of tragedy and heroism from the attacks on schools on Monday. Flowers had been laid at school gates and candle lit vigils held in nearby churches. What had jarred Robert the most, was the continuation of the usual structure of the news cycle, as the end of the terrifying reports was bookended by news that an English football club had made it into the next round of a European tournament, followed by the mundanity of the national weather report.

His grim mood, after his fear ridden sleepless night, had grown darker. The events of the week, added onto the morning news of ordinary psychopaths tearing at the edges of the order that the British public were so proud of, made Robert sincerely fear for his sanity. What on earth was going on out there? What was going on in his head?

'I'm fine, Aileen. Really, I am,' he lied in return. 'It's just...all happening so quickly, out there. Don't you think?' He put the documents neatly back into the folder and closed it, placing his hands, one on top of the other onto it.

Aileen shrugged non-committally, 'Well...'

'The news is blaming terrorists and Russia and some form of chemical or biological warfare, but...' he tapped the folder, 'it just seems so...'

'Random? Organised? Unlikely?' Aileen offered, shrugging again to emphasise that she had no answers herself.

She needed to be careful and steer the conversation to allow Robert to come to a conclusion himself. She touched the corner of his folder containing the lock down procedure, leaving her hand close to his.

'It makes this a more urgent necessity, doesn't it?' she began to ask leading questions.

Robert tapped the folder again and looked uncomfortable, he shook his head, not in disagreement with Aileen, or her statement, but against the world where primary school children needed to be supervised and educated on how to hide from 'danger' in school.

'Schools have and always should stand out as a place for children to be safe from harm and free to learn and grow without impediment,' he blurted out, 'We're in bloody England, not

Yemen or Somalia. If children are not safe here, now, then we are all bloody up the swanny.'

He looked up to Aileen to make sure that his outburst had not elicited an unforeseen reaction. He felt mildly angered that she was smiling benignly at him. He had had enough.

'I agree, but with the way the world is...' she drifted off, hoping he would finish the sentence for her.

'The adult world is a steaming pile of crap, Aileen. We vote to replace liars with liars. The most corrupt get promoted to the top of every industry, present company excluded,' he qualified, 'and here we are now. Adults polluting the child's world with fear of the 'unknown' danger. Instead of teaching them about Monet, Chopin, the Lumière brothers or Claudette Colvin and Greta Thunberg, we are teaching them to hide in terror behind desks in their schools. For some of these kids, school is the only safe place they have,' he paused as he began to teach Aileen to suck eggs, and caught himself mid-rant.

Aileen was becoming more than mildly amused by Robert's outraged middle-aged, middle class righteous ire. But, he had mentioned a name that she couldn't place.

'Claudette Colvin?' her interest piqued, she couldn't resist, despite the tangent possibly not assisting her cause. She checked her watch to make sure that she had time to indulge Robert.

Robert looked up in surprise. Aileen was a fervent feminist. He thought that she would know about each and every one of the legion of women who had fought injustice with diligence, patience and bravery.

'Claudette Colvin,' he repeated. 'She was the first Black woman, girl really, I think she was fifteen, who refused to give up her bus seat to a White woman in Montgomery, Alabama.' the girl's story made her a bit of a heroine for Robert. She was an ordinary girl, who was going about her ordinary day, when she decided that enough-was-enough and made a stand against the segregationist, racist institutions of America.

'That was Rosa Parks, surely. I seem to remember reading a lot about Rosa Parks, Robert,' she corrected him. It was time to bring the conversation back to the here and now.

'No, the Rosa Parks incident was later. The same year, I think. But the Rosa Parks protest had been contrived by the leaders of the Civil Rights movement. Claudette Colvin was one the five original complainants that brought about the ruling that segregation on buses was unconstitutional,' the debater returned.

'So, why haven't we all heard of her, then?' Aileen asked automatically and kicked herself for wasting time. She glanced at her watch again. They had about ten minutes before the morning briefing to staff.

'The leaders of the Civil Rights movement didn't like that she was fifteen and pregnant out of marriage,' he waited, knowing that the leaders were all men.

'Oh, well that sounds about right, doesn't it? Anyway,' she brought the discussion back to the pressing matters of the need for a lock down in her school full of children between the ages of five to eleven.

'There appear to be monsters and terrorists roaming the country and there are no rules and everyone and everything is a target. So..." she once again left a pause, hoping that Robert would fill the space that she left open.

'Monsters? Terrorists?' he questioned as he took the bait, they had both heard the same news. He looked at Aileen, hoping to find an answer, or a prompt. A reassurance that she was in complete control of the school buildings and that nothing, nobody, could enter with the intent to harm children there under her watch. She was still. She looked at Robert, her eyebrows slightly raised, inviting him to continue.

'Terrorists?' he repeated, 'or just ordinary people doing monstrous things?'

'Ordinary people? Doing monstrous things? Those people in London on Monday were monsters. They were evil, Robert. Pure evil. As for the rest of the terrible things happening this week...' she tailed off, but did not leave the space for Robert to take over – yet. 'How could people become monsters, Robert? How could they do that?' Aileen's face was the picture of outrage, but inside she was cheering and laughing. It couldn't be going better if she had scripted it.

'I don't think people become "monsters"...,' Robert accented the word monsters and used the first two fingers on each hand to indicate he was quoting Aileen, without agreeing with her. Aileen noted the annoying habit, '...on purpose. I think people become capable of monstrous things,' he shrugged, 'accidentally. It's something that happens incrementally, over time. Hitler, for example, wasn't born a racist, war mongering, psychopath. I'm sure his mum loved him.' He paused, wondering if mentioning Hitler or using him as an example was going too far. He decided to style it out.

'He became a total nutter in response to events, over time, that happened to him. As well as his perception of injustice to those around him.' Robert began to wonder if he was being interviewed for a post for the position of hand-wringing Leftie apologist. For some reason he was justifying the inhuman, monstrous acts that had dogged the week's news and fed the nation's fears.

'Look, I'm just as horrified by the things happening this week as you are,' he tried to change tack, 'but I just don't think a knee jerk reaction and labelling every unexplained crime and act of violence in the country as "terrorism",' he flipped his aerial quotation marks again, 'is useful. That's all,' he ended and hoped that Aileen would now let him leave.

He had to set his room up for the Cover Teacher, who would be releasing him to read and fill in all the required Risk Assessments required for him to Marshall the drill today.

'But, Robert, they are terrorists, surely. If their intention is to strike terror into us, into the children and their families. Then that's what they've done.' Aileen glanced at her watch, five minutes left. 'Haven't they?' she remembered to leave the question open. Dangling the fly in front of Robert, waiting, hoping that he would be well and truly hooked.

'I'm not sure I really want to carry on with this conversation. I don't want to say anything that will get me into trouble, please,' he had just had enough.

'No, please go on, Robert. Say it. Get it off your chest.' she smiled sadly, opening her arms with a sweep around the room. She looked at the walls that she had told him last night regularly closed in on her.

'This is our safe space. What is said in between these four walls, does not leave, Robert. OK?' again, she made sure that she finished with a question.

'OK. If you insist. What is terrorism? Who is a terrorist?' he relented and posed a question of his own to Aileen.

She knew the answer he needed, 'Terrorists are people that... that blow up schools, kill the elderly in hospitals. Terrorists are people who commit random acts of arson. The goal of terrorism is to strike terror into ordinary people.' She had heard so many stories of the troubles further north when she was younger, that her grip on the the idea of terrorism and terrorists felt pretty secure.

'So, were Claudette Colvin, or Rosa Parks, or ...' he thought, 'Nelson Mandela. Were they all terrorists?' Robert had had this argument many times with Elle. It had never really ended well and Robert continued reluctantly.

'The American establishment considered the Civil Rights movement to be more than just civil disobedience to begin with. The South African regime certainly imprisoned Mandela for terrorism. But the common thread is that they all wanted to effect change from the established order of things. To challenge the status quo. Terrorists are often labelled in order to turn public opinion against a cause. Che Guevara and Fidel Castro, in Cuba; Ben Gurion and the Zionists were considered by many in the international community to be terrorists. However, many of these people with radically different views on the world see themselves as freedom fighters, liberators. Challengers to oppression. The difference between those like Claudette Colvin, Rosa Parks or Mahatma Ghandi, who used peaceful methods, civil disobedience, to reject and overpower institutional structures of oppression, used the legislature of the so-called enlightened democracies against themselves. For those others. Perhaps they didn't have that luxury. It all depends on who you choose to stand with and what you choose to stand for,' he paused, 'or against. I suppose. Does that answer your question?' He paused again to think through the logical conclusion of the debate.

'I guess, that maybe, the people who are committing these extraordinary acts might think themselves to be disempowered and disenfranchised somehow. The usual methods, like voting or protesting, haven't worked for them. Disobedience is not enough and they think that their actions are justified to challenge the powerful.' He ended his grim summary. He was not any happier now than he was when he walked into the Head Teacher's office.

Aileen stood, time was up, 'God, I'm glad you're here today, Robert. I need you.' She held her hand out to Robert to shake it.

Robert stood and accepted the outstretched hand. Her grip was firm, her eyes were rock-solid and stony. He couldn't read the expression on her face, again, as she walked him to the door.

Aileen opened it, inviting Robert to leave, 'You'll be great today. It's just as well I poisoned Charles, to get rid of him,' she said flippantly, stopping Robert in his tracks. 'I'll join you in the staffroom shortly. I just need to pick up some things,' she said and smiled as she closed the door in his astonished face.

45

Lewis woke to find himself engulfed in an enormous, marshmallow like, thick fluffy blanket in a huge bed. The blanket was really thick, but not heavy at all. Charlie had said it was a 'doovey'. Lewis had never heard of it. He had never slept in a bed so big and wide and warm.

With a start, he reached down to see if he had wet himself overnight, but found his new pants dry. They were soft and smooth and bendy, they weren't like his old pants at all. Alysha had told him that they were called 'Boxer shorts'. She said that he had to have them after knocking Charlie out with one punch earlier and laughed. Charlie hadn't laughed. She told him that only strong, brave boys wore them and had given Charlie a long hard look after saying that, with a very amused smile on her face. Lewis had seen the smile in her eyes too. He liked Alysha. Charlie still hadn't laughed. It was funny, but he had felt braver and stronger when she told him that. He certainly hadn't had the bad dream that night. Maybe wearing Boxer shorts was the key. He decided to tell his Mum when she came back.

He wriggled across the bed, under the tent-like voluminous blanket and got up. Taking the towel that Charlie had placed on the radiator for him, to dry it out, he went straight back to the shower.

Following the instructions to turn on the water as he had been shown last night, Lewis expected the water to be cold, like it always was at home in the morning. The jets of water raced out of the shower head and splashed all over the enclosure. It was immediately warm and soon hot. The water seemed to be hot all the time! Lewis jumped in and danced under the rain of hot water, laughing as he poured the contents of the shower gel over his head.

In the living room, Charlie could hear the noise from the bathroom. The boy was awake and cleaning himself for the second time in twenty four hours. Charlie had spent the last couple hours drinking tea and tidying the main living room of the flat up. It had become a bit of a tip, even by his standards.

He had emptied the various ashtrays around the room, he found one under the mattress and one, somehow, had managed to be placed behind the TV, into a black bin liner. To fill the rest of the bag up he had cleared the coffee table, thrown the remains of Alysha's half eaten cheese toastie from the night before out and then thrown out some out of date food from the fridge on top of it.

The black bag was placed surreptitiously in number Fourteen's green landwaste bin. The old dear who lived there ate like a shrew and rarely put anything in it. After that, he had quietly cleaned the kitchen and the washed out the pipes of the large Hubbly Bubbly, the centrepiece of his smoking den's equipment. Once cleaned it was stored in a cupboard. Charlie didn't think it was right to have all of his drug taking accessories on show to the kid. So he then searched the rooms for any other small pipes or remnants of materials used to consume illicit substances and tidied them away, out of sight.

Now that the boy was up, he decided it was OK to get a hoover out and start to vacuum the floors. After running the nozzle over the rug under the coffee table he realised that it wasn't dirty, just covered in burn marks. The table was moved and the small rug rolled up. He would carry it downstairs and dispose of it later.

The revealed carpet looked nice; he considered whether it was time to go and buy a new off-cut from a carpet store to cover the room again. After finishing, he surveyed the room, hands in the pockets of his hoodie.

The bean bags had been stacked up in the corner, the coffee table had been moved over to the TV, the mattress had been doubled over and hidden in the airing cupboard. The floor looked clean and the room looked much bigger. As a finishing touch, he lit some sandalwood incense sticks to fragrance the room.

Sniffing his armpit, he wrinkled his nose. The last thing he needed to do was wash himself and put on some clean clothes. The boy was making a racket as he bounced back to the bedroom to get dressed. Charlie took his chance and hoped the boy had left him some hot water.

Once both had cleaned and dressed, Charlie and Lewis sat together on stools in the kitchen eating toast and drinking tea.

Lewis was dressed in the same hooded top and tracksuit bottoms combo and thought that it looked much better than the awful school uniform he normally wore. Charlie had thrown on a pair of black combat trousers and wore another designer black hoodie. This one sported the word '*Plank*' in elaborate gothic, Olde English red font across his shoulders on the back and the slogan '*Total Plank*' on his chest over his heart in white. Lewis decided Charlie was alright, he looked proper Gangsta, even if he was a wimp.

'Can I go to school wearing this?' Lewis asked innocently, he munched happily on the toast smeared with real butter and chocolate spread. His smiling lips were covered in the sweet brown greasy goo.

'No school t'day, mate,' Charlie replied.

Lewis sat stock still, stunned by the news that he was going hook off for another day!

'We're gunna see your Uncle Mickey soon. 'E wants our 'elp to find your Mum. OK?' Charlie thought it best to let Lewis know that his Mum was still missing.

'Aww, Oncle Mickey's the best!' The information that there was still no sign of his Mum passed Lewis by. His head was full of clean smells, clean clothes, a new haircut, not being hungry and being driven around in a cool car by the larger than life Mickey Butcher.

Charlie sipped his tea and watched the boy eat. He was a cute kid, really, he thought. Punches to the nuts aside. Maggie had given him her most attractive facial features, the almond shaped eyes, the long lashes, the perfect cheekbones. Lewis was going to be a real lady-killer when he grew up. The girls were going to fall at his feet, after one look into those hazel eyes. Alysha had said that Lewis had Charlie's eyes last night, but he was too wasted to wonder what she meant by that.

He looked down at the formica worktop. The style was called 'Lava Dust' and it looked like one of those images that a telescope produces of distant stars, except in inverse. The background was all white and it was covered in thousands, millions of variously sized black dots.

Charlie had sat on the stool some nights, after particularly heavy sessions, with a cheese toastie and just watched in amazement as the dots danced around on the surface. Dark matter solar systems and galaxies performed feats of intergalactic evolution for his entertainment. He had lost hours just staring at this manufactured infinity, hallucinating and letting his empty mind wander through the impossibility of existence; he always pondered the pointlessness of chasing unattainable material goals and felt satisfied with his lot. He was, he always concluded, content. As long as he was wasted. An indolent immortal that didn't waste time trying to better the perfection of creation.

'When?' Lewis asked.

'When, what?' he answered, Charlie was already getting tired of the never ending stream of questions the boy had. It was easier when Alysha was here. She was clever and knew how to answer them so that the conversation ended. He always seemed to encourage more questions.

'When is Oncle Mickey coming?' Lewis provided further detail to his enquiry.

'Bout, Eleven. Soon,' Charlie hoped that he had provided enough of an answer to end the conversation so that he could return to his train of thought. He found it difficult to think of too many things at once and preferred to process things in a sequence. 'Finish your breakfast.'

'Where?' Lewis persisted.

'Oh my God. Where wot?' Charlie let his head sink over his mug of tea and felt the steam heat a circle of his forehead. Little droplets of water condensed and formed quickly on his skin, making it look like his head was leaking as he turned and looked imploringly at Lewis to stop asking questions.

'Where's Oncle Mickey taking us?' Lewis elaborated, licking and sucking at his lips to remove the smear of chocolate on them without the wasteful gesture of wiping them on his hand. Besides, Lewis decided, he didn't want to risk getting these clothes dirty.

'I don't know, Lewis,' Charlie whined. He really didn't know. But, after a moment's thought he considered where Mickey would want to take them to. 'Probably his snooker club,' he opined.

'Why?' Lewis was now sucking the butter grease and the last remains of the spread from his fingers. His face the picture of concentration.

Charlie tutted his disapproval, 'Mate. Wots wiv all the questions?'

Charlie could take no more. He had totally forgotten what he was trying to think of. Instead, he stood and picked up Lewis's plate and his half empty cup of tea and walked over to the sink, emptying the tea down the drain. He placed the dirty plate beside the sink and looked at the clock on the oven. It said Nine-thirty. 'How about a game of Mario Kart?' he offered as a distraction.

'Oh! Really? Can I? Can I be...?' Lewis was really excited, but had absolutely no idea what Mario Kart was, or any of the characters in the game. But he really wanted to play.

'Yes, you can be Mario!' Charlie smiled. At last, he had found something to end the questions and a way to keep the kid quiet.

46

Robert had begun the day in a dour mood, the morning's outlook had become increasingly bleak and confusing. His attempt at cool professionalism, to keep his concerns about Aileen Byrne under control failed miserably at the first hurdle. He had responded with a dark implacability his inter-galactic anti-hero would have been proud of; he had left his class in the care of the cover teacher, after twenty minutes of increasingly infantile questions about the procedure and purpose of a lock down drill.

He had started the exposition of the morning's drill clearly and sensitively, despite his mind reeling in turmoil from the implications of Miss Byrne's comment about poisoning Charles Syndale. The mysteriously ill Deputy Head's sickness had begun about the same time that Robert had noticed aberrant behaviour by Aileen. His uneasy paranoia, a feeling and a suspicion that had become more intense throughout the previous days, that resulted in his panic attack and loss of consciousness in the Mouldy Cupboard, seemed to have been legitimised.

In light of the national events on the news, Robert decided that he needed to broach the subject of a lock down carefully with the children. He did not want the class of eight year olds to spend ten minutes in a darkened classroom screaming and crying in hysteria. Nor did he want them going home and telling their parents that they were never going to go back to school again because they had hidden under the tables in terror. Afraid that they were being attacked by a killer in the school, like in London, or in America.

He had begun by asking whether the Year 4 children thought the fire drill was stressful or a waste of time, and the children had responded positively. The more eloquent pupils explaining in reply that no, even though none of them had experienced a fire at school, it was good to know what to do in the event of an actual fire occurring. It was neither stressful nor a waste of time. So far so good.

Robert had continued by detailing the arrangements of a new procedure that pupils needed to practise, including all the steps that he would take to lock doors, close shutters and turn off the lights and the projector for the interactive whiteboard. When the bell rang five times with two second intervals, all the pupils had to do was put their pens or pencils down, close their books and close their eyes.

Robert went through the focused meditation breathing exercise with the children again, the one that had allowed him to compose himself after his 'episode' the day before (he imagined the sound of breath being sucked through the shiny, black Bakerlite faceplate and its hissing expulsion and wondered what the effect of the sounds would have on the children of the class if he imitated it).

All the children breathed in, held their breath and breathed out slowly. The children had opened their eyes and smiled, relaxed.

Robert continued by explaining to the children that, just like the fire drill, that they had to practise what to do in the event of the school being locked down so that they would not be scared if they had to do it for real. It then became a circus.

'How is locking the door and closing our eyes going to help us if someone lets a big bomb off outside the classroom?' asked Will, his hand raised. 'And what if someone walks up to the window or the door with a big gun and just starts shooting through it?' he continued.

Without hesitation, half the class raised their hands and bombarded him with hypothetical scenarios that were more in keeping with Hollywood Action Blockbusters or First Person Shooter games with PEGI rating 18+. Robert had raised his hands and counted to five loudly to calm the class.

'This is Falmbourne, not a Post-Apocalyptic wilderness, or a spy strewn Los Angeles. This lock down procedure is much more likely to be triggered by a stray swarm of bees. Do you remember last year? Reception class had to be moved into the hall for an afternoon, because bees had swarmed into the tree outside their their classroom?' he noted the open mouths of concentration and the odd nod of the head.

'It is much more likely that we have to close the doors securely because a pupil is over excited and running around the school,' everyone knew about Ronnie in Year 5, he had ADHD and regularly dodged his medication. The pupil in question had been known to spit at, swear at and bite staff, when the mood took him; his condition giving him a strength and acceleration that the adults who 'supported' him could not always contain.

It was always a source of entertainment for the children of the school when he exploded into a classroom and ran, crawled and jumped around the furniture like a competitor running a Tough Mudder obstacle race, to the cheers and adulation of the other children, as staff tried to corner or corral him. Although, Robert was wondering whether the procedure would be likely triggered by their psychotic Head Teacher roaming the corridors and picking off the staff one-by-one with a sniper rifle.

'By closing the doors and turning off the lights, we are not adding any extra stimulus to a pupil who feels a bit, I don't know, out of control,' he paused. 'The last thing that we, as adults looking after all of you,' he swept his hand around the class, 'is for any of you to get hurt. Especially if all we have to do to protect you is lock the door. You all lock your front and back door at home right?' Thirty odd heads nodded, 'That's all we are doing here.'

'Yeah, but that won't stop a bald, axe wielding psycho who wants to mash you up, Sir, will it?' Toby had recalled the incident in the playground and thought it was time to have a realistic conversation with Mr Carpenter. 'I mean if that man who talked at you yesterday, after school, brought a big dog with him, like a Rotweller or sumfink, and carried a chainsaw. Locking the doors aren't gonna help you are they, Sir?'

'What if a dog with rabies gets in the school?' chirped a girl's voice from the back of the room.

'What if a rampaging sheep or goat gets through the fence?' a voice from the left, one of the brighter children added, to a chorus of giggles and cheers.

'What if a farmer comes on the field and tries to shoot a rampaging sheep?' more laughs welcomed this comment, as Robert decided that it was time to go and leave the class in the hands of the nervous looking cover teacher. The last comment he heard was definitely Will's shouting: 'Get orf my land!' to a cacophony of raucous laughter.

He paused outside the classroom for a moment, wondering whether to go back and calm the children down, but yawned and left the chaos to the Supply cover, wondering why he had put so much energy into addressing the lock down procedures in such a subtle and sensitive manner. The class were no shrinking violets, many of them were engaged in several hundred campaigns on Fortnite a week.

Shaking his head at the vague indifference he felt towards a colleague who had obviously had enough of full time teaching and had settled for the paltry hundred quid a day offered by agencies that didn't value teacher's professional qualifications, he walked with numb purpose towards the School Office, where he was to meet the Head to begin the lock down drill. He was trying to work out whether she had been trying to be humorous earlier, to set him at ease or on edge, considering the context of the week's events, or whether she was merely signalling her well known dislike for her Deputy by indicating that she would have wished that she could poison him? Was she just making a sick joke? He didn't know. He realised that although he had worked with Aileen for about seven years, in reflection, he didn't know her at all.

He paused as he turned the corner. Ahead, with her back to him, was the Headteacher, who was talking through the drill with one of the Governors. Not a hint of the criminal malice or the fleeting glimpses of near insanity required to intentionally poison someone that she was responsible for keeping safe could be gleaned from her prim posture and the cool, calm professionalism with which she addressed the Governor. Both wore the bright fluorescent yellow high visibility personal protective vests that were worn to ensure that a crazed terrorist or infuriated parent would single you out as the first target to exterminate from the health and safety obsessed culture of the UK. There was an additional vest on the Office counter waiting for him.

'I am just a fucking Year 4 Primary School teacher,' he mumbled to himself.

The week was proving too much. He shook his head slowly as the Governor looked up from the sheaf of paperwork that had been thrust into his hands by Aileen. The look on his face indicated that he was eager for Aileen to be distracted by anything at all.

'Ah, this must be Mister Carpenter,' the Governor interrupted Aileen's detailed and precise break down of what would begin in about five minutes time and placed the papers on the counter next to the high vis armour that awaited Robert.

'Tom,' he held his hand out and walked towards the still motionless teacher, and paused half way. An open and welcoming gesture that required Robert to join the pair of school leaders.

'I have to say that I am very grateful to you for stepping up, today,' he explained, 'Miss Byrne has filled me in with the unfortunate illness that seems to have struck Charles down. Noro-virus, was it?' he half turned to Aileen, forcing her to take a step towards the middle of the corridor.

'That's right. Unfortunately, Mr Syndale has been taken ill with a bad dose of a stomach bug that causes vomiting. I can't be sure it is Noro-virus.' Aileen smiled to Tom, the Governor, but didn't meet Robert's questioning look.

'No problem.' Robert replied, 'Always happy to help out.' For some reason, to fill the silence as he approached the welcoming and charming Governor, he continued, 'You can't refuse a request from Miss Byrne. She doesn't take 'no' for an answer,' cringing on the inside again as he said this, he wished that his brain could be disconnected from his mouth.

'Indeed not,' Tom smiled.

Aileen watched as the two men shook hands vigorously, but briefly, in disdain at how easily men superficially bonded. An acquaintance, a friendship, an alliance. She could always observe such social conventions, but had failed to initiate or respond to them herself for quite some time. Except, she thought, with Robert these last few days.

She considered him, watching Robert put on the ridiculous yellow vest while Tom filled him in on the Risk Assessment paperwork that he needed to counter sign. Since her failed attempt to poison him on Monday, she had spent more time being human with him than she had with any other single individual in, what? Years?

'Gentlemen,' she cast sentimental reverie aside. 'Shall we begin?'

47

The drill was a success, according to the e-mailed report written by Tom later that afternoon.

The intended alarm sounded after the school Secretary triggered it on her computer. The distinctive sound of the alarm ringing intermittently, warning everyone of an existential threat somewhere on the school site was received with unexpectedly relieved smiles and a high five between the Governor and the Secretary.

The trio left soon after, on an inspection tour of the school to ensure that all external access points were secured and all classrooms were locked and quiet, a process akin to the Blitz blackout procedures, leaving the Secretary with printouts of the morning's registers for each class as she began to ring around the rooms investigating whether all children and staff could be accounted for.

Overeager support staff had not only locked the doors to the playgrounds, as well as their classrooms, they had also managed to bolt the doors in the corridor between classrooms. Stuck between the locked front access at Reception and the School Office and Aileen's office, the three milled about.

'Well, erm..' ventured Tom, who silently cheered at the prospect of his Governor duties being cut short, in favour of a well earned lunch time pint.

'Jesus, Mary and Joseph,' Aileen muttered, ducking into her office.

Robert stood by the locked door, head down and motionless. He wished he had just crashed the car into a hedge, or a stationary bus, or something, on his way to work that morning. A bump that would need an insurance claim for the car, and a trip to A & E, but no serious, long term injury. Just something to have got him out of where he was.

Shortly, Aileen returned with flushed cheeks and a large set of keys, which proved to be the master keys for the entire building. She turned immediately to the bolted door that was obstructing entrance to the KS1 classrooms; after flipping through half a dozen colour coded brass keys, she jammed the appropriate master into the lock and twisted it forcefully. To no avail. The bolts were not on a deadbolt and the door remained secure.

'Oh...' Aileen contained the desire to let rip a tirade of profanity. 'The doors to the other corridors,' she instructed Robert dismissively, thrusting the set of keys, the blue tabbed key outstanding, into his hands.

48

Robert watched a tall, solitary cumulonimbus cloud drifting across the horizon, heavy and laden with moisture ready to drop, somewhere, as the trio ambled around the perimeter of the building.

The school site seemed unnaturally quiet, like it did in the school holidays when only the staff were in, tidying, marking and putting up new displays ready for the next termly onslaught of thirty or so daily marathons.

The other two internal corridor doors had also been bolted, obstructing any intruder, or leadership team from gaining entry to any area of the school, other than reception and the Head Teacher's office. Tom had made light of the situation with a quip about a ransom for Aileen's release; the gag was greeted with tumbleweeds of silence from the two employees of the school.

'So,' Tom began as, undaunted by the embarrassed gloominess of the two teachers, he peered at his own reflection in the closest pane of the Victorian arched windows of the Year 2 classroom. The dark blue blinds were fully closed and with the interior light from the room off, nothing of the interior was visible.

'I think that we have clear evidence of the strength of security here at Thresher Street,' Tom continued, taking large strides to speed the pace of the pointless inspection parade up, as Robert wondered whether the lock down of the building kept children safe from any external threat or trapped them without any hope of escape.

'I think your lock down procedure has proved to be even more efficient than we thought possible,' he smiled at Aileen. A little charm never hurt, even with this icy queen, Tom thought. He could almost taste his pint of IPA that was waiting in the barrel of the *Toad and Lemon* public house.

49

Harley Otterden had been the apple in his mother's eye. He had been over-nurtured and overindulged throughout his gilt-edge youth.

As a boy, he had been skinny and considered a bit of a wet blanket by the other boys at both primary and grammar school, because he was never any good at football, rugby or cricket, in any position he tried to play in. What was worse was that he always went home on time and left a team short handed before the end of a match. Girls had rarely paid any attention to him. He wasn't cool, good looking or particularly smart, and so was of no use to any of them.

His adolescence had been one of lonely frustration and unrequited lust. Life changed for Harley – Lee to his new friends – when he discovered steroids and a boxing gym. Ending his education much earlier than his family, especially his mother, had wanted, instead learning an age old craft from an older night-club bouncer, who always had an eye for an outsider.

Youthful bitterness had given him a mean streak which was developed and channelled in his new, chosen vocation. Life as a strongman on the door had imbued him with a kudos that he had never before experienced. The authority to grant or obstruct access gave him a power that he could abuse any time he liked.

Especially when an old school acquaintance needed a favour, or an attractive group of women agreed to meet his price for entry to the packed nightclub.

He quickly gained a reputation for using violence efficiently, without hesitation or fear, as well as for being a bit of a lady killer: he used sex powerfully without mercy. His supercharged ego quickly controlling young or vulnerable women, who would capitulate to any degradation in an attempt to please him more than any other woman could.

Lee vainly checked his tie in the full length mirror by the front door before leaving the house. His boss, Mickey Butcher, was a stickler for appearance.

'Look smart, think smart,' he said to his reflection as he jerked his arms a la Tommy Cooper, to make sure that his shirt fit across his steroid and bench press enhanced shoulders, and with a flick of his wrists he made sure his sleeves were even.

Turning the key to unlock the door, he took a last smirking glance up the stairs where he had left Laetitia, one of his part time girlfriends, who was also incidentally a married Police Constable, asleep, exhausted, and a bit sore.

Reaching back to the post ending the bannister, he grabbed his casual suit jacket, before theatrically swinging open the door to welcome the morning scene of the street. It was a desirable area, lined with Edwardian terraced townhouses where Laetitia had previously lived with her family. Until Pete, her husband, had discovered her philandering with Lee and had taken the kids to his parents.

Lee shrugged the jacket on as he swaggered cockily across the deserted, but car crowded street, pivoting and pirouetting past the closely parked vehicles. Commuters used the street as it was only a couple of minutes walk to the train station.

' 'Bout bloody time the Council made this residents only!' he declared to the pigeons, in his nasal warbling, bird-like voice

His hand caressed the car keys in his jacket pocket. His thumb and index finger gently traced the soft curves of the small moulded plastic lozenge that remotely controlled the car's locking mechanisms with a sensuous, almost timid care that Laetitia and his other self loathing, but submissive girlfriends would not recognise.

The opposable digit paused and circled over the metal button that stood bevelled out, like an aroused nipple, that opened the flip key folded into the housing, intimately. Without taking the key fob out of his pocket, he pressed the button that emitted the radio signal in every direction along the tube like street, searching for the right gamete to receive and decode the signal and unlock his pride and joy. Parked on the opposite pavement, a sleek, black Audi A4 responded with a double beep and flashing yellow indicators. It was unlocked and ready for its master to enter.

Mickey had called Lee the night before with a pick up. He had to collect the two-bit drug dealer and a kid, who Mickey had warned, might smell a bit like shit, from the place he had sat outside of the afternoon before and take them to a lock up at the edge of town. There they would all wait together until Mickey arrived. It had been stressed that neither of the parties had wronged Mickey and that no harm should come to them.

Lee was known as an assiduous bouncer at the town's late night boozer, that doubled on Friday's and Saturday's as a makeshift club. Mickey had owned it after buying out the previous landlord, who had developed a bit of an expensive habit of having posh birds on his arm. The driver's door opened with a muffled click, after the handle was pulled with a gentle reverence. He marvelled at the silence of the hinges as the door glided open. Its shadow swept the drab grey paving stone, adding a touch of German engineered style to an otherwise unremarkable foot path.

The smell of new car leather exploded out, intoxicating Lee as he entered the open cavity; the atmosphere enveloped and penetrated him as he pushed on the surfaces of the interior with as many sensitive areas of his body as he could. Absent mindedly, he pulled the door closed with his finger tips, to give himself the privacy that the moment demanded, before reaching again into his jacket pocket, this time taking the mechanical tool out.

It sat on his upwardly turned palm, the metal button inviting gentle pressure to release the bonds restricting the short metal member. His thumb snapped down and the small, grooved and symmetrical ignition key shot out like a switchblade from a fighting dance sequence in West Side Story.

Lee thrust the erect phallic ignition key into the waiting slot, giving it a dominant quarter twist clockwise. The machine came to life with a gently throbbing purr that coursed through Lee's body and soul. With a stroke of the steering wheel and a tentative pump on the accelerator, he pulled out of the tight spot and moved into the carriageway with poise and control towards his desired destination.

50

'Are we nearly there yet, Charlie?'

'No, not yet mate.' Charlie replied for the umpteenth time.

It seemed that Lewis never tired of asking the same question. Lee turned the car off a back road onto what seemed like a dirt track, flanked on both sides by tall and voluminous hedgerows. Small dark birds flashed across in front of the bonnet of the pedigree car, as proof of their daring - part of a modern mating ritual - modern avians adapting to the fast, ever changing technology of the hairless bipeds. Or, perhaps as a warning, a desperate attempt by millenia old species to attract the attention of the simple hairless bipeds to the poison gas being spewed out of the noisy, ugly metal contraptions? Neither Charlie nor Lee had any idea.

'Is Oncle Mickey gonna be there?'

'Not sure, to be honest, mate.'

'Charlie, will my Mum be there?'

'Dunno, mate. 'Ave to wait and see.' Charlie's voice finally began to rise in irritation, partly because he seemed to know very little himself, the boy was shining a light on his ignorance.

Lee slowed the car to a stop on a small square of gravel that provided access to the row of shambolic and neglected looking garages beside a double wire mesh gate that was overgrown by Jasmine and Wisteria vines. He gently pulled the handbrake up and put the car into neutral, turning the engine off with a gentle twist of the ignition keys.

'Is Oncle Mickey gonna take us out in his Jag?'

'I dunno, but this is a nice car, right?'

'Wot are we 'avin for lunch, Charlie?'

'We just had breakfast, Lewis. You can't seriously be hungry already.'

Lee had had enough, 'For fucks sake. Will you two give it a rest for a minute?' He turned his head to look at the long haired skinny ponce in the passenger seat. 'Does that kid ever shut up? Didn't you teach him any manners at all?' He stretched to face the small hooded bundle strapped into the passenger seat behind him.

'Children,' he paused and nodded his head towards Lewis, 'should be seen,' he became uncomfortable with the exertion of twisting his over developed torso around, so he turned and sat back into his luxury heated driver's seat and watched the child flip him a silent two finger salute in the rear view mirror. 'And not bloody heard,' he finished, glaring at Charlie in indignant accusation over his piss poor parenting.

The car fell silent for just a moment, before Charlie leaned across, 'Is there any need to swear? You know, in front of the boy?' he jerked his head at the now silent and sullen child.

Lewis waited, hood up, arms crossed. He had sunk back inside the hoodie so that only his eyes and forehead could be seen in the aperture of the shadowy garment.

Charlie had understood the insult about parenting and considered whether to disavow any responsibility, but thought better of it. In the circumstances.

Lee just shook his head and turned the radio on. The sound of the 'Pop Master' jingle introduced the DJ and quiz master Ken Bruce, as he tested listeners and contestants on their music trivia knowledge, predominantly from the 70s and 80s. No one in the car had any idea what any of the answers were, and each sat in their own awe at the super human genius's who kept answering correctly.

The engine quietly ticked, as it cooled down and the thoroughbred parked car rested. The lock up was part of a group of cottages that had been built to house farm workers between the wars. The garages had been added later.

Behind them was a large plot of land that had been bequeathed to the council by a grieving mother and widow many years before. It had been divided up into allotment plots that had been loved, worked, tilled and nurtured to produce some of the best vegetables seen in local village fetes in Kent. It was quite a remote spot, with little or no passing traffic, with the occasional and oblivious arrival and departure of the dedicated gardeners and small holding entrepreneurs.

Slowly and silently, a car approached the line of pebble-dashed garages. The gravel of the untarmaced, track gently crunched under the tyres, as Mickey Butcher arrived.

Slowly cycling up behind the incongruously out of place classic car, was Mrs Fincher, once a very important local magistrate and accountant, now a retired, septuagenarian gardener, with a penchant for homemade Gooseberry wine and listening to her rhubarb creaking to Desert Island Discs. Although, she wasn't sure about Lauren Laverne. Not enough gravitas for her liking.

The occupants of both cars sat waiting for her to arrive and unlock the gate to the allotment, which she did totally oblivious to the two out of place cars sitting outside the garages adjacent. She had her headphones on and was lost in a podcast of Woman's Hour that she had downloaded at home. With the gate securely padlocked behind her, she walked her bicycle along the path to her allotment. It was a prime plot, next to the field with a southerly aspect.

Once the old woman had left sight, Mickey got out of his Jag and produced a set of keys, which he was thumbing through to find the one that opened the shabby garage door.

'Stay in the car and wait 'til I tell you to get out. Got it?' Lee instructed Charlie, an index finger punctuated the question.

After a pregnant pause, he followed Mickey, leaving Charlie and Lewis alone.

'Don't like 'im.' Lewis commented after the driver's door had clicked closed , the boy watched Lee's back swagger over to the impressive old gangster. It was the first time he had spoken since Lee had told him to shut up. 'E's a prick,' Lewis concluded.

Charlie turned to face the boy, who was still hidden in the hood of his tracksuit top, 'You shouldn't say things like that, Lewis.'

Charlie paused and wondered how best to encourage the boy to keep quiet without offending him. He was a bit scared of Lee.

'You shouldn't use language like that,' he considered, 'your Uncle Mickey wouldn't like it.'

He turned back and looked at the two gangsters through the windscreen. 'Not about one of his mates.'

'I'm not scared of 'im. Mum says most men are pricks,' Lewis replied, 'they're 'bad news' and 'not to be trusted', like. Except, maybe, you. You're alright, Charlie.' he mumbled.

Silent tears trickled down his cheeks. It had been a while since he had really thought about his mum, and he was missing her familiarity. It was strange though, he felt safe with Charlie. He wasn't hungry, or thirsty or afraid of his mood, the way he was with mum. He wiped the tears away with his hand. He didn't want Charlie to notice.

51

Mickey swung the thin aluminium garage door up, and stood talking and gesturing with Lee. They both looked at the Audi and laughed, Mickey put his arm paternally around Lee's shoulder and walked him into the empty gloom of the garage.

Charlie was getting a bad feeling about this. It was not the kind of place to reunite a mother with her son. This was the kind of place to 'make someone disappear'. He looked nervously over his shoulder at the boy in the back trying to put his fear and nerves back in Pandora's box. Mickey wouldn't do them both, would he? Not a boy, surely.

Lee returned to the mouth of the garage and pointed at Charlie and indicated that he should come alone, as Ken Bruce asked his Three in Ten question to name three hits by 10CC.

Charlie nodded, 'Wait here, Lewis,' he heard himself say as the contestant named *I'm Not in Love* and *Donna* and then agonised until the jingle played at the end of the ten seconds. Ken's commiserations were replete with adulation of how great the contestant had been and how it was not as easy when it's your ten seconds.

Charlie swallowed and left Lewis in the car. The door clicked gently behind him, leaving the tearful and lonely Lewis behind. The air was crisp as chilly gusts of wind pushed the large, dark grey fluffy clouds across the sky. Charlie's legs turned into licorice sticks as he approached Mickey and Lee.

'Alright Charlie? How's the Little Man been? Not causing you too many problems is he?' Mickey said as he stepped out of the shadowy interior of the empty garage.

'Lee,' he chuckled, 'tells me that the kid don't stink like he shit hisself,' the two tough men shared a look with each other, 'so I guess you're not a total waste of space, then. Probably for the first time in your life!' He broke into hacking laughs at Charlie's expense.

The tension of the covert meeting place was broken for Charlie, as he realised that he wasn't about to be 'bumped off' in a Scorcese-like hit to tie up loose ends, and he exhaled explosively and laughed at his own misfortune. Recalling the punch in the jewels and the stress of cleaning the lad up, he shook his head and looked between the two.

'No sign of her then?' he asked.

'You were right about the teacher,' Mickey growled. 'E,' he announced, ' E, is a proper noncey twat. He knows where she is, or what she's playing at.'

Lee hunched and rolled his shoulders, 'I say we pick the kiddy-fiddling faggot up and give 'im a pastin'!' Miming an upper cut and a left jab to emphasise his physical prowess.

'It might come to that, Lee,' Mickey considered. He reached up and toyed with the dangling pull cord that allowed someone to close the door to the garage from the inside. Using the small wooden dongle, on the end of the cord, as a punch bag and rolled his arms through the beginning of a training routine that was well in his past.

'Can you get your hands on a kitchen chair, with no finger prints of course, and a pair of handcuffs?'

Lee let his shoulders relax and smiled, nodding his affirmation. The kitchen chair was easy, just a second hand store with no CCTV he knew, the police grade handcuffs would take a little more effort. Laetitia's shift didn't begin until tomorrow morning, so he had plenty of time to distract her while he borrowed them.

'Good, but lets hope we don't need 'em. Kidnapping a school teacher will not go unnoticed. While you sort them out, and bring 'em back 'ere. Me, Charlie and the kid will follow the twat and see if he leads us straight to her. Job done!'

Mickey ushered the pair back out of the garage and pulled the cord, closing the door and dismissing Lee, who walked directly to the car and opened tits rear passenger door, pointing away from it and uttering the single instruction: 'Out!' to Lewis.

'Mr Butcher,' Charlie began hesitantly, 'what are you gonna do to her? When we find her?'

Mickey followed Charlie's gaze to the boy who had been unceremoniously ejected from the Audi and who was fronting up fearlessly to Lee.

'We'll cross that bridge,' he put his hand on the bony shoulder of the small time dealer as he spoke gently, 'when we get to it. Alright?'

52

Robert watched the Governor pull away through the automatic gate in his muddy people carrier. Tom hadn't wasted any time taking his leave.

Aileen's mood had been foul. Her plan had largely been ignored by the staff, who locked every single door they could find, including a cleaning cupboard containing a broken hoover that had been left open for weeks by accident, obstructing her from conducting a proper assessment of the classroom conditions during the procedure.

She had gone straight to her office, leaving Robert to conclude the pleasantries, with the ever complimentary Tom.

Robert stood staring at the car park through the glass door at the entrance and wondered how best to voice his suspicions to the Head Teacher. He was tired of the strange game of cat and mouse they had played with each other, the last few days. He had kept quiet throughout the morning, but he had to challenge her about Charles. Why would she say that she had poisoned him? It was much more plausible that he was suffering from some gastro-intestinal bug. Then there were the other moments, in her office, in the staff room. The look of...what? Panic, claustrophobia, insanity? He had been the one who had a panic attack and passed out in the art resources cupboard, after all.

'You alright, Mister Carpenter?' the school secretary asked, as the phone began to ring, breaking him out of his immobility.

He breathed deeply and smiled, rocking onto the balls of his feet and then back on his heels, he turned and nodded, walking purposefully back to Aileen's office for a showdown.

Behind him he heard the normal life of the school continue, 'Good morning, Thresher Street Primary School, how can I help you?' the efficient and cheerful voice tinkled from the other side of the reception desk. 'Certainly, I'll just see if she's available, please hold.'

Robert picked up his pace and tried to beat the call to Aileen's office, but arrived at the open door to find her sitting at her desk, holding the receiver to her ear and nodding.

'Yes, uh huh, you're sure...it's the whole unit definitely leaking then? When can you fix it? How long until the part is available? Today?' Aileen's voice became increasingly tense, it was clear that today was not a good option.

'Yes, I know it's urgent, but I can't just turn off the gas to the school, now, can I?' Aileen looked at Robert implacably and shook her head. 'No,' she refused, 'you will not carry out work during a school day, and I will not pay you overtime to complete the repairs in the evening. Saturday will be fine. The boiler has lasted this long, I'm sure it can last a couple more days.'

She nodded her understanding, as her conversation partner provided a detailed disclaimer, absolving him from anything, should the boiler have a fault in the interim.

'Yes, I understand. You have informed me and I am making the decision. Yes,' she became exasperated, 'I know that the insurance may not cover us now. Thank you.' She ended the conversation suddenly, slamming the handset down on its cradle, 'Good bye.'

Aileen placed her head in her hands, her raven black hair curving across her shoulders and face, appearing, to Robert to look like feathers on wings, curling protectively around her. The silence was broken by a low growling mewl of frustration from Aileen, who then slammed her hands down on the table as she turned to address her stand in Deputy.

'You have something on your mind, Robert. Come in and close the door.'

53

She had better, more important things to do. The main focus of her attention had been the murder and disposal of the malignant parent who had harmed the child that she should have protected and loved, in Aileen's humble opinion.

The frustration at having to nursemaid the governor throughout the morning's questionable security and safeguarding test had taxed her patience. The sound of the fire-alarm's intermittent ringing had brought jarring visions and memories of sensations from recent memory into sharp focus. A sharp pain in the heel of her right hand commenced when the ear-splitting alarm began its first ring. The sound stabbed at her as a reminder of the resistance that Maggie Tracey's unsuspecting brain tissue had provided, to the intrusion of her disposable pen, misused to penetrate and butcher.

The brief silence had allayed only the physical repercussions of her actions. Images of bloody clothing and a tear and blood streaked face replaced those of Tom and Robert, who had stood beside her in the school reception.

The alarm sequence provided a further four aural floods of ninety decibel shocks, triggering torturous recollections. The memory of crunching bone and sinew jarred up her forearm. A remembered feeling, as she had sawed and cut the cadaver, through the squelching soft tissue and dripping wet messiness of dismemberment into the small 'bite size' pieces of flesh and bone that she later roasted on last night's bonfire. The smell of the charred body brought bile to her throat. The deafening silence that followed the end of the alarm reminded her of the peace and tranquillity that she had felt, despite the horror, as she watched the stars slowly roll across the sky, the fire spitting and sizzling its way through the piecemeal cremation ceremony, in her back garden.

Her temper had frayed at the humiliation of not being able to conduct the brisk inspection of the corridors and classrooms. She had railed against her idiot staff as she had walked the gently protesting buffoon of a governor around the perimeter of the school building. In no way had she been mollified by his protestations that it was evidence of her wonderful leadership; strong protective instincts that had lead to the even more efficient lock down than even she had proposed.

Now, standing before her was Robert Carpenter. He was holding out her keys. It was the master set that she had almost thrown at him earlier.

'Leave them on my desk,' she uttered, as her hands drummed the desk's surface.

Robert stepped gently forward and placed the keys on the edge of her desk. Sitting there, she seemed both vulnerable and volatile. Feminine and violent. Like a Black Widow spider: enticing, beautiful and deadly.

He was once again unnerved and on edge in her presence and wanted desperately to be anywhere else. Any thought of confrontation with her concerning his suspicions and anxiety over the mystery illness of Charles and the weird behaviour that he had observed was pushed firmly from his attention.

'Coward!' his subconscious Elle voice yelled at him.

'Are my duties for the lock down over?' he asked hesitantly, 'Is it OK if I return to my class?'

He had decided that the easiest route out of this was to demonstrate his professional duty to the children of his class.

In his mind's ear, he could hear Elle chide him laughingly: 'Why are you asking her? Tell her you are returning to class, you wimp!'

There were times when he hated his subconscious. However, he hated it even more when it was right.

'No,' Aileen stood and looked out of the window. The die was cast and she had to win Robert today to make her plan work.

'We're going to make a visit to that boy in your class,' her icy, emotionless eyes met Robert's again, sending a shiver down his spine. 'Lewis, wasn't it? Lewis Tracey? And his Mother, that,' she spat the words out, 'that Maggie Tracey, who I met with earlier. The woman who beats up her own son and abandons him to...' she wondered whether to play the Catholic prude for him.

She left the sentence unfinished, as she shrugged on her jacket and collected her handbag.

'You know she's a drug addict? she asked Robert as she placed the school's master set of keys back into the lockable drawer, hidden in the filing cabinet.

She turned to face him, 'No? Did you know that Lewis had been taken into care last year?'

Robert stood silently, his head shaking, indicating that he had no knowledge at all of the character of Lewis's mum. He had only met her briefly on the playground. She never stopped to chat or ask after Lewis's progress after school.

'No, but I am surprised that Lewis has such severe hygiene problems, because she seems so...' he hesitated considering the pretty, young single mother that Maggie Tracey seemed to be. He was sure that there were several of the parents of the children in his class that regularly abused illegal substances. He had even caught the odd herby smell from Toby's clothes. Mrs Hedgecock was definitely a bit of a pot head.

'Clean for a prostitute?' Aileen interjected with a haughty laugh as she rummaged in her bag. 'Oh yes, I know what you mean,' she smiled as Robert winced at the mention of Maggie Tracey's chosen vocation.

'She is guilty of extreme neglect of the poor boy. He has had to compete with her desire for illegal drugs and her compulsion to degrade herself and sell her sex to get the money to buy them.' She pulled her car keys from her bag and walked straight past Robert, out of the office. 'We'll take my car,' she called over her shoulder. 'Find out the address from the office there, will you?'

54

The journey passed by uneventfully and silently. Each of the occupants was lost in their own deliberations.

The dulcet tones of the Radio 2 DJ soothed the listener and failed contestant alike, the latter replied with a crackly voice. The DJ spoke gently consoling platitudes to the former contestant, offering a consolatory, but rather poor prize, and the chance to mention the names of near and dear ones on a live broadcast.

The traffic was rather heavy, as the roads were currently being dug up by a company laying new gas pipes that were being routed to a new housing estate, being built just outside of town. There were temporary traffic lights everywhere. This month it was gas. A couple of months ago it was water or electricity, digging up exactly the same stretches of road.

Angry residents had put up temporary road signs declaring: "Stop the madness!" and "Dig it once! Do it right!" One humorous household had simply put a sign up at the edge of their driveway: "Welcome to Falmbourne! Home of the traffic jam" with a big smiley face under it.

Robert was always surprised at how many people were not at a place of work, or whose job it was to just drive around finding traffic jams to sit in and get paid for attending them. He rarely saw the world beyond his classroom in term time. Incorrectly assuming, that as he was trapped into a single fixed location for his working life, that everyone else in the country was too.

The lines of cars and vans wound their way through the busy town, passed rows of traffic cones and temporary protective barriers that provided a plastic shield between the slow moving vehicles and the workmen sitting in holes, drinking from flasks and talking about the strange events from the news. Passed signs written in chalk on blackboards declaring that businesses hidden by the giant mechanical diggers and large gas pipe carrying lorries were 'Open as usual', despite the roadworks resulting in trade that was anything but.

Aileen barely noticed the candy stripe flashes of day glow orange and white on the cones and fencing that separated the traffic from the planned deconstruction as she passed the roadworks. Their appearance only enhanced the unreal atmosphere that her life had taken on. Her hands and feet did not seem to be her own as they manipulated the vehicle's controls. Some part of her brain fought to keep hold of familiar and sane activities.

Mostly, Aileen was happy. Plastic workman were frozen in place; moulded hands clasping nothing in their cylindrical grip. The world flattened into a two dimensional children's play mat as she followed the white lines on the black tarmac. She wondered whether the giant child pushing her car along had blonde or brown hair, was a boy or girl, as she wound her way round the traffic bound one-way system.

She wondered too, how to break the news to Robert that she had killed his pupil's mother. That the remains of her were stashed in school and he should dispose of the evidence for her. She was placid and serene as she watched the Victorian and Edwardian properties replaced by far more modern monstrosities. The carefully crafted red-brick buildings, built with care, pride and attention, were replaced by grey box-like terraces and chunky blocks of flats.

Adored by some and neglected by those who lived in them. The social housing was slowly falling into disrepair and decrepitude. A long dead architect's dream of a perfect worker's Arcadia had become the disaffected, unemployed and socially dysfunctional's right-angle edged nightmare of mediocrity and unsatisfied ambitions.

She drove without much conscious thought; her feet reacting to the changing speed of the car by engaging the clutch or depressing the accelerator whenever needed. She only required an occasional touch on the brakes if a driver ahead of her made a mistake, or had to stop quickly for a changing light. This allowed her to let her mind wander. Again, she mentally prepared herself for a variety of eventualities that she may encounter, once they arrived at the address Maggie Tracey had given the school. Would the place be empty? Would the child be there alone? Would the mysterious grandparent be around? Would the police be waiting for her?

Aileen reached a T-junction and slammed down hard on the brakes, stopping the car sharply. A horn blared behind her, as the following driver made an emergency stop. She stared straight ahead, paying no attention to the fact that there was no traffic coming from the left or right; the road was empty and she was free to pull out and continue on her way.

She had barely considered the illegality of her actions. The consequences of breaking so many taboos were being locked up in a cell measuring six by six. It not really been a pressing concern in her previous mania. The thought that she could be moments away from being discovered by the authorities sent panic racing through her mind.

The sound of the beeping car horn faded into the distance as her stress induced panic attack reduced her vision to a fuzzy tunnel. Her wrinkled knuckles, that had been deep inside the dead mother's abdomen only hours ago, were the only visible anchors holding Aileen in the world. They transformed in her mind's eye. Slowly they changed, morphing from the rictus grip of terror, with which she held onto the steering wheel, holding onto the last shred of solidity and sanity left to her, into the yellow claws of a bird, perching carefree where-ever it chose. Ready to fly.

'...OK? Miss Byrne? Is everything alright?' a male voice intruded into Aileen's chrysalis. A car horn beep, beep, beeped. The last beep followed by a distant curse intended to offend her.

'Miss Byrne? The road is clear, Miss Byrne. We're clear to turn. It's just over there,' the male voice continued.

An arm, pointing, came into view. The direction it indicated was clear, her flightpath was open. There were no white cars with bars of blue lights on the roof. No officers in stab vests waiting. Just an empty space outside a pigeon-shit covered block of nondescript flats. Some balconies had washing visible. Most windows were closed. The car horn blared behind her and an angry engine revved.

'Miss Byrne?' Robert's urgent voice awoke her and she turned to him and blinked at him to acknowledge that she had understood.

She smiled weakly and pulled the car across the road, turning right and quickly pulled over left, into the curb to park. An angry man in a baseball cap pulled up next to her, gesticulating his displeasure and wheel spun away.

'Sorry..I..' was all she could say as she turned the engine off and released her seat-belt.

They sat together in the car, silently. Each embarrassed for very different reasons. The engine ticked gently as it began the process of cooling down after managing the thousands of carefully planned and controlled detonations within its casing. Robert couldn't look at Aileen any more. Instead, he chose to watch the unchoreographed dance of daily washing on tiered, cheap wire framed racks, left on several of the balconies. The pulse of each gust of wind inflated arms of shirts, legs of trousers and jeans flailed and cheap knickers, bras and pants were blown on the concrete bases of the balconies. There to sit damply, a disappointing end to a cleaning cycle.

Aileen pulled herself together. Her heart beating like the captive bird of her favourite Roberta Flack song. She began to hum the tune, reassuring herself that there would be no-one in the flat. She knew it would be empty. Turning to Robert, humming the tune melodically, she blinked twice to indicate that it was time. Without offering any further explanation for freezing at the junction, she smiled and got out of the car. She had collected her hand bag and removed the keys from the ignition smoothly. Almost rolling out of the car door like a dancer. Still humming, she turned, almost pirouetted, to close the door behind her.

Slowly, achingly, awkwardly, he followed her lead. He swung the door and it closed with a dull thud. He stood waiting, head down. Eyes firmly fixed on the ground examining the cracks between the paving stones, his hand closed around his mobile phone inside his coat pocket. Silently wondering who he could call for help.

Elle would be on her way to Manchester by now. All he could ask for there was moral support. His Union representative would be on call. But, he didn't really know how he could explain Aileen's behaviour without sounding like a madman himself. He knew he would be told to take a week off and then get a GP to sign him off for stress.

Robert noticed that Aileen had walked over to the block of flats, the home of Maggie and Lewis Tracey, without him. Her hair and coat gently billowed in the breeze and made her resemble a poster for the fictional inter galactic anti-hero that he had tried so hard to encapsulate.

'A Phantom Menace? Really? Now?' he muttered to himself.

He decided that he had to take some time off for stress and followed her to the buzzer panel, humming the ominous overture in response to the atmosphere of the moment.

'Dum dum dum, dum de dum, dum de dum,' he strode in cadence with the rhythm, as he always did; he needed to get this over and done with before he started running down the street screaming.

Aileen stood waiting at the glass and steel framed security door that barred entrance to non-residents, the blue paint peeling away from the metal, waiting for Robert to catch up. She didn't know which of the inset steel buttons to press to call the flat. She looked up at Robert and blinked once to indicate that he should be the one to call on the Tracey residence.

He waited beside her, waiting to see if she would take the lead. After a moment, he realised that something had changed. Aileen wasn't the commanding figure she had been at school. The journey to the Tracey home had been something more to her than it had for him. Why had she frozen at the last junction? He supposed he would never know. Here they stood together, each waiting for the other to act. Meekly, he reached out and pressed the button beside the flat number the secretary had given him. A brief buzz was followed by the crackly echo of the speaker, but no voice answered their call.

Aileen felt giddy. Another moment had arrived. She had managed to create this situation. Her imagination, her creativity, her determination. He was here beside her. She had to take the next step. He had to follow her lead.

'They're not here,' she said simply. 'She won't answer.'

'There doesn't seem to be anybody home. Maybe we should've called ahead?' Robert offered. 'We could have saved ourselves the drive,' he turned to face her. 'We are wasting your time, Miss Byrne. There are no Senior Staff left at school, should something happen.'

He once again tried to return to a little bit of reality. 'It's time we headed back, don't you think?'

Aileen looked up at Robert, blinked twice. Her smile was cold and her eyes twitched in their sockets.

'I know where she is, Robert,' she spoke slowly, her tone a little more shrill. 'Would you like to come and meet her? Will you come with me?' she invited.

55

Laetitia sat at her dressing table and looked out the window, overlooking the garden. The grey clouds scudded across the sky without any known purpose.

In the distance, the rooftops were sprouting a rainbow. The blurry multicolour edges washed the light and gave the town a fairy-tale quality. But, she thought as she looked at her distorted reflection in the small magnifying mirror, her life felt anything but a fairy-tale.

Her short cropped hair was wet from the shampooing, the towel that she had wrapped around it like a turban after leaving the shower had been discarded on her bedroom floor. On the corner of the table sat a photo, her two children. A boy and a girl. Both smiled up at her happily. A reminder of better days and sunshine, ice-creams and roller-coasters.

She opened the drawer to select her make-up for her day off. Between the bottles of nail varnish, lipstick and foundation brushes sat a half empty bottle of vodka. It's red lid was the same colour as her favourite lipstick shade. She slumped back in her chair, her bathrobe, a Christmas present from her soon-to-be ex-Husband, rubbing luxuriantly on her skin.

She didn't seem to be able to say no any more. She wouldn't say no to an extra shift, couldn't miss a night in the pub after work, couldn't leave a bottle unopened. She picked up the bottle and unscrewed the lid, drinking the liquid neat, with barely a wince. She had worked long hours, mostly shift pattern, and she had seen some awful things. People could be so hideous. The power that she had to wield over them felt unnatural. She had to spend her days in control.

Phil hadn't understood, but didn't question the increased drinking. He didn't understand the guilt she felt for missing out on the kids as they came home from school, or not seeing their club performances or football games. The dance and flute recitals. So she drank and spent time with others who had understood. Her colleagues.

She noticed that most of her married colleagues disappeared with the single, newly qualified officers. Or spent more time with some of the girls on the game than they should have.

She couldn't say no to him. For some unknown reason. She had met him on a Friday night. The club he was a bouncer at had called them because there was a particularly rowdy crowd out, from an office party, or something. He had chatted and charmed her as she stood in her uniform, as a warning to anyone drunk enough to start trouble.

He had joked about her arresting him for crimes against love, or some such cheesy nonsense. But she did have a car to herself that night. She had waited for them to close up. She had waited for him to be alone, her cuffs spinning on her finger tips.

His shoulders were broad enough to fill the back seat alone. He had followed her.

After that, they met regularly. Secretly at first, but then more blatantly. He began to call the house. Phil had threatened to leave with the kids and she had promised it was over. But it wasn't. Now, he had asked for a divorce. The papers were downstairs. He was going to get custody too. She was losing her kids.

She heard the keys in the door, as she took another swig from the bottle, before returning it to the drawer. She recognised the slow heavy tread of him as he took each deliberate step up. Slowly. Her heart began to beat heavily, butterflies tickled her stomach and a desperate wanting made the hair on her arms stand on on end. The door opened, pendulously.

'Good, you're awake,' was all that he said, as he walked behind her to the built in wardrobe where her uniform hung neatly. He slid the doors open and rifled around until he found what he wanted. She didn't turn, barely breathing. He took the handcuffs that he needed and held them out to her. She obediently held her arms out. He smiled, flicked the keys in the air and caught them in his fist, placing them in his trouser pockets. In the distance, the rainbow had vanished from view.

56

The sweet smell of the burgers were all that was left over from the picnic in the Jag. Mickey had gone to a local Drive Thru after the meeting at the Lock up had ended.

There was nothing unusual about the trio as they had sat in the car, parked down the street from the school. The gate to the staff car park clearly visible. Mickey had passed his untouched burger and fries back to the boy, who seemed to have an insatiable appetite. Mickey also noticed what a messy eater the boy was in the rear view; his cheeks smeared with mayo and ketchup, dribbles of the red sauce had trickled down the collar of his new hooded top. Mickey had bitten his tongue and decided that it was probably a good idea to take the motor for a full valet, rather than admonish the etiquette deprived child on eating habits.

Charlie, on the other hand, ate like a mouse. He had been carefully dipping his chunks of breaded chicken into a BBQ sauce, nibbling the coated fraction attentively. No crumbs, no drips. He was grateful for small mercies there. A fine drizzle had fallen outside, briefly followed by a sharp downpour. It had drummed on the roof of the car and coated the glass with droplets, obscuring the view into, and out of the car.

Charlie had been given instructions. Once they had nabbed the teacher, he was going to be dropped off by Mickey to pick up the ingredients to a rather strange cocktail. The poor bloke was not going to have a good night ahead of him.

He sat munching his nuggets thoughtfully. He was wondering what Maggie could have been thinking. Trying to run off with a local teacher. Her son's teacher at that. Something didn't quite add up for him. He knew that Maggie was a bit scatty, but she wouldn't thumb her nose at Mickey like this. She wouldn't leave her son alone this long, without contacting someone. This teacher was holding her somewhere. Had he fallen in love with her? Wanted a bit more than just a girlfriend experience?

He just wanted to get Maggie back safely. Maybe, he thought, he could use some of the money he had stashed up above his ceiling to take the two of them away. Somewhere like Ibiza. Charlie let his daydream carry him away: sunshine, sunsets, cafes, nightclubs and morning sessions as the sun rose. Just the three of them together. Maggie's obsession enticing almond eyes locked on his. Her lips, wet with a Margarita, brushing his as a DJ played Balearic chilled out beats to the select crowd.

He looked through the rain misted wind-shield just as a nondescript SUV pulled up beside them, indicating that they wanted to turn into the school car park.

Lewis sat up, between the two front seats, his attention suddenly focused on the two people in the car opposite.

'That's 'im. That's Mista Carpenter. 'E's wiv the Headteacher. 'E's wiv Miss Byrne,' he pointed animatedly at the pair in the car that had pulled up to the closed gate.

A woman's arm had appeared out of the window, holding something in her hand that resulted in the automatic gates opening.

'What are they doin' out of school at this time?' Charlie asked.

'That..dirty..bastard,' Mickey opined. 'He's only knocking off her as well!'

He shook his head incredulously. He hadn't thought the poncey twat had had it in him. 'And they work with kids, too,' Mickey finished his thought.

As far as he was concerned, the country was going to hell in a handbasket. What with all the weird news lately.

'Well, at least we know he's in there now,' Charlie settled into the leather front seat for the stakeout. He twisted round to Lewis. 'You better put your hood up and sit back. We don't want any of your mates spotting you while we're waiting out here.'

'That is a very good point, Charlie,' Mickey chimed in. 'You sit yourself back now, Little Man. Just have a nap or sumfing, OK?'

Lewis shrank down on the backseat, pulling the hood close around his face, 'Can you put the radio on Oncle Mickey?' he paused, 'Please?'

Mickey turned the radio on, just as the broadcaster had finished with the traffic updates. The news would be next. The jingles soothed Lewis, he found the silence to be too oppressive at times.

The flat was always silent when his Mum was out. Only the muffled sounds of other people's TVs and stereos had broken the vacuum of his loneliness. He even welcomed the angry sounds of arguments and fights outside. It always meant that there was someone, somewhere. Now, as he listened, the newsreader talked about people who had done lots of bad things.

'Police are continuing their investigations into the seemingly unrelated crimes against the public, which seem to have been perpetrated by those entrusted to serve and protect us,' a velvet voice intoned commandingly, silencing the listening public. Partly in respect, partly in entranced awe at the deep, rich voice of the radio. 'Evidence of the disappeared suspects have been located in various, isolated parts of the country.'

'About time they found these crazy bastards,' Mickey's gravelly voice provided the sentiment of an outraged nation.

'Items belonging to a nurse, wanted in connection with the mysterious deaths at a Geriatric care department, have been found at the entrance to a disused and long abandoned, Tin mine in Cornwall.'

'Well, they're a bit weird in Cornwall. I had a mate from there. Took too many pills and got Sectioned.' Charlie considered being from the West Country to be a more likely cause of mental instability than the ingestion of hundreds of pills of Ecstasy over a period of just several years. He thought their accent made them all sound a bit simple.

'In addition, the uniforms of the missing members of the Fire Brigade, wanted in connection with a number of fires in Liverpool, have been found on a beach in the Wirral. No sightings or bodies have been found in connection. The public are warned that the individuals are considered to be dangerous, and advised not to approach suspects, but to immediately call the Emergency Services.'

'We trust these people, and what are they up to?' Mickey, a pimp and racketeer shook his head in disgust.

'In other news,' the newsreader continued, 'there have been reported sightings of individuals wearing little or no clothing, running in the New Forest and across Salisbury plain.'

'Weirdo's from the West Country again!' Charlie chimed in.

'These naturists, as yet unknown persons, have been spotted hiding, particularly in the woods, in what seems to be a 'return to nature' fad. Camps of makeshift shelters have been discovered by Woodland Trust and RSPCA staff, who are concerned that the activities of these, as yet unknown persons, could endanger local wildlife...'

The last sentences were drowned out by the laughter of the two men in the car. The newsreader then delivered a bland

and oversimplified weather report that could have been true on any given day.

On the back seat Lewis allowed himself to drift into a light sleep. He could hear the conversation between Mickey and Charlie as if from a distance, it had something to do with going easy on his Mum. He let the sound of the light rain drumming on the roof of the car carry him away to a far away forest where he could hide in the trees and live in a home high in the branches: hidden and safe.

57

After a torturous couple of hours, back with his class, Robert returned to Aileen's office at three thirty, as requested.

During the intervening time, he had made a couple of simple decisions. He had been at Thresher Street Primary long enough, it was time to move on and start looking for a new school. He was stuck in a rut, with the same old faces and the same old problems. This, he decided, was the root cause of the instability he had felt throughout the week.

This was notwithstanding the fact, that the entire country seemed to be going through a nervous breakdown. The news he had heard on the return journey to school seemed to be out of the Twilight Zone. People committing horrendous acts then vanishing into thin air, people running around in woods naked. On top of the national madness, the events and stresses in school had been too much. He decided that the only thing to do was get through the day and then call in sick tomorrow. Get a GP note citing that he was not fit for work due to stress.

Once he told the entire tale to Elle, he knew that she would agree that he had to take some time off. His absence would not raise alarm bells, or seem out of place, as the Deputy Head - the Great White shark himself - Syndale was off school, too. For whatever reasons, Robert didn't care. He knew if he tried to stay and ride the strangeness out, he would soon be running out of the classroom and the school screaming. That would be the end of his teaching career. He just needed to get through the day.

Aileen had told him, cryptically, that she knew where Maggie Tracey, and subsequently, Lewis were. That she would take him to them. But then she just drove, without incident, back to school. She requested that he meet her at her office after the children had gone.

So here he was, standing looking at the door again. He felt sick. Like the feeling of something falling in his insides that he got every time an Ofsted inspection was announced, or when the dreaded inspector called into the classroom. Knowing that his being, his quality, his effort, his humanity, was being weighed, measured and judged. All those days, nights, weeks, years of hard work ignored. Just a snapshot moment. Judged by the Gods. He felt the same way about knocking on the door now. As soon as he created the sound waves with his closed fist, he knew he wouldn't be able to take them back. There was nowhere to hide. No way to turn back.

Aileen had waited in her office. Laptop open, emails unread. Unanswered. She had waited. She was different than before. She was unsure. She was worried.

She knew what she had done would be considered very wrong. She wanted to erase it all. Not to undo it. Just to get rid of it. Memories flooded through her all afternoon. Of her descent into madness.

She remembered every night sitting at her computer at home, writing insanely. Unholy recipes and concoctions using poisons, roadkill and even the human body itself. She thought about the confessions that she had written as introductions to each section of her sick, sadistic cookbook.

She thought of the vicious, desperate hours she had spent on this endeavour. Her hands had been shaking, so she had sat on them, to keep still for just a moment. To find peace for just a moment. To find a rational thought in her head, for just a moment. It had to stop. There had to be an end, somehow.

His knock at her door shocked and surprised her. She had nearly forgotten him, remembering only needing him to do something. Aileen stood, walked to the door and opened it silently. She blinked up at Robert, who stood pensively waiting for her call to enter.

He looked disappointed to see her. Aileen decided to just take him there directly. To speak to him honestly. To try to explain why. To determine what she needed.

She turned right from her office and led him through the dining hall. Passed the gossiping teachers, who were avoiding their marking and preparation tasks for the following day by talking about children and parents. Passed the Science and Technology resource cupboard, out to the Boiler Room.

Robert had sighed repeatedly on their walk, he followed two steps behind her resentfully. He just wanted the day to end so that he could go home, close the curtains, lock the doors and fall asleep on the sofa with the Chairman, lulling him gently with his authoritarian purring.

58

The hinges of the Boiler Room's warped and bent wooden door creaked as he closed it behind him.

Aileen had flicked the switch that turned on the room's only light. An unshaded, bare, ancient tungsten bulb glared, casting the room in a fierce eye-squintingly bright light, with deep shadows behind the enormous boiler housing units and cobwebbed pipework. The green paint that had begun to peel away from the door was evident in poorly maintained patches of fading and flecking paint around the walls.

Aileen stood in the middle of the room, looking directly at the bulb, her head turned away from Robert so that all he saw was her silhouette. The black hair shining.

'You've been here, how long Robert? Five, six years?' she asked him, her back still turned to him.

'Seven, it's been seven years,' Robert replied meekly and quietly.

He thought her voice sounded even more shrill than it had before. Like she had aged and become a much older woman in the course of the day.

'Seven years. That long?' she shrugged, her shoulders seemed to jerk, but he couldn't see her face.

'Well, then in the seven years that you have taught the children fractions and Shakespeare and Roman history,' she paused. 'You wouldn't know, but in that time, you have taught a child who was raped by her older brother. There are children who have been here who have terrorised entire neighbourhoods, selling drugs to other children here and setting fire to their parents' cars if they didn't pay. Or, smashing their windows with bricks, if their parents owed them money. The police just used to shrug and say that they couldn't do anything because they wanted to catch the London gang that controlled them. I know that there are girls who have left here, and just a year or two later have been arrested for prostitution, pregnant and destitute. You have taught a child that was living with strangers, who had pretended from birth to be its biological family, but in reality were just given a baby by a stranger in a park. No idea who the real mother was. But they had kept the child and loved it, but still had the child taken away from them and they were given a criminal record. You have taught a child that saw his mother break the arms and legs of his newborn baby brother. Seen her arrested and taken away in a police car. There have been so many children here that watched as their mother was beaten by the new boyfriend, just a line of bruised of despair. You have taught a child who was addicted to drugs from its first breath.' She chuckled. 'ADHD my arse. That kid is just crazy.'

She breathed in deeply, letting her head drop to look at her feet. Robert still had no idea of her facial expression or the purpose of being in the Boiler Room for her disclosing this confidential safeguarding information. He knew she shouldn't be telling him though, and almost interrupted her, but she began to speak again. Her voice became as shrill and sharp as a razor.

'You have no idea at all, how many times I have had to intervene because parents are beating, neglecting and abusing their own children. Lewis Tracey is the tip of the iceberg. Bruises on his shoulder? I have seen welts on backs, legs, arms and arses. I've seen burn marks from cigarettes, scars from the buckles of belts that would make you cry,' she absent-mindedly soothed herself by lifting her hand to her cheek.

'Year after year, Robert. It never ends. No-one helps. We're supposed to deal with it all. Left alone to cope with it all. Over and over and over...' She raised her other hand, her shoulders hunched like dark, folded wings.

'Who are these people? Where have they all come from? Why do they do it? Why won't they just stop?'

She turned to face Robert at last. He could see tears streaming from her eyes. He had no words for her.

Robert stepped forward and put his arms around her. He held her as she sobbed into his chest.

'I had to save one,' she mumbled into his jumper through the sobs. 'I had to try to stop her, the only way I knew how.'

She looked up imploringly, hoping that she could make him understand just through her expression. She blinked twice and regained a sense of her composure, breaking the consolatory embrace, clenching her fists at her sides defiantly.

He could hear the whirr of the pump, the gentle hiss of a mechanical device operating. The soft sound of something igniting in a continuous stream. He felt cold in the room that was meant to provide warmth to the school. His bones sensed that he should walk out of the Boiler Room now, run through school and go to his car. Drive home, not looking back and leave this strange, alluring, terrifying woman to whatever fate awaited her.

'What have you done?' he asked in a low, desolate and resigned voice.

He had crossed the Rubicon days before. There was no turning back now. Whatever die had been cast, he had to find out what Aileen had been up to. He was compelled to find a reason for his own unstable emotions.

'She's there,' Aileen pointed to the old winter salt bin, against the far wall.

Robert walked over to the salt store box, took the shovel and stood it against the door that led outside and lifted it open. Inside was a cardboard box marked Accounts, a plastic petrol can beside it .

He shook his head in misunderstanding, 'Aileen, I can't read the files. I'm not Safeguarding trained,' he turned to look at her, 'it's not right.'

He stopped shaking his head as she shrieked and cawed in deranged mirth. It was something out of a horror story. Aileen's legs remained rooted to the spot, but her face wrinkled as she bent over double. She wrapped her arms wrapped around her own shoulders and neck, as if forming a hangman's noose from her own body. As suddenly as the macabre dance began, it stopped, as Aileen straightened up with a deep breath and pointed to the box.

'No, Robert. She's there. I've done something monstrous,' she blinked, hoping that this would make Robert understand.

59

Robert drove without a destination in mind. He hadn't decided what to do. He knew what he should do, what Elle would implore him to do, what he, in his right mind, would do. But in his stunned and confused condition, he hadn't figured out whether he was already implicated and in trouble.

He just followed the road and when he had to make a decision, kept turning left. It was easier than crossing the line of traffic, until he finally got out of the town's one-way system and reached a main trunk road. It was straight and had been based on the old Roman road that became known as Watling Street.

The repetitive, cloned landscape, with carefully constructed banks of stunted bushes and trees that were traps for occasional plastic bags to get caught in, that waved to the passing traffic in the breeze, looked the same everywhere. The familiarity of the road lulled him.

Traffic eased and he looked at himself in the rear view mirror. He looked pale, gaunt, even to himself. The large purple rings under his eyes made him look a little haunted. He thought that was apt.

He didn't notice the classic Eighties Jag that had followed him. Hadn't seen the adults arguing in the front seats as Charlie tried to convince Mickey that he couldn't follow the teacher wherever he was going by being the next car behind him. It was too obvious. The pair argued, based on Mickey's personal experience and Charlie's observations from TV cop shows and the game Grand Theft Auto. Mickey had finally relented and dropped back at a junction, warning Charlie that if they lost him, he was going to get the pasting of a lifetime.

Robert was too busy trying not to think about what was in the box in the boot of his car. A sign ahead informed him that he was three miles from the seaside town of Tankerville. He had already driven for ten miles without even realising.

The dreamlike white lines on the black tarmac blurred by in a hypnotising prayer of procrastination. The town he was approaching had once been a Georgian destination for the wealthy denizens of London. A retreat with clean air and pebbly beaches. The Victorians turned the quaint seafront's spacious town houses and secluded beach front views with understated grandeur, into a meticulously organised and glitzy retreat for the well to do. They had constructed new shopping arcades and large hotels; now it was a mere shade of its former glory days. It still had a few independent shops, selling pointless knick-knacks at much inflated prices, and cheesy postcards that were hopelessly out of touch with modern sensibilities, but mostly it was home to a range of care homes for the elderly. The ones who had saved their entire lives and lived frugally, just to ensure that in their twilight years that they could congregate together to get blue rinses fortnightly and eat cheese sandwiches and drink lukewarm tea.

As good a place as any to make a decision, he thought. There would be a police car parked somewhere near the town centre. Near the cluster of pubs that offered 'Happy Hour' discounts at clocking off time for the local care workers, self employed brickies and part-time shop assistants at the local supermarket to get temporarily smashed before going home to the kids. He could take the box to the officers stationed there.

He turned left to join the coast road. A more scenic and less travelled carriageway with a thirty mile an hour speed limit imposed on it. It would give him more time to think about what he would do next.

The sea came briefly into view; a murky and dank grey coloured expanse on the horizon between the gaps of the hedgerow that allowed a glimpse of the open patchwork of small green fields and white, weatherboarded cottages and converted Oast houses along the coast. The road twisted and turned; junctions offered Robert opportunities to turn off the road, that began to edge closer to the open sea. It took him away from the recently built housing estates, the last main centres of civilised certainty.

To his left, the fields finally fell away, giving in to the relentless, creeping, fluid giant that lapped reassuringly against the shore. Always there. Always ready. To his right, the hedgerows gave way to the Georgian palaces that had once welcomed the grand families of the capital. Now, many of the grand mansions had been subdivided into tiny parcels for holiday rental, an occasional traditional guest house or B & B had survived the *Air BnB* revolution. White picket fences gave way to iron railings and newly rebuilt brick walls, demarcating public and private spaces. He still had not made a decision.

The road ended its reptilian slither as the coast levelled out and it began to rise onto the cliffs. Robert drove slowly along the esplanade, cars were parked nose to tail.

Passed the magnificent Nautical Hotel, a Victorian meringue masterpiece overlooking the busy shipping lanes. The lobby proudly contained a plaque commemorating the visit from a notable local author of a popular spy novel series, who immortalised the bus route number between Dover and London. Robert remembered a hot summer's day and visit to the beer garden with Elle and her parents who were visiting from London.

As he rolled along the road, the parked cars thinned and the grand hotels and guest houses gave way to shabbier care homes for the elderly. A lone pub, the *Fisherman's Nets*, punctuated the change between the postcodes. The further along the cliffs he drove, further away from the centre of town, the fewer the properties and the shabbier they looked. He still had not decided what to do.

Robert indicated left, and pulled over, parking about two-thirds along the long cliff edge, next to a path that led to a weatherbeaten shelter and steps down to the water's edge. Taking the keys from the ignition, just as the street lights came on, he sat alone his car.

He didn't notice the XJ6 that pulled into the car park of the Fisherman's Nets, or the three occupants who hastily entered the pub, gathering at a table in the large bay window, which provided an enviable view of the whole clifftop. They sat, drinks untouched: watching, waiting.

60

Aileen had never experienced such a sense of relief. Robert had taken the box from the school. She saw him place it in the boot of his car with her own eyes.

She had told him everything. Well, almost everything. She hadn't told him about the cookbook, or the use of Maggie Tracey in her cooking, days before. She didn't think he needed to know that just yet. A confession to the crime of murder, but with justification for her actions. Qualifications for her decisions. Somehow, they convinced him of her motivations. Persuaded him that she had needed his help. He had stood there silently. Accepting. She assumed, understanding, even sympathising.

She had a monkey off her back and she felt great again. Once he had left, she had stalked around the school, speaking to staff, calming their anxieties about the week's news. About the new lock down procedure, and no she wasn't disappointed or angry. If there was anyone to blame for the mix up, it was her fault for not explaining herself, she reassured them. Joining groups she gossiped about parents, about anything really. It had occurred to her that he might go straight to the police. That was OK with her. She was confidant that she had covered her tracks, at least well enough to buy her time for the finale.

Aileen breezed past the Year 3 classroom. She still couldn't quite face Mr Parminster after her vision from lunchtime in the staffroom. Looking into the Year 5 classroom, she saw Suzy Tallister, at her desk, head in hands, books stacked neatly beside her.

'Hi Suzy, you OK?' Aileen poked her head in the door, her feet remained in the corridor. The room was Suzy's territory.

With a brave face on, Suzy smiled at Aileen, 'Miss Byrne. Thank you. I'm fine, really. It's just been..' she shrugged with open hands, gesturing to the books and the room a voila!

'A trying day,' Aileen finished her sentence and with a nonchalant swing of her leg, stepped across the threshold, entering the classroom cautiously.

'No, it's been a trying week, so it has,' she walked over to Suzy at the front of the room, casting approving looks at the neat, up-to-date classroom displays.

Speaking gently, she placed a comforting hand on Suzy's shoulder, 'You seem troubled. A problem shared is a problem halved!' she smiled. 'Believe me, I know how good it feels to confide your troubles to someone.'

She smiled at the pretty young teacher. Aileen squeezed her shoulder, looking into her eyes. She was trying not to notice the firm swell of cleavage visible as she looked down.

Suzy shrugged and gave a deflated and tired sigh.

'Meet me in the Staff Room in five minutes. I know just what you need,' said the spider to the fly, she thought.

Aileen turned and marched purposefully to the door, pausing and throwing back what she thought would be a winsome and attractive smile. Walking down the corridor to her office, she felt a stirring that she thought she would never feel again. She gently bit her finger in the excitement of the chase. The pleasure and pain of the sharp sensation crystallised an idea. Well, she thought to herself as she walked to the drawer containing the chocolate brownies that she had baked, laced with the bags of powder and herb that she taken from the dead mother's coat. She found a clean and attractive plate to arrange the cakes.

'Well, I've got nothing to lose, there, have I? I might as well go with a bang!' she informed the empty office, shaking free her hair and tousling it with her fingers, she prepared herself for an unexpected opportunity.

61

The late afternoon light faded quickly, the scudding clouds had gathered and obscured the last of the Sun's rays. The dull Autumnal twilight was a harbinger of the grey winter days ahead.

He left the car and walked slowly along the path to the cliff edge, crossing the grassy verge towards the dishevelled shelter. It had clearly been blasted by years of chilly horizontal gusts from the sea, from which it offered little protection. He continued down the steps to the beach, seeking a place to think. A way to make an unthinkable decision. Missing the almost invisible shadow at the top of the cliff behind him. The large hulking presence of Mickey Butcher had followed him and watched from above.

The parade of after work joggers and dog walkers had thinned as the light had faded; a sharp on-shore breeze had put off many casual promenaders who may have wanted to enjoy one last long lingering walk, determined to insist that Summer wasn't gone just yet.

As he approached a lone bench, he felt consumed by the rhythmic booming of the breaking waves pounding the shore. His ears were filled by the hissing and ripping backwash, a sound that made him think of a thousand blind witches, scorned and abandoned as the spent wave drew away again. The white foaming, curled liquid fingers clawed at the shoreline with all the malice the spent wave could muster, before the next rolling ridge of water jabbed in.

Sitting, hunched over, he replayed the events of the day, ending in the discovery in the Boiler Room. Was he an accessory already? He had suspected that Aileen had been behaving suspiciously all week. But he had thought that it was his own paranoia; his response to the bombings and attacks around the country. Now he had the remains of a murdered parent of a child from his class, who may just happen to have been a prostitute, in the boot of his car.

Just thinking about going to the police with this made him feel sick. He was guilty. Even if he had not perpetrated the crimes himself. He thought about all the strange events occurring around the country that week, and the disappearance of the main suspects, knowing he would be questioned and that he would undoubtedly be a suspect himself.

Would Aileen disappear too? Who would they believe? Aileen was a well respected Headteacher with an impeccable reputation. He knew he would act guiltily straight away. The police would probably suspect that he had done something to Aileen, too. The strain of the last few days had been too much already. Robert just wanted to go home, pull the curtains and lock the doors until Elle came back.

An elderly lady, with a long dark overcoat and a woolly tea cosy of a hat drawn close over her head approached the steps down to the beach. Behind her was a small brown and white dog on a long strung out lead that sniffed at the stained edges of the shelter, before it cocked its leg and pee'd copiously. She walked past the imposing gangster quickly, she didn't like the look of him at all, and hurried down to the beach front.

62

To Edie, Robert's silhouette looked like a soul in need. He sat, elbows on shaking knees and head hanging.

'Come on Rissoles, let's go and see if he's alright', she spoke to the grizzled old Fox Terrier that never left her side, as she ambled over to the bench where the bedraggled Robert sat.

'Hello dear, I don't think it's the right weather for a dip tonight, really. Did you bring a towel? Oh, you do look a sight.'

Edie sat next to Robert. She watched him for a moment and decided to take her coat off and began draping it over his shoulders, despite his rather weak protestations. Insisting that her thick three quarter length cardigan was more than adequate, she settled herself down next to him. Putting her hands into the cardigan's low slung pockets for extra protection against the chill. Rissoles sniffed at Robert's feet suspiciously before taking his post at the old lady's feet, on guard.

She leaned forward and scratched behind the dog's ears absent-mindedly, 'My name is Edie, and this little fellow is Rissoles. Bless him.' The dog rolled his head in gratitude. 'And, who might you be, young man?'

Robert had not been called a 'young man' for quite some time. He turned his head and examined the old woman who had disturbed his deliberations, as she shrugged against the cold wind and returned her hands to her pockets with a shudder.

She had a distinctly 1920's flair about her. Her woollen cloche hat had a rather elaborate flower on the side, he suspected that she had knitted it herself. The coat draped over his shoulders had a fur collar, which he assumed was fake. Still, she had been cut from a rather well-to-do cloth.

'Er..Bert,' he half lied. 'My name is... Bert.'

'Ah!' she leaned against Robert in a familial, trusting manner. 'My husband's middle name was Albert.' She gave a short nod of approval.

'Now. What on Earth are you doing, sitting in the cold on a miserable evening like this? Hmm?'

'Well...' Robert began before Edie interrupted him.

'You're not...' she did a double take and looked up and down the beach front. 'You're not one of those people from the news are you?'

She edged a few inches away, further along the bench, disturbing Rissoles' guarding posture. The dog stood and barked briefly into the wind, before returning to territorial sniffing around the perimeter of the bench.

'No..I,' Robert cast his mind for any kind of excuse that he could think of, as the dog stood squarely in front of him. 'I have to..' he looked at the kindly old woman, his face wracked with guilt. 'I have to...' he stumbled towards a lie. 'Our dog died.'

He saw her mouth form a consoling O shape.

'We had him cremated...at the vets.' Robert stared at the concrete at his feet. He couldn't believe that he had lied so easily to someone who had shown him kindness so freely.

'And, you came to scatter the ashes here.' Edie stated Robert's possible crime. The pair sat in silent reflection for a moment. It seemed that his offered excuse had provided reason enough for Edie.

She considered a much loved pet to actually be a member of the family. Scattering a dog's ashes at a beach was not that an unusual an activity. There were so many dogs and walkers that frequented the beach that it was not surprising that it might be the place for a treasured memory. To her, there was no difference between the company offered by her now dead husband and Rissoles. In truth, she rather preferred the unquestioning love and devotion of the dog. Robert's distressed state was easily mistaken for grief.

'Of course,' Edie broke the silence. 'Of course, if you were one of those people,' she nodded, staring out into the gloom. 'I shouldn't judge.' She turned to look at Robert and leaned in again. 'Should I?'

He paused and took a breath, 'Why not? They've killed people,' he answered shortly. This was neither the time or the place for a debate about current affairs and he needed space to make his mind up.

'Ahh,' Edie warmed. 'Now, Bert,' she didn't often get a chance to meet new people nowadays. 'but why did they?'

'Why did they kill people?' he replied, adding a note of sarcasm, hoping that the old bat would bugger off with her dog. He thought about giving the animal a bit of a kick to get it barking so that she would be embarrassed and take her leave.

'Well, precisely! Now, my husband, God Rest his Soul, always used to say that one day those idiots at the top would push people too far. He always used say, "Edie, one day all those wonderful people, who work their socks off to make all those buffoons rich are going to realise that they have had the wool pulled over their eyes." '

She gave a tug on the lead to bring Rissoles back towards her. Her eyes twinkled in the darkening evening as she looked at Robert.

'He was such a wise man. He used to say, "Edie, they govern with the consent of all those people out there." ' She pointed into the middle distance to emphasise her point.

' "Edie," he said, "one day they will turn around and withdraw that consent. Then where will we be?" Well Bert, where exactly indeed!'

They sat together quietly. Each listening to the regular boom and hiss of the heart beat of the Earth's circulatory system. Robert could feel the rumble of each wave; feel the palliative static hiss as it washed his exhausted conscious thought clean.

Edie took his silence to be agreement and continued, 'An eye is only useful if it can see. Isn't it really?' She reached into the pocket of her overcoat, nudging Robert, to retrieve a bag of treats for Rissoles.

'Sit!' she instructed.

Rissoles dutifully sat on his haunches at attention, chin up and eyes on Edie. She opened her palm and he gratefully gulped the cube of cheese up.

'Good boy!' she smiled.

'He's a good dog,' Robert observed. 'I don't think the corruption of the ruling class justifies the indiscriminate murder of innocent men, women and children,' he contributed. He just couldn't resist. Although he hated himself a little more for it.

'Ah, you're right Bert,' Edie assented. 'You are right, Bert. It's because it's wrong isn't it?' Edie held another treat in her closed hand and leaned over to her dog. She hesitated and opened her hand, Rissoles ate greedily.

'It's just that we seem to have become so extreme lately. Don't you think?' She looked at Robert for a response and carried on when he gave none.

'We buy things without any thought to the cost of them. It doesn't matter if we don't have the money for anything, we just buy them 'on credit',' she emphasised her disgust of the idea of borrowing money to buy things.

'People have no idea of the value of anything any more. If something breaks, they just throw it away!' She saw a smile cross Robert's lips.

'You're laughing at me,' she admonished him. 'You think I'm silly.'

'No! No,' he began to defend himself.

He didn't want to cause offence, especially as she was the first person to show him any true kindness in long time. Well, he corrected, the first stranger. Elle was always endlessly kind and patient.

'It's just that I'm sure that I have said the exact same thing at some point to my wife. I agree with you, that's all.'

'Well,' she retorted, 'I don't want to teach you to suck eggs! It's just that when I was a girl, we never had any of these things. Electronic gadgets and credit cards. It took us all morning to get to London on the train.'

'It still does,' he interjected.

'Ha! I suppose it does,' she agreed, 'But we used to make do with what we had. We appreciated everything, and everyone, a little more. My point is that it seems that the way of showing how rich we have become is not to make our families and communities better places to be. It's just to throw things away!' She stopped and leaned forward, closed fist held out straight in front of the dog. 'Maybe that's how we show how wealthy we are. We just throw people away.' Robert's breath caught in his throat.

'Paw!' she instructed.

Rissoles raised a leg and tapped her closed hand with his paw. He had learned that when he did it, he got his reward. She opened her hand, palm up and he gobbled and chewed the cheese happily. He liked this game. He sat at attention hoping for more.

'I haven't seen my children for an age, you know. One moved to Australia and the other to Edinburgh.' She sighed sadly, remembering family breakfasts and picnics on this very beach on hot summer's days.

'I wonder, after I've been thrown away, what is the point of me?' she looked at her dog. 'Rissoles knows,' she smiled and scratched his head lovingly.

'You see, Bert,' she smiled down at her obedient and loving companion. 'Rissoles here knows that I love him. Knows that I will feed and walk him. Pet him and keep him warm and safe. Paw!'

Rissoles raised his other leg and tapped Edie's closed hand with his other paw eagerly. More treats! The old dog licked his lips and smiled at the old lady in gratitude.

'So he consents to me restricting his freedom. I put a lead on him and stop him chasing the neighbourhood cats.' She looked at Robert and winked. 'If not I would have some very angry neighbours.' She returned her attention to Rissoles, who had laid down facing Edie, his eyes never left her face.

'I am his benevolent tyrant. Aren't I, silly chops?' she stroked the dog's head gingerly, before leaning back. She turned to face Robert once more.

'Do you think I am a responsible owner? Hmm?'

Robert nodded silently. He didn't need to answer. There was clearly a strong bond between the two.

'But what if I stopped feeding him? What if instead of walking and petting and looking after Rissoles' needs, I left him in a room, alone?' she paused, but expected no response. 'What if all I did was occasionally walked into the room and gave him instructions that he didn't understand and couldn't follow. What if as a result I beat him with stick or a whip?'

She looked down at Rissoles, his tail thumped gently on the concrete. He was clearly hoping for another chance to earn a cube of cheese.

'Would you blame him for biting me? Would it be wrong of him to do so?'

Robert looked at the happy dog, still thumping its tail, hoping for a chance to earn more tasty morsels and thought about the news and the insane acts of random violence that were being perpetrated by seemingly normal, law abiding people. He thought about Aileen. In the boot of his car was her bite back in response to being left in a room and abused by everyone she sought to serve.

Was he the epitome of this sick society, after all? Was he rich enough to throw someone away?

He looked over and examined Edie's face. Her twinkling, gentle eyes were surrounded by wrinkles that told the story of her life. Inscribed into them were the years of smiling and laughter. He wondered why providence had delivered him such a messenger.

In this moment of indecision and despair for him, after years of impotent observation and moral hand-wringing, he had met Edie with her simple counsel. He stood and thanked Edie for the loan of her coat, he held his hand out for Rissoles to sniff as she put it back on and then he trudged back up the steps, without looking back once, to his car to wait.

63

He had sat in the car too long. His cold, stiff fingers had gripped the steering wheel, as evening had darkened into night, leaving only the inadequate intermittent yellow glow of the street lamps, weak candescent islands in the darkness that couldn't compete with the blackness emanating from the invisible sea.

'Never, ever, ever, ever step foot in that...fucking.. school again!' he emotively instructed himself as he unclipped his seat belt and opened the driver's door. His haggered mind made up, he just had to act quickly and decisively and not get caught.

In the Fisherman's Nets, Charlie had done his best to entertain the bored Lewis with eye-spy games and he had found some colouring sheets and pencils beside the bar, which he found strangely comforting to complete himself.

Mickey had returned from the cliff even less garrulous than usual. His eyes did not leave the parked vehicle that sat alone a few hundred yards further up the road. After making a call to arrange things with Lee, he scrutinised every jogger or passer by, looking to see if he could recognise the missing Maggie. He had decided that this had to be a meeting place, that Maggie must be hidden somewhere in one of the guest houses along the cliff. He wondered what, if anything, the old lady with the dog had to do with it. Had she passed on a message? He had followed the old lady's progress along the beach with her dog after the teacher, Carpenter, left her, before giving up and circling back to the pub.

The thought that Maggie might be about to just do a runner with this bloke and leave her kid behind incensed the paternal instincts of the childless gangster. He sat silently as twilight had turned to dusk, and dusk fell into night, his pint of lager untouched.

The sudden and swift actions of the teacher caught him completely by surprise, as the subject of his surveillance disappeared out of the pool of illumination afforded by the street lamp, into the shrouded gloom of the cliff's edge.

'Charlie!' Mickey snapped the attention of the man-boy back to the here and now.

'Go and stand right there and find out what 'e's up to,' Mickey grabbed hold of Charlie's shoulder with one hand and pointed at the dark cliff's edge with the other. 'And don't get seen! You 'ear me? No 'eroiks if she's there,' he let go, 'Just see what they're up to and come back 'ere.' He returned his sweeping gaze to the cliff top and dialled Les on his mobile.

64

Robert wasted no time at all. With barely a glance along the empty cliffs, he opened the boot and took the cardboard box out; holding it under his arm, he hurriedly slammed the hatch down and locked the car before rapidly striding along the path leading to the cliff's edge. He almost skipped down the dark steps leading to the promenade that ran parallel to the emergent, pebbly beach.

The on-shore breeze felt icy as the gusts cut through his thin pullover and work trousers. The thin strip of concrete, laid to separate the natural beach from human endeavour, was cracked and uneven. Robert looked up and down the beach to make sure that there was no-one coming.

With no sign of any possible intrusion, he dropped onto the backshore; the pebbles crunched under his shoes as he landed awkwardly. The weight of the box dragged him forward a staggered step. Without hesitation, he dropped the box and knelt down to untie his shoes.

With socks stripped off and trousers rolled to the knee, he took a last look towards and away from town. There was no sign of walkers or beach fishermen, so he picked up the box, shoes and socks balanced on top, and continued, tracing the route down to the water's edge beside a half submerged, seaweed encrusted groyne, for protection against the wind and to merge into its thick shadow.

He was still several feet higher than the shoreline as he set off, a berm, a high ridge of glossy stones, had been maintained as the first defence against flooding through a high storm tide. Robert leaned back as he descended, the pebbles pounded the soles of his feet like an angry reflexologist, stubbing toes and and crashing against his heels. The salty tang on his lips tasted like supper, as the hair on his legs shivered against his skin. Two steps away from the water's edge he hesitated. The open water ahead seemed to whisper to him through the wind that blew grit into his eyes. He stopped.

In the box were the last remains of a real person. She had lived, smiled, cried and died. This was her funeral. He wrapped his arms around the box as tears began to stream down his face. He had been right. Aileen Byrne wasn't just a bit crazy, she had murdered someone, and now here he was getting rid of the evidence. He was more than guilty himself.

He stood and watched as gulls circled, each gust lifted them enough to just glide down towards the sea for a few moments before the next gust lifted them back up again. Over and over. But, he wondered, what if the wind just stopped? Would the birds just fall gracefully down, accepting their fate? There was a metaphor there somewhere for him. A message about determinism and choice. He was in no mood for philosophy, though. Aileen had been desperate. What he had always mistaken for a cool, calm exterior had been a mask that had hidden her knowledge of the acts of evil perpetrated by monsters. Acts that had shredded her sanity. Resulting in her snapping. Did he blame her?

There would be no family visits and last lingering good byes for Maggie Tracey. No funeral procession or emotive music to help her loved ones let go. No memorial readings or celebrant eulogy. With eyes closed, he placed the box carefully onto the sloping and undulating beach.

Robert listened to the boom of each wave breaking as it met the land, hinting at the hidden power behind it, followed by the timid backward hiss as the swash retreated back into the next foaming wave. An endless and timeless cascade that would grace Maggie's funeral. An epochal monument to her that Robert would not forget as long as he lived.

Taking the lid off the first tin, his tears spilled on the broken fragments of bone and teeth, mixed with the ashes and dust of last nights final cremation. The faint whiff of the fire that consumed the contents was snatched by a blast of wind that preceded the next crashing wave. With blurred vision, he walked, stiff legged into the sea.

The water had not retained any summer warmth and the shock of the cold arced up his body, making the hairs on his arms and neck stand on end. His tear ducts instantly dried, allowing his vision to clear. The shock forced him to take five or six rapid breaths before he could control himself once more. He pushed forward through the dark, until the waves crested just above his knees.

'I commend this...' Tin? This victim? This part of a body? This abusive parent? To what? He wondered.

He heard the hiss of the swash and the pull of the water on his legs, urging him to join it. Walk further in and become one with it, it pulled persuasively. He felt the comfort that letting go of his worries and just heading further away from shore would bring.

Ahead he saw the rolling mass of the next wave pushing in. He held the tin up, safely away from the reaching wave as he jumped. A gasp against the cold escaped him, as the wave crested against his belly. His soaked clothes stuck to his skin. Coins in his pocket pressed into his thigh. His car keys suddenly felt like an anvil pulling him down.

Waiting until he found the moment of stillness through the noise and motion the water seemed to stop for a moment and find peace; balance. Tranquillity. He held the tin a few centimetres above the eddying water and slowly tipped the contents out. The gentle pull of the retreating water became an insistent rush as he tipped the tin upside down and watched as the heavier fragments were swallowed eagerly into the dark mass below. Davy Jones' locker had not dined for quite a while, he thought. A moment later, wading back in distress, stepping, almost falling over backwards in a mockery of baptism, as the ash and dust mushroomed on the surface, reaching out in all directions before succumbing to the call of the deep and disappearing like a miniature fog into the darkness beyond his vision.

Breathing heavily in the cold of the night, he felt an odd moment of relief that his legs had not been coated in the ashes. His clothes were soaked, sucking the warmth from his skin. He felt disgust with himself and stood, empty funereal tin in hand. He hurled his pathetic and cowardly frustration into the dark. Quickly followed by the empty tin and its lid. His night's undertaking was not yet done. Turning sluggishly as the last ebb of water tickled his numbed feet, he returned to the box to collect the next tin urn for scattering.

65

Charlie shivered in the sharp breeze, hood pulled up over his head and hands thrust into his trouser pockets. He had arrived to witness Lewis's teacher stagger across the beach carrying a box, his trousers rolled up and bare footed, in a hobbling walk.

The chill cut through the thin fabric of Charlie's cult couture clothes, he watched as he felt a shiver. The teacher took something out of the box and strode hesitantly into the breaking water.

'You've chosen an odd time for a paddle, Mister Carpenter,' he muttered to no-one in particular. Standing alone on the cliff-top, watching the teacher stagger, knee deep, as a wave retreated. The tiny figure's arms punched the air and waved like a mental raver to some banging Techno beats. Then, Charlie saw the teacher throw something as far into the open water as he could.

The cold began to penetrate through his clothes deeply, and Charlie was not resilient to suffering hardship, but knew that he should wait and see whether Maggie turned up. Still he watched, as the teacher began to repeat this strange watery ritual over and again, until he decided to return to the pub's warmth and report back to Mickey.

Robert had repeated the process until all that remained in the box was a disassembled phone. By now he was chilled to the bone, tired, hungry and thirsty. The breeze was already moving the near empty box across the stony beach, so Robert quickly collected the electronic items, noticing that he was shaking quite violently and that his teeth were chattering, and cast the box to blow away on the wind. It would be gone by morning, he mused, perhaps fate would see it join a plastic bag on a twisted branch on a roadside.

Retrieving his socks and shoes, he returned up the berm and struck out along the parade to find a suitable bench to sort himself out. To put his socks and shoes back on, before he could return to the car and set off home. He walked away from the town, to the nearest bench he could see. He recognised it as the same bench he had sat on earlier. He didn't want to remember the fateful conversation that had made his mind up. Didn't want to remember what had just happened. He didn't care any more.

He sat down and managed to unfold his sodden trouser legs back down over his frozen calves and drag the thin material of his socks over his numb feet. He thought about the loyalty and love that Rissoles had shown the old lady and it occurred to him that he needed to get home and feed the cat.

A formless, fleeting shadow of thought crossed his mind as he considered his and Rissoles fate not to be too dissimilar. It passed without his conscious acknowledgement. He had far more important things to worry about.

Had he been seen? He needed to get back to Falmbourne as quickly as he could. He thrust his feet back into his shoes, he had hoped for some relief from the hypothermic sensations. Sitting alone on the bench, he had made for a sorry sight. He was not at all dressed for a nocturnal visit to the sea.

Setting off for the steps back to the clifftop, his tear streaked face betrayed the anguish and emotional turmoil that had just ravaged him. Returning up the steps that would lead up to the car and home, he climbed, walking with a horse-riders gait. The sodden seams of his trousers were rubbing the skin of his cold legs raw.

66

Aileen poured her companion more of the acidic red wine, that was bar's best attempt at Merlot, listening to the young teacher's gushing angst about being in love with a married man. The married man, in this case was her nemesis, Charles Syndale.

She had met a timid Suzy in the empty staff room as arranged, leaving the plate of brownies in the middle of the small, circular table in temptation. They had sat together and chatted blandly for about ten minutes, before Suzy began to make her apologies and got herself ready to leave.

In desperation, Aileen had played her last card and asked if Suzy knew how Charles was, hoping to extend the dialogue and find an opportunity to get Suzy to eat a brownie. What Aileen had not expected was for Suzy to burst into tears. Aileen had moved beside her young colleague and put her arm around her, oozing warmth and empathy. When Suzy had finally stopped crying, Aileen moved the plate of cakes in front of Suzy and encouraged her to begin eating.

Now the pair sat, side by side, in a secluded booth of a bar in a local hotel. On the table in front of them was an empty bottle that had contained the bitter and acidic red wine. Both Aileen and Suzy's dishwasher scratched glasses were full.

However, Aileen was still on her first glass and Suzy had already drained two.

After the first brownie, Suzy had begun to open up to Aileen. Words began to tumble out of her, a self demeaning explanation of how stupid she felt for getting involved with Charles, mixed with appreciation for just how good the brownies were. She ate two and half of them before Aileen offered to buy her a drink.

Aileen had driven them to a local ramshackle hotel and leisure centre, on the outskirts of the town. Fields of sheep flanked the long drive-way to the remote and secluded buildings. The gym and squash facilities were frequented by many of the locals, but the bar and hotel that they subsidised were empty. Aileen and Suzy sat alone and undisturbed.

For Aileen, as she listened to Suzy, every atom of her being seemed to be vibrating. She existed only in the moment. She wanted only one thing, watching the super animated motion of her companion, following every pout, every lick of the voluptuous and full pink lips and wanting. Desperately wanting.

Their thighs touched and rubbed as Suzy bounced her leg uncontrollably under the table. Their hands brushed against each others, every time that Suzy picked up and replaced the glass of wine. The sensations made Aileen bite her own lip in longing. Minutes felt like hours as Suzy continued to drain her glass, between self flagellating and self indulgent introspective pronouncements until, finally, she noticed Aileen.

When their eyes finally met, Suzy couldn't help responding to Aileen's dilated pupils. She had only experimented with kissing another woman once before. Dancing, drunk in a club with a friend, when a Katy Perry song told her that the celebrity had kissed a girl and liked it. The two had looked at each other and laughed. The kiss that followed had been fun. It had driven the men around the pair wild and as they broke the kiss off they took their pick of the bunch for the rest of the night. Now, the prospect was entirely different.

The kiss, when it happened, was tender, urgent and ignited a desire in both of the women. It was only broken off when Aileen went the to the empty hotel's Reception to take a room for the night.

67

Robert reached the top step and unsealed his trouser pocked as if it were a sandwich bag, rummaging in the twisted material that harboured his car keys with his right hand. His trousers were still plastered to his legs, and they had begun to steam as his body fought to warm the skin under them. In his left, he carried the separated parts of the phone from the box.

He walked awkwardly along the path on the cliff top, his crotch was flaming agony as each stitch and seam sawed away at the sensitive area with each stride, approaching his car gingerly. He hadn't noticed the black Audi parked close behind him. The last thing he remembered seeing was his hand reaching for the driver side door handle, when the world went black and pain exploded, a freight train slammed into his stomach.

He knew he had doubled over onto his knees, as he briefly felt the solid tarmac under him. Something covered his head, obscuring his vision, but not blocking all of the light. Was it sack or a pillow case or something? He didn't know.

Desperately, he tried to call out, in panic and in pain, for help from someone. Despite the brutal assault, he tried to call out to whoever was doing this to him to stop. The pain in his arms, as they were twisted behind him savagely and restrained, was agonising. Something hard slammed across his wrists with a click.

However, he couldn't make a sound, except for dry heaving breaths as he tried to recover from the hardest punch he had ever felt. Succumbing to his capture or arrest, he was lifted and dragged from his car. A crunch underfoot indicated that the phone of the recently deceased parent had been dropped, the screen giving way as he stood.

His assailants dragged him back away from his car and bundled him, he thought into the back seat of a police car, but actually he was unceremoniously tipped into the boot of Lee's Audi. He managed to cry out as he landed with his whole weight onto an arm that was trapped beneath him. He thought it had broken.

Robert knew he wasn't being arrested when he received another impossibly hard punch in the face to silence him. The boot hatch was slammed down hard, almost deafening him and left him alone in complete darkness. In just moments, Robert's world had been turned upside down.

The car heaved and pitched as his two captors settled into the front seats. Their doors thudded as they closed. Not a word or a sound had been uttered by either of them. Robert wriggled to relieve the pressure on his arms as the engine gently purred into life.

He felt every bump and pothole in the road as he was driven a short distance, before he felt the car's suspension lift in relief, as the passenger got out and stepped away from the car. He heard the car's radio as it was turned on. It was muffled by the stuffing of the back seats, but he could just make out the tune of a hit from the 90s. Shortly, his journey to an unknown destination began again in earnest as the car revved and he was driven away.

68

He didn't remember passing out, but he was certainly waking up. He could feel that he was sitting upright, on a chair with his arms behind him. His wrists were still restrained and his arms shrieked in suffering. This was not the boot of the car. It was cold and it was dark.

He couldn't see anything and he still had something cloth like over his head. It felt like he was alone. He could breathe again, but the pain in his stomach was still a dull ache. Swallowing, his mouth tasted like copper, and his cheek hurt. He remembered the punch in the face. Wriggling carefully, he tried to move his feet, but there were sharp, tight cords around his ankles and he figured his legs were tied to the front legs of the chair.

A wave of undiluted, sheer terror and panic washed over him with more power than the sea had earlier. He remembered the moment where he had felt the insistent invitation to just walk further in, as the waves had retreated, with a desperate frustration. He wished he could transport himself back to that moment, knowing what was about to happen to him, and just accept the invitation to join oblivion in its loving embrace.

A guttural, prehistoric cry of fear was impeded by the soft cloth that had been stuffed into his mouth at some point. Images of torture victims, abducted by serial killers, flooded his imagination. No-one knew where he had been. No-one, including him, knew where he was. He was the plaything of some sadistic psycho, free to inflict whatever pain they wanted on him, for as long as they wanted to.

Robert strained every muscle he could in a vain attempt to break the bonds that held him, giving up very swiftly, noting to himself that he had quite a low pain threshold. He hoped that this was a good sign and that he would just keep passing out, until the killer got bored and just ended it.

He pictured Elle's crying face at his funeral and all the people that would miss him.

His dark fantasies were cut abruptly short by the sound of crunching footsteps approaching, followed by a loud grating sound of metal screaming against metal. Robert felt the air pressure change as he was exposed to a bigger, more open space as a blast of air brought the sound of distant cars and the gentle rustling of nature. A loud click introduced a bare light source in front of him. The indistinct globe above him enabled him to make out the shape of three people standing in front of him.

'Ave you got it ready?' a gravelly voice spoke. He vaguely recognised it, but couldn't place where from.

'Yeah,' another voice, a little further back replied. The tone made Robert think that whoever it was was uncertain, but doing what the first voice said. Gravel man was in charge, he decided.

'Alright, lets do this,' intoned Gravel man. A shadow loomed over Robert. He could feel Gravel man's breath on his cloth hood.

'Wait,' Uncertain man had issued a surprising instruction. Gravel man hesitated. 'Maybe we should just ask 'im first, like. 'e might just tell us.'

There was a pause and Robert could hear feet shuffle. He imagined them all looking around at each other and just shrugging. It bought him some time to think and prepare himself. They weren't serial killers who wanted to eat his liver with a tasty bottle of red. That was a relief. They wanted some information. That was bad. As he didn't think he had any, being a school teacher. He briefly hoped that this was just a case of mistaken identity and that it could all be cleared up quickly. His abductors would realise their mistake and free him. They could all have a bit of laugh about it over a nice cup of tea.

'Where's Maggie?' Gravel man asked.

Robert made a muffled sound, 'O Thif.'

A hand reached under the cloth hood and removed the rag in Robert's mouth, 'Wot you say?' It was Gravel man again.

Robert began to place the voice and remembered the stranger danger he had reported to Aileen.

'I said: 'Oh shit',' Robert replied smartly, before regretting it immediately. He felt the open palm slap sting his face and snap his head to the side.

'Wot 'ave you done to her? Tell me now or you'll regret it you...' Gravel man trailed off.

Robert felt his face being held by his jaw, forcing his mouth open. The hood was lifted up over his nose which someone's fingers held shut. Something was stuffed into his open mouth, pushed back over his tongue to the back of throat, followed by a water bottle tipped up and his mouth soon filled and it forced him to swallow. Whatever it was, it was ingested in the first gulp.

'Give 'im an hour or so and 'e'll be off his trolley,' Uncertain man said proudly. 'He'll talk then.'

Robert heard the screaming metal again as he surmised, a door was closed, followed by footsteps fading away. He heard the dull thud of car doors closing, remaining alone, tied to the chair, in the small room with a hood over his head. His abductors had left the light on, but it didn't help him at all.

69

Suzy sat on the toilet long after she had finished peeing. The muted golden lighting in the en-suite bathroom didn't cast any shadows at all. It was comforting and womb-like.

She had never experimented with any drugs at all and didn't comprehend the tell tale signs that she had been spiked. All she knew was that she alive in a way that she had never thought possible.

She had just had sex with the Headteacher, a woman, and she had never had orgasms like it. Almost from the first stroking caress and probing investigation, Suzy had been overwhelmed in ecstasy. Aileen had made her feel more intensely than anyone, any man, had ever done.

She sat staring at the basin opposite. She had had her fair share of partners and enjoyed them all. They had all been men. She couldn't remember ever looking at another woman and thinking 'phwoar' before. The way she had when she saw a fit bloke. So how could this be possible?

Aileen wasn't even that attractive a woman, Suzy thought. She was good looking for her age, but when she took her clothes off, she was all angled, pointy bones. There was little in the way of soft curves or tender, smooth muscle.

A gentle thump on the floor of the bedroom beyond the door let Suzy know that Aileen had stirred. She stood, flushed the toilet and washed her hands in the sink opposite, regarding her reflection in the mirror. The soft golden hue of the light softened the bruises under her tired eyes.

'Well,' she said to herself, 'you weren't expecting that were you?' She dried her hands and returned to the bedroom and found Aileen standing at the end of the bed, half dressed already, searching for her shoes.

'Oh,' was all Aileen could think to say when Suzy emerged from the bathroom completely naked, turning awkwardly away, not wanting stare.

'I've lost my shoes somewhere, ah,' she found one under the dressing table opposite.

'I can give you a lift back to school, or home, if you prefer.' She glanced at Suzy who had foregone the hassle of underwear and just put on her skirt and was just lifting her blouse from the floor. 'I can pick you up in the morning, to save you the trouble, like,' Aileen felt like the teenager in the girl's locker room again. But that was a long time ago. 'If you would like?' she asked.

Suzy smiled over at her hopelessly embarrassed and awkward boss, she always felt comfortable in these moments, being young, free and single. There was no guilt or embarrassment for her to feel, that was left for her girlfriend or wife cheating partner. She was also supremely confident in her own skin, being very attractive and knowing it.

'Home, please,' she yawned. 'I would be very grateful of a lift in the morning, too. If that's OK with you?'

Aileen nodded her agreement and the pair finished dressing in silence. They made the bed together and left the room without speaking again until they reached the car park.

'Miss Byrne,' Aileen looked across the bonnet. 'Aileen,' Suzy continued, 'I just wanted to say, to reassure you, I mean.' Suzy shifted, feeling awkward now herself. 'I mean, I am ...discreet.'

She looked down at her feet. The shingle gravel car park crackled slightly as she shifted her balance from one foot to the other. The older woman just looked blankly at her and blinked, once.

'I had a really good time, I just wanted you to know,' Suzy smiled her winning smile and got into the car.

Aileen stood alone in the dark and felt the hollowness inside her as Suzy got in her car. She had felt like a spectator to pleasure and intimacy as soon as the love making began. Her initial lust was merely an echo from her past. The passion a mechanical imitation of her youthful vigour. She was grateful it was over. It hadn't been Suzy's fault, she had turned into one of Aileen's most enthusiastic lovers. It had surprised her. Aileen reflected that the anticipation of something was always better than the actual thing. She blinked twice at the night sky and got into the driver's seat. She hoped it wouldn't take long to deliver Suzy home.

70

It didn't take long for Robert to notice that something was changing as he began to relax about the whole being bound up on a chair by strangers thing.

The tingling sensations in his arms and legs, became his sole focus, with concentration he began to twitch individual muscles in a sequence that meant something only to him. He even began to hum a tune that was normally associated with strongmen in a circus performance. He felt remarkably calm and relaxed, considering. His perception of the light through his cloth hood began to intensify. The frequency of sound changed according to the where he positioned his head. He also felt sleepy, but wide awake at the same time. Whatever Uncertain man had given him was good stuff, he mused.

Outside several dull thumps in the distance, followed by the crunch of gravel and stones heralded his jailers approach. The idea of guests coming to see him in his lonely abode made him quiver with anticipation. Under the hood, he waited with a wide mouthed smile. If he concentrated, he could hear bits of what the men, who were soon-to-be-guests, were saying to each other.

'...if he doesn't know anything? What then?' one voice, Uncertain man he thought, asked.

'He'll talk when we apply the right pressure, don't you worry,' a new nasally voice responded.

Robert hadn't heard this voice before and tried to picture who it might belong to. He pictured a cross between Frankie Howerd and Willie Rushton with a jittery laugh and couldn't wait to meet him.

'We see if your truth serum works first, don't we. We don't 'urt 'im, unless we 'ave to,' Gravel man said. 'And if we 'ave to, I'll do the 'urtin' got it? You," a pause, "keep your 'ands clean. Got it? Put these on, so 'e doesn't see yur boat race,'

Robert wondered why Gravel man couldn't pronounce his aitches and considered what teaching strategies he could employ to assist the man with his diction. He really liked the idea of going to a boat race though!

'Why can't I have the Panda? I found the bloody things,' Frankie Howerd asked.

'Cos you're a Rabbit, got it?' Gravel man seemed to stop any further discussion on which animal they were.

A click was rapidly followed by the worst sound that Robert had ever heard in his life. A million screaming harpies filled his ears and mind with a pain and suffering he couldn't imagine as the unoiled rollers travelled along their runners. He writhed on his chair in absolute agony as the garage door opened like the gateway into hell itself. The veneer of frivolous humour that masked his predicament was torn away from his consciousness, as he became intimately aware that he was trapped and at the mercy of these unknown strangers. This horror was compounded when the cloth hood was snatched off his head, blinding his sight with the blistering incandescence of a single burning bulb.

As he looked up at it, the thin, superheated filament left an indelible image imprinted on his retina every time he blinked. His vision was quickly obscured by two, then four, then eight, then sixteen burning elements that turned twisted and grew to fill the small space that he and the strangers occupied.

He began to sweat uncontrollably. Droplets rapidly formed into rivulets on his skin. Suffocating, unable to supply his body with the oxygen it needed to survive his new environment, he hyperventilated. In what seemed like seconds his underarms were soaked and his besieged eyes began to sting as the sweat swept over the natural dam formed by his eyebrows. Robert could only find succour from this discomfort by rolling his head from side to side, making the ground around him roll back and forth. He was a sailor on rough seas. No, he thought, I am an astronaut on re-entry.

'Help! Help! We're going to burn up! We're not going to make it! Major Tom!' he screamed at the top of his voice, floating in space without a tether to take him back to the ship.

'Well, he is deffo off his tits,' Uncertain man said, with certainty. 'He,' there was a pause like a delay in transmission between the Earth and the Moon, 'is all yours. I'll wait in the car with the kid.' Uncertain man's footsteps crunched quietly away.

To Robert the footsteps sounded like meteors hitting the outside of his ship. Cowering in terror, he waited for his head to explode. Frantically searching for his helmet, the only protection he would have in the event that the hull was breached and the atmosphere vented into space, he looked around the cabin, but couldn't find it. There had to be help somewhere. Why weren't Mission Control helping? For some reason his companions were animals. He wasn't sure why a Panda and a Rabbit would be in space.

The Panda slapped him across the face: it really hurt. The stinging sensation just kept amplifying until it felt like his teeth were going to explode. It was a really mean Panda. Robert looked to the Rabbit for assistance and found none.

'Alright now, cupcake. Tell me where Maggie Tracey is and all this will be over,' Robert recognised that the voice coming from the Panda was Gravel man. Lewis's grandfather. This realisation totally blew Robert's mind. Lewis's grandfather was a mean space Panda!

'She's gone, the Blackbird took her away and I sent her to Davey Jones's locker,' Robert quite reasonably explained. Given the circumstances, he thought he had provided a full answer. The Panda didn't and punched him in the stomach, hard.

The punch pushed Robert's chair over and he landed on his restrained arms behind him. He screamed. He screamed very loudly. It carried out of the garage, to the parked car outside. It woke the sleeping Lewis up with a start.

Robert rolled over on his side to try to quell his angry nervous system and stop it sending bullet train signals of pain up to his brain. He couldn't cope with any more. Laying on the floor, open mouthed, not even able to enunciate the exquisite agony he felt with prehistoric grunts or whimpering squeals. He tried to twitch his muscles again, to check that everything still worked. Every tiny movement caused him to feel like he was falling and tumbling, over and over. It was nauseating. His life was in an uncontrollable spin and he would be re-entering Earth's atmosphere without his helmet. Spaceman Robert was beside himself.

'Please,' he whispered through strained lips, 'please, make it stop.'

'I would love to, cupcake.' The gravel voiced Panda replied. 'But, you see, I have a little problem. A problem I hope that you can help me wiv'.'

The Panda moved closer to Robert and bent over to make sure that they could see eye to eye. It looked terrifying to Robert.

'You see. A friend of mine should've gone 'ome to 'er kid, a few nights ago. But she didn't. And no-one. I mean, no-one, has seen or 'eard from 'er since. So I would like to know where she is.'

'I told you,' Robert panted, 'She's gone and won't be coming back. The Blackbird,' he saw dark wings flapping around the Panda's head. 'The Blackbird took her life.' Robert whimpered now. His complicity couldn't be kept from the Panda.

'I took what was left to Davy Jones.' Robert cried. 'It's not just your friend. The Blackbird poisoned The Great White Shark, too! She might have tried to poison me,' Robert nodded frantically, trying to make the Panda understand, so that it wouldn't hurt him again. 'She tried to poison me, but I was too clever! Ha! Too clever for the Blackbird!'

Robert heard the Rabbit complain, 'Blackbirds and Great White Sharks. This bloke is off his trolley. I should've brought the Guy Fawkes masks. I did try to tell you, animals are a bad idea. We should just beat the crap out of him and then we'll get some sense, you'll see.'

A new voice entered Robert's world. A high pitched voice that he knew.

'Blackbird's what we call Miss Byrne.' Robert placed the high pitched voice as Lewis Tracey's.

The voice got louder as the boy approached, 'I've heard them all talk about a shark at school. The teachers, like. It's what they call Mr Syndale behind his back.'

'The Blackbird took Maggie and poisoned the Great White Shark,' the Panda with Gravel man's voice repeated.

'Charlie, take the boy to the car. Lee, gimme those keys quick. Drive 'em both 'ome. Then get these cuffs back to our friend on the force before she misses 'em. I'll deal with this, 'ere. Go!'

The group of teacher-nappers leapt into action and before he knew it Robert was freed from his restraints. Not that he could escape though. He writhed on the floor like he was being struck by invisible snakes, as the blood flowed back into his beleaguered, oxygen starved limbs.

'Alright, cupcake. Just rest a while. It'll all wear off and you will be right as rain by the morning,' Gravel man pulled the Panda mask off his head in view of the horrified Robert, who thought Mickey was peeling off the Panda's face.

The night passed slowly for Robert, once he had been pushed off down the lane, away from the garages, by Mickey. He ran in the dark as the hedgerows either side of him rippled mysteriously in the cold night's breeze. Their green glow kept him moving, an ancient anxiety and fear of all things natural at night kept him going, although he had no clue where he was.

Ahead, laser beams of light clashed, white flashing like light sabres to his right and red punctuated blasts moving to his left. His hallucinations leading him to believe that he was in fact on an alien planet in the midst of an epic battle. The sounds of foxes, badgers and owls in the looming shadows surrounded him, as the wildlife continued their nightly routine, unaware of the intruding human, they gathered, chatted to each and hunted their prey and had him running, tripping and staggering through the fields and undergrowth in abject terror.

The shape shifting shadows of trees left him paranoid. He feared being mutilated and consumed by ravenous, hideous alien beasts. He kept running towards the lights of a settlement in the distance, in a meandering zig-zag across newly ploughed fields. Hunted. Haunted.

For Aileen, the night quickly passed .

She had showered once she had got home. At first she just soaped herself, washed the scent of her encounter with Suzy off. Gradually, as her thoughts turned darker, she scrubbed her skin harder, using her nail brush until it hurt and her skin was red raw.

At least she could still feel pain, she thought.

What would become of the boy, Lewis? She wondered as the deluge of water cascaded from the shower-head. He had been one of the catalysts. The mist and steam of the hottest shower setting fogged the bathroom entirely leaving her in a formless cloud. His neglect and abuse the trigger that she had waited for. What would become of him?

She had been a little disappointed that the police weren't waiting for her when she pulled up to her house. The panic she felt earlier had gone. Now, she just wanted someone to stop her. To save her from what she must do. Robert had obviously not gone to them. He may even have disposed of the ashes as she had begged him to. Why on Earth would he do that?

After drying herself off and wrapping herself in a bathrobe, slipping her feet in the soft, fluffy scuffettes, she sat at her computer and wondered how she could repay her debt to him. He would have to live on knowing what she had done, and live with his part in what was to happen next. Opening the file *The Sick Teacher's Cook Book.doc* on her desktop, she selected *File* and *Print*.

The sound of the robotic printer chugging and whirring its way through its task obediently, filled the room in the dead of night. Its final clank was abruptly followed by a thunderous silence, indicating that its job was done. The void roused Aileen from her stupor. She collected the pages, hole punched them meticulously and placed them in a cheap, frosted ring binder.

She flipped through the pages, with more than just a little pride that she had written such a tome. Sure that a copy would exist somewhere, she returned to her computer and moved the mouse pointer over the little icon indicating the disk drive. Clicking the right mouse button, a small pop up menu appeared immediately. Aileen moved the little arrow on the screen down to the *Format* option and clicked it. A box with a more complicated menu appeared. Aileen chose the *OK* button. Once clicked, the machine began to shut down. The computer obediently began to erase itself, washing itself clean and giving itself a brand new beginning. Aileen watched in jealousy.

73

Mickey waited for Lee at the train station. The roads were quiet and the station was all locked up.

He thought about the young mother as he last saw her. She had flipped him the finger when he had told her that he had a punter, a man in his sixties, who he wanted her to look after. Once a week, at his place for a couple of months. He had told her that she should be pleased. The punter had picked her out personally. Said she reminded him of his wife when they first met.

When she complained that he was too old, Mickey had told her that it was a guaranteed two hundred quid a week, which would go a long way to help her pay back the money she owed him. He passed her the punter's address and warned her not to fuck up, again. This was her last chance. He had watched her strut off, wiggling her hips.

Lee got into the car without a word, the two men shared a serious look. Lee nodded to indicate that he had been successful. The cuffs had been returned to Laetitia. In fact, Lee had managed to sneak in and out without even waking the police officer, his girlfriend, up. As Lee clicked the seatbelt in, Mickey started the car and pulled away. The journey to Charlie's flat would not take long, even with the traffic lights and the road works, at this time of night. They had a plan to make and a score to settle.

74

Charlie was woken by the buzzing of his mobile phone. He had slept on the mattress in the living room again, as he had given his bed to Lewis.

He looked at the illuminated screen, it displayed a number he didn't recognise, so he ignored it. He had missed three calls from the same number, but there were no messages. Stretching, he got up and organised his morning, by first going to the bathroom, quietly, he didn't want to wake the boy. Then he mooched around the kitchen, making a cup of tea. This process was interrupted by the sudden bombardment of fists on the door downstairs. He knew who that had to be.

Mickey waited impatiently. He had tried calling Charlie several times using one of his burner phones from the boot of his car. The lazy twat hadn't answered.

There was nothing else for it but to go and knock him up. He and Lee had hatched a bit of a plan, but it needed Lewis to work. They needed to go separately into the school during the morning drop off and manage to get themselves on the grounds.

Lewis would appear and show himself to the Headteacher and then run off and hide somewhere around the school building. He, Lee and Charlie would then follow the Headteacher, until they could get her alone. Charlie would take the kid back to the car, whilst he and Lee had 'a chat' with this 'Blackbird' about the missing Maggie. It seemed simple and straightforward. The fewer the details, the better. They could improvise if they needed to.

When Charlie finally opened the door to Mickey, the big man's patience had run out.

'Get the kid up and ready,' Mickey barked the instruction. 'Be in the car in ten minutes.'

He left Charlie with the clear impression that it would be better if they were both in the car in five.

75

Aileen had spent the night cleaning, hoovering and bleaching every surface in the house and scrubbed the whole place clean. All the bedding had been changed and fresh towels and linen put out in every room. It was spotless. Lastly, the kitchen had been scrubbed and scoured as if the worktops were her soul; she had attempted to wash and cleanse away the stains accrued from her past.

Once she was satisfied that she had done her very level best, she prepped for the day. Her only copy of the cookbook was in her laptop bag, the bins were out and the doors were locked. Keeping her word to Suzy she collected her, early, to get to school. The young teacher had appeared wearing large, dark sunglasses. Apparently, not enjoying the come down at all.

There had been a very awkward moment, when Suzy had hesitantly and nervously, leaned in for a kiss when she first got in the car. Aileen had shied away, the look of horror had sent a clear message that the intimacy of the previous night was over.

Once at school, Aileen placed the ring bound cookbook into Robert's pigeon hole. He would find it at some point. She hoped it would explain everything clearly and give him a sense of closure after the ordeal that was to come.

The Secretary had informed her that Charles had called in sick again and that he had been referred to the local hospital for some blood tests. Aileen thought about the little blue pills that she wished she had slipped him ruefully. She wouldn't get the chance now.

She went to the staff room and left a message on the board that there would be a brief meeting at eight fifteen to prepare for the day and to give feedback regarding the lock down. Care needed to be taken to make sure that staff didn't bolt the doors again. She wanted access to the whole school building from the Boiler Room. Everything was in place. Now she just had to wait.

76

Robert's world began to retake shape as he reached the outskirts of Falmbourne and dawn broke.

The hallucinations became less frequent and he began to recognise road names and places that were familiar. A recalled visit to a friend's house who lived down that road. A familiar shortcut through to another road that would take him closer to home. He patted his trousers, looking for his keys, and remembered dropping them by his car in Tankerville when he was attacked the previous night.

Sleep-deprived, drugged and anxious beyond medical measurement, it was a struggle to remember what was real and what was a hallucination. He separated the events that were most likely to have really happened: the kidnapping, the imprisonment, the beating, the drugging and the interrogation.

He remembered that there was a Rabbit and a Panda, but thought that must have been hallucinatory. They had asked him questions about a friend of theirs. Maggie. They had asked him about Maggie Tracey. He knew he had babbled something. He obviously hadn't taken responsibility or he would have been killed there and then, he assumed. An image had stayed with him. It had been so vivid. It was of black wings flapping around the Panda's head. He had told the people that had taken him about Aileen. He was pretty certain. Although it was all a bit hazy.

He couldn't go home. His keys were probably still laying on the tarmac beside his car in Tankerville. He couldn't go and get his car, because his wallet and his phone were in his car, in Tankerville. He only had a couple of quid in his trouser pocket. Reaching into the trouser pocket to check it was still there, he found it empty. The coins must have fallen out in the Audi's boot or in the place that he had been tied up in.

There was only one place that he could go. He needed to tell Aileen what had happened and warn her that Maggie's friends were onto her. He looked at his reflection in the large picture window of the house he was passing and didn't recognise the figure looking back at him.

77

Laetitia sat at her breakfast bar in full uniform, ready to go work. Open in front of her was the letter from Pete's solicitors, requesting that she sign the divorce papers and return them to the court addressed, using the envelope that they had provided.

She noted that the reason Pete had given was her adultery and unreasonable behaviour surrounding the home life of the children. She sipped her tea and took a bite of toast. There was no contesting any of it, so she just signed it and placed the forms in the pre-addressed envelope that his solicitors had handily provided. It was heart-breaking, but for the best. Her shift would end at five, so she was going to go out with some of the girls and get absolutely smashed tonight. No men. No families.

Her phone buzzed with a message. Kevin, her partner for the day, was waiting outside. It was time to go on duty. She left the tea and toast on the breakfast bar, with the unsealed envelope containing her divorce papers. She would have to deal with all of that later. She locked the door and got into the passenger seat.

'Mornin' Kev, how's the Missus?' she began the day's banter amiably. There would be plenty of time to rib him about his wife's condition.

'Ha, bloody ha. I don't why you're taking the piss, Tish. You're gonna 'ave to go through the menopause at some point as well. I expected better from you.'

Kevin took the moral high ground before confiding, 'I get a better night's sleep on the sofa with the dog, than I do with her.' He shook his head and released the hand brake, pulling away down the road, away from the train station. 'And as for mood swings!' he glanced across and raised his eyebrows to emphasise that his wife was experiencing pronounced symptoms.

'Poor you,' Laetitia commiserated and patted him on his arm.

'Anyway,' Kevin changed the subject. 'We've got a call,' he began.

'Already?' Laetitia looked at her watch. She hadn't finished her breakfast and now she wasn't going to get a chance to stop for a coffee.

'Yup,' he replied. 'Mother and child have been reported missing. Haven't been seen or heard from in over forty eight hours. Bill and Kelly are checking out the address and canvassing neighbours. We get to go to the kid's school and find out what they know.'

'Huh,' Laetitia was unimpressed. 'Bet they are taking advantage of cheap holiday deals and that they turn up again with a great suntan and a sombrero. Which school?' she asked.

'Thresher Street Primary,' Kevin informed her.

'Oh, Christ almighty,' Laetitia's morning just got worse. 'That's means..'

'Yeah,' Kevin interrupted, nodding, 'the bloody roadworks!'

78

Kevin parked in the school's car park in a space marked 'Guest'. They had arrived in the middle of the morning's drop off rush. The street outside had been packed with cars, SUVs and people carriers as well as with with pedestrians of every age, shape, size and colour.

They walked to Reception and asked if it would be possible to speak to the Headteacher. They were politely asked to take a seat by the Secretary, who was inundated with parents, who cast quizzical glances at the two officers.

The parents were unperturbed by the presence of the Law and bombarded the poor Secretary with questions and requests, asking how to fill out forms for trips; forms for after school clubs; or to how pay their arrears for school dinners. It was organised chaos. The two seasoned police officers sighed together and sat down on the uncomfortable looking sofa to wait until the madness calmed down.

For Aileen, the day was progressing well. She had delivered her briefing, feeding back to the staff about what went well and how to improve for the next lock down practise that was due to occur at some point during the morning. There had been a groan. The internal doors would not be obstructed for her today! Suzy had stood at the back, glasses remained on her face.

Aileen noted that Robert was not there so had checked his room and asked the Secretary to establish whether he had called in. He hadn't been heard from. Quickly, a Cover Supervisor was arranged to step in and take his class. She would check up on him later.

For now, she was occupied at the Parent and Child gate, where she smiled and greeted the families coming in. Surrounded by happy faces, Aileen failed to notice the three men who had tagged onto random children as they entered the gate. Too busy thinking through her plan for the morning, she had one or two loose ends to tie up.

Early Help and the Social Services needed to be made aware of her concerns about the safety and well-being of Lewis Tracey. Care of the child had to be arranged rapidly and wheels needed to be put into motion, before she was finished.

Now, Robert needed to be contacted as well, to find out what had happened and make sure that he knew about the copy of her confession in his pigeon hole. It was strange but she felt compelled that she say goodbye to someone. A need for that human connection for closure. Then she would be free.

A commotion grabbed her attention. Just outside the gate. Shouts and screams of indignation and abuse were being hurled at someone, from both adults and children. A bruised and battered scarecrow of a man appeared, dragging a child dressed in a tracksuit by the arm. The tramp saw Aileen and made a bee-line for her. She recognised the scarecrow man was Robert Carpenter, except that he looked like he had been half-drowned, dragged through a hedge, or several hedges, and spat out of a meat grinder. She gasped at his appearance. He looked awful. She looked down at the child he was holding and recognised him as Lewis Tracey.

'Get off me! You drugged up paedo!' Lewis struggled, 'Get off!'

'My office, now!' she exclaimed, directing Robert to move into the school behind her, before moving into the throng of parents and children who had gathered to watch the strange spectacle, to calm the scene and get the children into class as quickly as possible. Her plans for morning would just have to change.

In the ruck, three men managed to detach themselves unseen and move around behind the school buildings where they couldn't be seen. They huddled underneath the window of one of the classrooms to confer and adapt their morning's plans accordingly.

Mickey had insisted that Lewis tell them the layout of the school. All the good places to hide, all the ways into the school that the teachers didn't know about or didn't check, like the Fire doors by the Boiler Room, or the window to the Art cupboard. Lewis was a master at sneaking in and out of school, with or without tradable contraband. After their brief conference, they split up and moved stealthily around the building to their allocated positions.

79

Robert had approached the school slowly, aware of the eyes that followed him down the busy street. He felt their gaze and remembered what Edie had said just yesterday afternoon.

'Eyes are only really useful if they can see,' he remembered how much sense that had made to him, then.

Now the meaning felt entirely different. Why hadn't his eyes seen, he wondered? What could all of their eyes see now? His anxiety was still heightened by the substances that Uncertain man had given him the night before as the blood buzzed around his veins, electrifying every muscle and sinew with each pulse.

His perception was still altered, as he walked among the surprised and staring children and parents, he heard his name whispered in hushed tones. The timbre of the voices echoed through his psyche, mingling with the threats, real and imagined that he had confronted throughout the long night.

In front of him, a short child in a grey tracksuit caught his attention. The child's eyes were impossibly large. His wide open mouth a giant 'O'.

It was Lewis Tracey. As quickly as he saw the child, he was on him. The child's arms were locked into a vice-like grip that he had never made using his hands before. This child knew the people who had held him captive and tortured him. The child knew who was after Aileen. Now, he had the child. There was no way he was going to let go.

He had pushed the child ahead of him roughly, to the disapproval of all those delivering their children to school. But Robert had not cared. He had managed to get through the throng and had found Aileen. He had managed to get the child into school, kicking and screaming, past his confused and concerned colleagues and into Aileen's office, where the two of them sat at the table.

'My Oncle Mickey's gunna kill you,' was the only thing that Lewis said, once they were sat facing each other, staring, sullenly and resentfully.

80

Aileen had successfully calmed the outraged parents and over-excited children down, promising that she would be looking into the incident personally. She reassured worried carers that the children's welfare and safeguarding was the most important thing at the school until it nearly choked her.

With the parent gate locked she rushed hurriedly to her office. As she passed the corridor leading to the main Reception, she noticed the two police officers waiting. With no time to waste, she flung the door of her office open and grabbed hold of the boy's arm.

'For Christ's sake Robert, what happened to you?' she asked as she dragged the boy out of the office, in the direction of the Boiler Room.

'Boiler Room, now!' she exclaimed to Robert, as her office phone began to ring.

The school Secretary was trying to contact her regarding the long arm of the law, waiting with decreasing patience and sore backs, on the uncomfortable sofa by the main entrance.

The three raced down the corridors, passed open and closed classroom doors. Thankfully, Lewis was too confused to call out, but he had spotted Lee through a window as he was dragged along. Eye contact was made for a brief moment, so

Lewis knew that he his Uncle Mickey was going to come and rescue him. Aileen fiddled with her lanyard, to find the key that opened the Boiler Room door.

Outside the floor to ceiling glass pane stood Lee, who was explaining to Mickey exactly how to find him on his mobile. Lewis fist pumped and tried to drag Aileen's restraining grip behind him in imitation of characters flying into a Battle Royale, from his favourite game. But, like Robert's grip, her fingers were an iron clasp. His reaction had garnered her attention as she found the right key; she stood eye-to-eye with the man who was trespassing on school property. She unlocked the door casually and passed Lewis over to Robert.

'Take him in there and wait,' she instructed.

She smiled at the stranger outside and walked back towards the main part of the school coolly, leaving the agitated and panicking Robert to deal with the child in the Boiler Room. She walked straight into the nearest classroom and picked up the room's intercom phone and dialled the number for the Secretary. As soon as he heard the Secretary's tinkling voice she uttered a simple set of instructions.

'Lock down, now. Stranger on site. Outside Boiler Room. Call the Police,' and put the phone down before she had to face any questions. She began her walk back to the Boiler Room counting.

'One thousand one, one thousand two, one thous...' the alarm broadcast its stop start message of danger and teachers sprang into action. She had bought herself some time.

81

Robert cast about in the dark trying to find the light switch. Once the light was on, he looked around. Everything was as he left it yesterday. The shovel against the door, the salt store open.

He let Lewis go and walked over to the salt store. There was an impression on the sand and salt mix, where the box containing the tin urns of Maggie Tracey's ashes had sat. Next to to it was the plastic petrol can. He picked it up to gauge how much was in it, dislodging the lighter that had been thrown in after.

The can was full. There was a way to light it. He smiled, sadly. The men who had assaulted and tortured him were here, for Aileen and him. There was no way that this was going to end well. He had procrastinated all week, and this is where it had got him.

If only he had been more decisive earlier, then maybe none of this would be happening. Looking at Lewis, he felt the guilt of the boy's loss and realised that he was going to go to prison for a long, long time.

'Lewis, you need to stand by the door, over there,' he pointed to the door that they had entered through.

'When I tell you to. I want you to run,' he watched the child's face to make sure that he had understood. 'But not before,

OK. I want you to run to our classroom and get everybody out through the Fire Escape. Can you do that for me?'

Robert opened the cap on the petrol can and walked over to the boiler units. He ripped the front off each of the units, exposing the internal workings and corroded pipework. Lewis nodded and walked over to the door.

Aileen walked in as Robert began to pour the contents of the can over the boilers and the rotten pipes that fed them. The liquid splashed haphazardly around, covering his shoes and trousers; spilling all over the floor.

'What happened to you?' she asked. 'You look terrible, Robert.' She approached him and placed her hand on his, stopping his tipping motions.

He turned and faced her, lowering the plastic can that was now less than half full.

'I didn't know what to do, so I just drove for a while,' he paused, 'to give me time to decide.'

'Whether to go to the Police?' she asked frankly, her hand still on his forearm. She could see that he held the lighter in his closed fist.

'Yes,' he hesitated.

'Why didn't you?' again, she asked with a disarming frankness as her hand soothed him, rubbing gently from his forearm down to his wrist.

'Because I don't blame you for biting back,' he stuttered. Breaking their physical contact, he returned to spreading the petrol around the room.

'I don't think you should be blamed just because you withdrew your consent,' with his freed hand he waved the lighter around airily, 'from all this,' he paused and looked at Lewis, 'nonsense.' He moderated his language.

'Give me the petrol, Robert,' Aileen instructed him.

He complied without question or hesitation, but kept the lighter for himself. He reached over and took the shovel leaning against the door, as it dramatically heaved in as if a massive weight had just been thrown up against it.

Robert and Aileen both backed away from the door that had once opened to the outside. They heard two voices counting down.

'Free...Too...One,' followed by another massive heave against the door. The wood supporting the hinges was rotten and splintered under the weight and momentum of the two body building men. The door was kicked until it smashed inwards, flooding the dimly lit space with natural morning light.

Robert recognised the two silhouettes as he experienced a moment of Deja Vu. He expected the two figures to have a Panda and Rabbit head, but this time they both appeared in their human form. A sinking feeling in his stomach and his knees weakened him as he remembered the force of the blows that he had suffered.

'Charlie, take the boy and get in the motor. Now!' the largest of the two men spoke to a diminutive companion who appeared from behind them and grabbed Lewis.

'Lewis, let's go. Let's go now!' the third man insisted, but Lewis dug his heels in.

'Where's my Mum?' he demanded of the group of adults. He looked each of them in the eye. He felt betrayed.

He turned to the largest intruder, 'You promised me!' There were tears rolling from his eyes.

'I know, Little Man. I know,' the roughly spoken older man spoke to the child with a surprising tenderness.

'I will make this right. I promise. But,' he pushed Lewis out of the Boiler Room, into Charlie's arms. 'You need to go now, OK?'

The pair left and sprinted towards a part of the field where a PE store up against the fence on one side and a shed in a neighbour's garden on the other, made it possible for an agile individual to climb over with ease.

82

Aileen stepped forward, in front of Robert, with her hands behind her back.

'I'll save you the time. I killed her on Monday afternoon,' she stated matter-of-factly. 'I killed her, then I cut her body up, removing some organs, from which I prepared a feast for the Governors on Tuesday. They thought she tasted delicious.'

She began to flick her thumb, knowing that only Robert could see the motion. She continued on to the dumbstruck professional criminals: 'I cremated her body in my incinerator at home and asked Robert, here, to dispose of the ashes, so I did.'

She turned to face him, her hands still miming the lighting motion. She mouthed the word 'now' and turned back to see the two men stepping towards her.

'Stop! Police!' Laetitia warned the two men facing the staff in the Boiler Room.

She had sprinted around the warren of a school, trying to find the incursion, finally approaching the Boiler Room from the field, seeing a broken door and the backs of two male suspects.

Her nose was filled with the fresh, sweet smell of petrol. Like she had just overfilled a tank and some of it had spilled back out. A woman stood at the rear of the room, with a man standing behind holding a shovel. She noted the open plastic can in the woman's hand. The man behind her began shuffling closer to the boilers. There was something else, too. Something a little too familiar about the broad shoulders of the man turning to face her. She flicked out her baton by her side and held her other hand out as a warning.

'Everyone, just stop and lets talk, OK? What seems to be the problem?' she instantly began with conflict resolution and mediation strategies.

Kevin huffed up, 'Two of the buggers just jumped the fence at the back of the field.' He smelled the petrol and felt the tension.

'Oh ho! What's goin' on here then?' he chirped up just as Robert lunged and swung the shovel against the rotten gas pipes until they ruptured, disgorging their pressurised gas out into the room. The odourless gas had been tainted with something to help engineers find leaks and the room instantly stank like a battery chicken farm.

Laetitia responded first and turned to her older colleague, 'Kev, evacuate the school. Now! I got this. OK?'

The four occupants turned and looked at her to find out what she would do next. She faced Lee directly, masking her surprise.

'Let Mister Butcher here go, Tish. He isn't a part of this. He was just helping me out.' Lee establishing the familiar relationship with Laetitia, tried to get his boss off the hook.

Mickey took his cue instantly and began to edge around the isolated police woman.

She couldn't corral them all and she let the old gangster passed her. He would be picked up later, she thought. Laetitia stepped forward, into the Boiler Room.

'Ma'am, could you please put the petrol can down?' She had decided who the power broker in the room was, and it wasn't Lee.

'She killed a friend of mine,' Lee interrupted by way of explaining what he was doing there. 'Maggie Tracey.' Laetitia stopped dead in her tracks. 'We were here to find out why,' he finished.

'It's true,' Aileen began to pour the petrol over herself, 'I killed her on Monday.' The can empty, she took a step back to stand beside Robert. He held up the lighter, for Lee and the police officer to see.

'They chopped her up and ate her, Tish. They're cannibals or something. They ain't right.' Lee told her all he knew by way of warning and began to back out into the sunlight.

'This is the end of the road for us,' Robert began, 'Tish, isn't it? I think you should just turn around and leave, before it's too late.'

'Is it true, then? Did you kill Maggie Tracey and chop her up and eat her?' she asked Robert as she continued to step slowly forward. Inching closer to the pair.

'No..I...I had nothing to do with that,' Robert replied.

He didn't want the police to get the wrong impression. 'Your friend there abducted me!' He raised his voice. 'Abducted and tortured me!' Began shouting. 'And...gave me me something. Some drug,' he held the lighter higher, at arms length. 'They beat me and drugged me and left me in the middle of nowhere,' he screamed at Lee.

Spittle hit Laetitia's face.

Aileen stood impassively throughout Robert's outburst. She was at peace at last. She felt the petrol soak through her clothes to her skin and knew that it would all end soon. She was grateful for it.

'If you haven't done anything wrong, sir, then why are you going to set fire to yourself?' she looked at the ring on his finger. 'Surely that's not what your wife...' she left it open for Robert.

'..Elle..' he ventured.

'...Elle..would want you to do, would she?' Laetita pleaded.

Robert consulted his inner Elle, the voice of reason that always gave him the right advice.

'You are well and truly fucked, Robert, my love. You better spin that bad-boy up while you still can.' Robert hated his Elle conscience, especially when it was right.

The emotional overload of his imminent incarceration or death split him through and through. He cracked as tears and snot and bile erupted from him and he fell to his knees, his arm with the lighter still held out.

Laetitia seized her moment and stepped up to Robert, taking the lighter from his grasp before the shocked Aileen could move.

'That's my good girl, Tish!' Lee said behind her as he stepped forward, confidently patting her backside and moving past her to land a solid jab onto Aileen's nose. Her face crumpled and the force of the blow sent her rebounding off the boilers behind her and onto her knees.

He turned, "Let's get out of..." but didn't finish his sentence.

Tish held the lighter level with her eyes and flipped the lid open. She spoke softly and slowly. The others strained to hear her above the whooshing gas from the leaking pipes.

'I'm going to lose everything, Lee.' She began. 'I'm going to lose everything.'

Everything seemed to stop. Time held onto the moment as each of the occupants of the Boiler Room realised that it was close to being their last. Aileen watched as even the dust hovered expectantly as the air thickened. The figure in the doorway held the lighter aloft in her hand, a living silhouette of liberty opening an aperture to the oblivion she now craved.

'My husband. My kids. My family. My home.' Her eyes were fixed on the lighter. Her thumb moved incrementally up onto the striker.

'I don't blame you, Lee,' she continued. 'If it hadn't been with you, I would have messed it all up with some other macho knob-head.'

She felt the self destructive urges that had been building inside her for some time. How long had it been since Pete had let her spend any real time with her kids? What kind of role would she play in their life? He had already met another woman to be their mum. She peaked as she realised that this was her way out. She just couldn't say no.

'If I die now,' she reasoned, 'then my kids will spend their whole lives thinking that I was a hero, won't they? This is my chance to not to spend my life, ruined. '

Her thumb spun the striker, as Lee lunged for her. Aileen threw her arms up in release to welcome the coming annihilation and Robert dived head first for the salt store.

Laetitia watched the tiny seed in her hand blossom into a flaming rose. The petals grew and multiplied into a bush that engulfed her arm. Her eyes widened at the beauty of it all. The flowers seemed to dance and leap towards the leaking pipes before the rushing stillness was broken by the appearance of a rapidly expanding sphere of super heated fire, and hesitated.

The explosion ripped the Boiler Room and a large part of the abandoned classrooms that had housed Key Stage 1 apart, killing the four occupants instantly.

83

Mickey was waiting at the car, when Charlie and Lewis finally found their way back through gardens and side roads. The explosion had shocked all of them.

'Oncle Mickey!' The elated Lewis had exclaimed, as the sound of sirens drew closer.

'Get in you muppets! Let's get...,' Mickey looked at Lewis, 'out of here!' He moderated his language for the boy.

They drove around the town aimlessly for a time, before Mickey returned them to Charlie's flat.

'Lewis, go and wait by the door,' he told the child in the back seat.

Lewis dutifully obeyed, and left the two adults alone in the idling car. In the distance, a plume of smoke marked the location of the burning school.

'Listen, Charlie. I had no idea that it would end up like this,' he looked at the man-boy ruefully. 'I mean, that was...' his voice trailed off and the pair looked first at the smoke and then at the boy waiting in the garden of the flat, stroking a stray cat that stood on the wall.

'I found something out, about Lewis,' Mickey began sensitively. 'Maggie, she told one of the girls, like. Now, don't think that you have to take responsibility. I can have 'im taken care of, like.' He hesitated. 'But, I thought you should know.' Mickey looked over to speak man to man to Charlie, but Charlie's full attention was on the boy.

'E's yours, Charlie. She never told you or wanted you to know. But, the boy is your son, Charlie. I can look after 'im though, if you need me to.'

'Thanks Mister Butcher. I think we'll be alright,' Charlie, stunned, got out of the car.

'Charlie,' Mickey called out, 'I think it's best if we both vanish for a while. You know, 'til this all blows over, like.'

Charlie nodded from the gate, before he and Lewis went inside, for a cup of tea and a cheese toastie. He was already making plans. He would collect the money and whatever belongings he wanted to keep into a bag and take Lewis to his Mum's. He was never going to return to the flat again. He told Lewis all about the legendary Sunday roasts as they walked through the empty streets, and hoped she would know how he could set about getting legal custody of the boy.

84

The wrinkled shirt collar and loosened tie of the officer facing her offended her professional standards. No one would hold any kind of interview looking so seedy and worn in her industry.

The coffee and cigarette breath reached all the way across the small square table between them, smothering her and choking her, despite the air conditioning unit's attempts to shield her from it. The officer placed a tape in the recorder that occupied most of the surface of the small square table.

The officer pressed two buttons on the recorder simultaneously, with a grunt. It was obviously a tedious chore. He watched the wheels of the recording tape turn as a high pitched buzz introduced the legal beginning of the interview under caution.

Once the buzz ended, he spoke: 'Interview with Missus Elle Carpenter, commencing at Four Thirty-Five p.m.' The officer placed a manila foolscap folder on the limited surface of the table as he recounted his and his colleagues full names and ranks for the record and then sat back, with a glance at his companion.

His colleague for the interview was a female uniformed officer who sat impassively, staring straight at Elle. There were bags under her eyes and smudges of uneven, hastily applied eye shadow and poorly accented blush that made her appearance somewhat ghoulish, he thought. She had been Tish's friend and he would have to tread carefully.

'You do not have to say anything. But it may harm your defence if you do not mention when questioned something which you later rely on in court. Anything you do say may be given in evidence.'

Elle looked between the officers and her solicitor, 'I have nothing to hide. This has to be a mistake. What you've said to me makes no sense at all.'

The scruffy officer rubbed his stubbly chin. Shaving stopped being a priority for him a long time ago. His dishevelled appearance hinted at the deep scars that he couldn't cover up. His sleep was broken every night by a pit bull, straining against its restraints. Sometimes it was bald and tattooed, sometimes it was pitted and pocked, framed by dreadlocks. The teeth were always the same. Incisors bared, reaching for his throat. The mouth full of baseball bats, hypodermic needles, serrated knives and broken bottles in a line. Too many broken faces and battered lives had left him cynical and weary. He was tired.

'For the record, Missus, ah, Carpenter is co-operating with police investigations voluntarily,' he looked at Elle with sadness, 'and if you wish, you have the right to remain silent or offer an answer of 'no comment" He followed best practise.

Opening the folder on the table, he withdrew a number of photographs. Some were of Robert from the previous morning, that had been captured on the CCTV cameras of local shops. One was of his car, with his keys and the broken fragments of a phone discarded on the ground beside the driver's side door. Another photo seemed to show two individual UHT milk cartons on a shelf, next to a ream of Mid-Year reading tests. The names that had been visible were covered with a black rectangle. The final few photos were of a document, four pages to a page. Elle read the title, shaking her head.

'What are all these? What do they have to do with Robert? Or me?' Shaking her head, she looked to her solicitor for support. She picked up the grainy image of Robert, staggering across a road as he had passed the local Co-op mini store on his way to the school for the last time. His shirt tails were ragged, his jumper and trousers looked dirty and he looked bruised. His disarray was clear.

Tears began to trickle down Elle's cheeks, her index finger traced the outline of her lost husband's figure, 'Rob, hon,' she sobbed. 'What have you done? What happened to you?'

Printed in Great Britain
by Amazon

61798240R00225